No More Terrible Dates

ISBN: 978-1692648336

Edited by The Letterers Collective

Cover design by Sue Traynor

Published by Wild Lime Books

No More Terrible Dates

A romantic comedy of love, friendship . . . and tea

High Tea Book 2

(Cozy Cottage Café Book 6)

Kate O'Keeffe

Wild Lime Books

Also by Kate O'Keeffe

High Tea Series:
No More Bad Dates
No More Terrible Dates
No More Horrible Dates

Cozy Cottage Café Series:
One Last First Date
Two Last First Dates
Three Last First Dates
Four Last First Dates

Fairy Tales in New York Series:
Manhattan Cinderella

Wellywood Romantic Comedy Series:
Wedding Bubbles
Styling Wellywood
Miss Perfect Meets Her Match
Falling for Grace

Standalone Titles:
The Right Guy
One Way Ticket
I'm Scheming of a White Christmas

Published by Wild Lime Books

Chapter 1

Of all the terrible, horrendous, completely diabolical dates I've been on in my twenty-five years—well, more like ten years because I didn't start dating until I was fifteen, like most normal people—this date has got to be the absolute worst. A clear winner of the much-contested "Most Terrible Date Darcy Evans Has Ever Been On" award. The Supreme Leader of the Terrible Dates World. No, the Supreme Leader of the Terrible Dates *Universe*.

Get the picture?

Sure, we met online via the dreaded swipe so my expectations were not exactly high to begin with. I've found the connection between an online profile and reality can be tenuous, and I fully expected this guy to be no different from the rest: all normal on the outside with some form of weirdness simmering just below the surface.

As I nervously wait at Cozy Cottage Café for him to arrive, I wonder how different he'll look from his photo. I have a bet with myself that the image of a hunky, athletic guy with messy mid-length hair in that Jason Momoa way I go weak at the knees for will only vaguely resemble his current physical state. What's more, I bet his list of hobbies that includes tennis, squash, yachting, and "working hard to keep my six-pack" is more like an unobtainable wish list than anything close to actual reality.

If there's one thing I've learned in the last month, it's that truth and the wonderful world of online dating very rarely coincide.

So, you can imagine my unadulterated glee when the guy walks in looking even better than his online photograph. He's dressed in a T-shirt and jeans combo that shows me his hard work on his six-pack has definitely paid off, and when his gaze locks with mine, my hopes shoot up into the clouds and I swear I hear a choir sing the *Hallelujah Chorus* for a full ten seconds.

Act relaxed, Darcy, like I meet guys who look like this guy every day of the week.

Hastily, I sweep my hair over my shoulders (to show just how relaxed I am) and shoot him a breezy smile.

"Are you Darcy Evans?" he asks in a voice that matches his appearance to perfection. Read: rich, low, sexy.

Yup, I'm pinching myself here.

I look up at the man towering over me. "I am," I squeak and immediately clear my throat, my cheeks heating right up. Why do I have to sound like I'm a close relative of Chip 'n' Dale at this crucial moment? Lowering my voice a full octave, I say, "I mean, I am, and you must be Devan." I stand up and offer him my hand, hoping he didn't notice my chipmunk impersonation.

If he did, he doesn't mention it. "It's great to meet you, Darcy. You look exactly like your photo."

"You do, too." *Only even better.*

His eyes rove over me. "Cute suit. You're totally rocking it. The navy brings out the color of your eyes."

Okay, so my eyes are brown, but whatever. I may just have

experienced a mini-swoon inside. If that's a thing. I look up at him and smile. Yeah, that is definitely a thing.

Self-consciously, I tug at my jacket. I'm not going to lie. I went through virtually my entire wardrobe to work out what to wear today. "Oh, this old thing?" I say, pulling out the oldest line in the book. "Do you, ah, want to take a seat?"

"I'll grab a coffee first. You want one?"

"I already ordered a coffee, but thank you. Sometimes I drink tea, though. I got into it when my friend got this job running a high tea place. Tea really doesn't deserve its reputation as an old lady's drink, you know." Why am I rambling on about tea and old ladies? "So yeah, I'm good." I shoot him what I hope is a winning smile and try to push my nerves away.

"Cool. BRB." He saunters over to the counter, and I've got to hold my chin up to stop my jaw from hitting the table. Everything on this guy works. He's the perfect build, perfect height, perfect look, perfect everything for me. If he orders an Americano, he might just be my perfect match, too.

But I could be getting ahead of myself here. It's only a first date, after all. Actually, I should be more precise: it's only an "Initial Meeting," according to the rules of the pact my friends and I have agreed to. The No More Bad Dates Pact. We came up with it a few months back. You see, we were all pretty darn sick of dating the jerks and weirdos of the world, and we figured, if we could help one another out in finding the right guys, we could avoid the pain of dating the wrong ones. And date the wrong ones we have all done. Repeatedly.

Under the No More Bad Dates Pact rules, once one of us has met a guy we want to date, we go on an Initial Meeting over a cup of coffee. If things go well, the guy then gets vetted by the other two Pact members to weed out the undesirables. Then, and only then, can a first date take place.

It might sound a little over the top, but when you've had as many terrible dates as we have, you'd be tempted to do the same. And anyway, it's a nice feeling knowing my girls have got my back.

A few minutes later, Devan arrives back at the table, and I get a pleasant waft of his aftershave as he takes a seat opposite me. "The guy at the counter told me he'd bring my coffee over."

His smile is dazzling. I mean, his teeth are so pearly white and perfect, NASA could use him to guide in the spaceships. Well, if they need bright, white things to do that. (I don't know if they do because I'm not an astronaut.)

"So, Darcy, is now the time I should 'fess up to you that this is my first online date? I'm a total novice at this whole thing."

"It is?"

He nods. "Yeah. Crazy, I know. This is the twenty-first century, right? What rock have I been hiding under?"

A happy giggle bubbles up inside me. "I know, right? Full disclosure?" I ask and he nods. "This is only my second online date. I'm pretty new to this, too."

"I guess that makes us both virginal. Well, me more than you."

"Are there degrees of virginity?" I ask and immediately blush once more. I'm so out of practice at flirting, I'm not sure how talking about virginity within five minutes of meeting someone new will land.

He shakes his head good-humoredly. "You'll have to ask a doctor about that. How did the first guy work out?"

I pull a face. "Badly." As in he was married and looking to cheat on his wife.

His eyes light up. "That sounds like a story."

Wow, this guy is cute.

"Not one I'll tell my grandkids, that's for sure." I toy with my hair and add, "Let's just say false advertising was involved."

He sucks in air. "Profile didn't match reality? I've heard that's a thing."

I look at him through my lashes. I'm pulling out all the stops here. "Not with you."

"Ditto." He grins at me and those zings return full force.

I sense someone arriving at our table and glance up to see Alex, one of the Cozy Cottage Café baristas, shoot me his characteristically cheeky grin—the one that makes me want to trip him when he's carrying hot coffee. And yeah, I know that makes me sound like I'm a very bad person, but believe me when I say he'd deserve it. And more.

But I'm determined not to let Alex Walsh burst my Devan bubble right now.

"Your Americano," Alex says as he places the cup of coffee in front of me.

I give him a tight-lipped smile. "Thank you," I say stiffly.

"And *your* Americano," he says as he places another cup of coffee in front of Devan.

We both drink Americanos? I have died and gone to heaven with this guy.

"Thanks a lot," Devan replies, offering Alex his dazzling NASA grin.

Alex tucks his tray under his arm. "You two look very cozy. Is this a date?" He looks from Devan to me. "You're all pink and flustered, and you're," he turns to Devan, "well, you look pretty normal. Yup, I bet this is definitely a date."

I shoot him a look that I hope tells him to scurry away. "Thanks again for the coffee."

"Hey, you're welcome." He doesn't move. Instead, he says, "I noticed that you both take your coffee the same way. Do you think that *means* something?"

Well, I did until you mentioned it.

"A lot of people drink Americanos, Alex. You should know that. You're a barista," I say, my (fake) smile firmly in place.

He leans his hand on the back of a chair tucked into our table, making himself quite at home. "I should do a study, you know. Work out what the top three ways to have your coffee are. It would be quite fascinating, don't you think?"

I grind my teeth. Why is this guy still here?

To my surprise, Devan replies, "I bet the Americano would be right up there. It's a classic."

I shoot Devan a look that screams *don't encourage him!* but in a completely sweet and "I'm trying to make a good impression" kind of way. I don't want to put him off. Jason Momoa look-alike, remember?

Alex raises his index finger. "You can't ignore the latte. Or the cappuccino, for that matter. Two very solid offerings right there."

I glare at him. Just *leave!*

"I do like a good cappuccino from time to time," Devan replies.

I know he's just being nice and humoring Alex, but really, I did not picture spending this Initial Meeting with both Devan *and* our barista. Particularly not when that barista happens to be Alex freaking Walsh.

"Thank you so much for delivering the coffee, Alex." I raise my eyebrows at him in a meaningful way. "See you later, Alex."

"Oh." The reality of the situation finally seems to have dawned on him. "Gotcha. I forgot this is a date. I'll, ah, leave you two to chat or . . . whatever."

Or whatever? What does he think we're going to do in the middle of a café at nine in the morning? Make out? I swing my eyes to Devan. Actually, that's not a bad idea . . .

Devan shrugs. "It's cool. Good chatting to you. And thanks for the coffee."

"No worries," Alex says to Devan before glancing back at me.

By now, my eyebrows are raised so high, I fear they'll permanently join my hairline.

"I'll get back to it. Enjoy your date." Alex finally leaves Devan and me in peace.

"He's a nice guy," Devan says.

The word "nice" is not one I'd use to describe Alex Walsh unless the word "not" proceeded it.

"Sure." I smile across the table at Devan. "Now. Where were we?"

"I think you were going to tell me about how much better I

am than the last date you had." His grin is cheeky and oh-so-adorable.

I let out a light laugh. "Believe me, you're a lot better."

We share a smile and both take sips of our coffees.

Placing my cup on the table, I say, "Okay, so tell me, Devan. What's life like as an advertising executive?"

"I love it. I get to work with some fantastic clients and super talented creatives. Some of the concepts we've come up with have been incredible, even winning awards at times."

"Seriously?"

"Yeah. I'm not one to brag, but . . ." As I listen to him talk about his work, his passion for it written across his gorgeous face, I begin to imagine what it'd be like to date Devan Smith. Going to awards dinners together, him looking resplendent in a tux, me in a gorgeous floor-length, strappy dress I can only afford in my daydreams. He's the kind of guy I could take to meet my sisters. It would make them super jealous, plus it'd get Mom off my back, that's for sure. No more "When are you going to find a nice man and settle down like your sisters?" questions. Or my personal favorite, "When I was your age, I was already married with a baby on the way." Yup, that's my favorite. And no arguments that women have more choices these days could ever dissuade her.

"—and that's going to be my next step, so long as I land the new client this week."

I snap my attention back to Devan. "New client?" I question.

"Yeah. Like I was saying."

Dammit! I've been so busy thinking about how great it'll be to date this guy, I wasn't actually listening to what he was saying. I can't tell him that, though, can I? So instead, I give a knowing nod and say, "You've got it all worked out, haven't you, Devan?"

He gives a self-deprecating shrug. "I guess I have. How about you?"

"Oh, as much as I'd like to, I don't particularly have my life worked out yet."

"I bet you do. What's your job?"

"I'm a personal assistant to a celebrity."

"Seriously? Who?"

"I could tell you, but then I'd have to shoot you. You know the drill," I deadpan.

"Wow," he chuckles, "that must be some celebrity. Come on, you've got to tell me now."

I shrug. I like talking about what I do. Sure, my boss can be demanding, but being a P.A. to a celebrity is never dull, that's for sure. "I work for Larissa Monroe."

"Larissa Monroe?" Devan's eyes almost pop out of his head as he utters the actress-turned-health guru's name. "As in made it big here, went to Hollywood and starred in that movie with Todd Milson, then came back to New Zealand to reinvent herself as our very own Gwyneth Paltrow? *That* Larissa Monroe?"

Could there be more than one? Gawd, I hope not, for my sake. And doesn't this guy know an awful lot about Larissa? "Yup. That's her."

His eyes are bright when he asks, "What's she like?"

I roll out my usual response. After all, she's my boss, so I'm not exactly going to say anything bad about her, even if sometimes she does drive me to insanity with her outlandish demands and hare-brained ideas. "She is so great. She's focused and super inspirational."

"Oh, come on. You sound like one of my advertising logos."

"I'm serious. Larissa is great to work for, and I'm lucky to have my job."

"Okay. We'll leave it at that, but you're gonna have to spill the dirt some time, you know."

Happiness bubbles up inside me. That means he wants to see me again. I knew today was going to work out great.

Ten minutes later, stories shared, our coffee drunk, it's hard to wipe the smile from my face. Outside the café, I take a deep breath, preparing myself to tell him about the next step in the No More Bad Dates Pact: The Vetting Process.

"Devan, can I ask you something?" I begin, ready to deliver

my prepared speech about the Pact.

"First up, I need to do this." He takes a step closer to me, and before I know quite what's happening, he places his hands on my shoulders, leans down, and presses his lips against mine. With his touch, I breathe in his wonderful scent, and although it's totally against the No More Bad Dates Pact rules to kiss during the Initial Contact—rules we all agreed for very good reasons—my knees feel like they could buckle right here on the sidewalk outside the café.

All too soon, he pulls back from me. Feeling as though I'm floating on a cloud, I open my eyes and gaze at him. But there's no look of pleasure I would expect to see on his face after a first kiss like that. Instead, he looks . . . well, vaguely revolted, if I were to be completely honest.

"Devan?" I question, suddenly unsure of myself. Was it my technique? Do I have bad breath? Oh, my God, I have bad breath! I knew I shouldn't have had that garlic bread with my dinner last night, dammit! What was I thinking?

I place my hand in front of my mouth and push a breath out to try to catch a whiff of garlic. It's pointless. I get nothing.

"What are you doing?" he asks with a frown.

"I, ah, thought I might have bad breath."

He crinkles his nose. "Your breath is fine."

"Wh-what is it then?" I ask, not sure I really want to know the answer. "You didn't look like you enjoyed that a whole lot." I let out a light laugh to show him it that it really wouldn't bother me in the least if I were the worst kisser he's ever kissed, which of course it would. Jason Momoa look-alike and all that.

"I guess kissing you does confirm something for me."

"Confirm what, exactly?"

I think I know what he's going to say, and I don't want him to say it. He's the first guy I've felt excited about in forever, and I've pinned my hopes on him. Making my sisters jealous, getting Mom off my back about being married? Yup, those hopes. And another hope, a hope that he's a good guy, the kind of guy I want to be with. The kind of guy who could make me happy. Because you know what? I deserve this. I've been on too many bad dates. It's got to be my time. "It's just…"

"It's just what?" I hold my breath.

He twists his mouth, lets out a puff of air, and says, "I'm definitely gay."

Wait, *what?*

"I'm sorry?" I'm not sure I heard him right.

Did he really just say he's definitely gay? As in not maybe gay, not a little bit gay, but *definitely* gay?

He shakes his head at me. "There's no need to be sorry, Darcy. You're a gorgeous girl. You're just not, you know." He gestures at me with both hands.

"A guy?" I ask, incredulous.

"Yeah. Exactly. A guy."

Flipping freaking *what?!*

He reaches out and pats me on my upper arm like I've been a good doggie and fetched the chew toy he threw. "Look, thanks for helping me work that out. I figured if anyone could show me my true feelings, it would be someone like you. The guys in the office said you were hot when they saw your photo, so I figured, why not give it a shot? One last-ditch attempt."

One last-ditch attempt? What am I? A battlefield? *Once more unto the breach, dear friends.*

I press my lips together, my hopes well and truly shriveled up into a hard little raisin that Devan's casually flicked away without a second thought. "Let me get this straight," I say, "no pun intended."

He laughs. "That's a good one because I'm not straight."

I grind my teeth. "Yeah. I got that. What I want to know is, did you only go out with me to confirm to yourself that you're gay?"

"Yeah."

"Well, I'm so glad I could help." I raise my arm and pretend to glance at my nonexistent watch. "Is that the time? I need to get back to Larissa. Busy, busy day today."

"Sure. Well, thanks again."

He's thanking me?

As I turn to leave, I feel his hand on my arm. "Darcy, can I ask you something?"

I lower my eyes to his hand and say, "I think you're going to anyway."

"I get it if you don't want to, but I kinda need a date to my brother's wedding in a couple weeks. Having you there would really put my mom off the gay scent."

I blink at him in disbelief. The gay scent? Is that even a thing? "You want me to be your date?"

His eyes light up. "Would you?"

I let out a puff of air. When I woke up this morning, I did not think I would go out with a guy who works out he's gay in the middle of kissing me, let alone that he would then ask me to be his date to keep his sexuality from his mother.

Not happening.

"No, I . . . Just no."

He shrugs. "Well, it was worth a shot."

As I shake my head in exasperation—how do I find these guys?—I notice Devan looking through the window into the café. I follow his line of sight and spot Alex chatting to a customer as he delivers their coffee.

"Hey, do you think that hot barista is straight?"

Seriously?

I lock my jaw. There's only so much a girl can take, and I reached that point a long time ago now. It's time to exit stage right, *pronto*.

"Goodbye, Devan," I say as I turn on my heel and plod down the street away from him.

And that is how my terrible Initial Meeting with Devan ends.

Ladies and gentlemen, I give you the ego-smashing, hope-dashing, not-quite-date of the century. Darcy Evans, the confirmer of gayness, the single and alone.

Forget the No More Bad Dates Pact. After this disaster, I'm a fully-carded member of the No More *Terrible* Dates Pact.

And I am determined that the next guy I date is going to be one of the good guys.

Chapter 2

By the time I reach the office, I've completely resolved that the only thing to do about the whole Devan thing is to put it behind me, pretend it never happened, and move on to the next guy. I'm telling absolutely no one. It's far too humiliating.

As I plunk my butt down on my desk chair, I pull up the dating app on my phone and begin to flick through my options. I wonder what the odds are that I'll meet another guy who'll kiss me to confirm he's gay. Oh, and then ask me to go to his brother's wedding *and* ask if the barista is straight. My guess is the odds are stacked against it, but with my luck, I simply can't rule it out.

I surreptitiously peruse the frankly depressing guy options in the app before I give up and place my phone on my desk. I look up at the blue wall and let out a puff of air. Everything in the office is blue, from the walls to the chairs to the floors. I'm "encouraged" to wear blue to the office, too, which really means if I turn up in any other color, my boss, Larissa, may blow a brain valve. And believe me, no one wants that. Larissa needs to keep all the brain valves she's got.

You see, in the world according to Larissa Monroe, as the color of the sea and sky, blue is the most spiritual, calming, and healing of all the colors in the rainbow. Apparently, if everyone wore the right shade of princess blue, we'd live in a perfectly balanced, harmonious world with no war and no conflict. Nothing but perfect blue happiness.

Do you think she needs some binoculars to see those (blue) flying pigs?

I know, I know. I'm being cynical. Erin, one of my BFFs and fellow No More Bad Dates Pact member keeps telling me to have an open mind when it comes to Larissa's ideas. Granted, she agrees that many of them are off the charts, bat-crap crazy, but she's always encouraging me to at least consider the less insane ones.

My attitude is that just because I work for Kool-Aid, doesn't mean I've got to drink the stuff.

Larissa comes breezing into the room. As always, she's dressed in the same blue of the walls and furniture. With her diminutive frame, you could easily lose her in here but for the fact she has long blonde hair.

I stand up and smooth out my skirt, knowing full well my entire wardrobe probably cost less than the dress she's wearing today. "Good morning, Larissa."

"Darcy, darling. How are you?" she asks without pausing for a response as she continues her breezy path into her office.

I collect my tablet, my trusty notebook with the cute Labrador puppy on the cover, and the opened mail from my desk and follow her. Larissa's office is stunning. A spacious, open-plan room with (blue) balance balls in one corner where she holds her meetings, and a large glass desk where she works, seated on her (blue) chair. We're twenty-three stories up in downtown Auckland, and her office has the most gorgeous view of the harbor and the volcanic island of

Rangitoto beyond.

She drops her (blue) purse, a couple of shopping bags, and her (you guessed it: blue) jacket onto the table and sits down on her chair. No need to tell you what color that is. (Okay, it's blue in case you weren't following). I trail behind her like the minion I am, collecting up her items and putting them away as I go.

"Tell me about my morning," she says as she looks out at the harbor littered with white yachts. Auckland isn't called the "City of Sails" for nothing.

I press on my tablet and the screen lights up. "Well, first up, you've got Therese Saldon from Usu coming in to show you some new stock she's recently acquired. She mentioned you'd already spoken and that you would be really excited by what she's got."

"Oh, that's the Guatemalan fertility charms." She claps her hands together like an over-excited seal. "I'm super excited about those. I've heard they're, like, amazing, and anyone who wants to have a baby has got to get one."

I'm a little more dubious about these types of things.

"Therese will be here in twenty-five minutes. Then you've got Jonathan Strangefellow, who needs to talk to you about—"

I stop when I see her waving her hand dismissively in the air. "Cancel him. I don't like his energy. Or his name. Strangefellow." She shivers. "Ugh."

"But, he's been in the calendar for weeks, Larissa. You've already canceled on him three times in the last month."

She presses her lips into a thin line and crosses her arms defensively, usually my signal to don the parent cap. Which is precisely what I do.

"Larissa, Jonathan is your accountant. You need to talk with him. It's important for the business."

This is what happens when you work as a personal assistant to a celebrity. You've got to be so many things. Parent, minion, counsellor, friend, punching bag. I do it all. They say Auckland has four seasons in a day, which is nothing compared to how many different people I need to be for Larissa, sometimes within a ten-minute conversation.

Really, I should get paid a lot more than I do.

"Why can't I have an accountant with a spiritually compelling name? Like Bliss? Or Flower?"

Because accountants are people, not brands of soap?

"Granted, Strangefellow does bring up a certain image of an unusual looking man, but Jonathan is a nice, sensible, traditional name." *Unlike Bliss or Flower.*

"I would meet with an accountant called Serenity every day of the week," she says.

"*Jonathan* comes highly recommended by Aroha Jones's people," I say, naming a well-known local entrepreneur I know Larissa is impressed with.

"He's Aroha's accountant?"

"Mm-hm."

She pouts, her already plumped-up lips looking like they could be used as flotation devices. Larissa Monroe would have come in very handy on the Titanic. "If I've got to," she grumps. "But you've got to be there, too. Promise?"

"I promise. Now," I pull out the pile of mail, "you've got some invitations here to events you may want to attend. I'm thinking it's a 'no' to the opening of the library's new wing?"

She pulls a face and nods. Reading isn't one of Larissa's things.

"And it's a 'yes' to an interview on *Good Morning New Zealand*? They want you to speak about how you transitioned from internationally successful actress to online health guru." I'm quoting them directly here.

She nods enthusiastically. Larissa loves to talk about herself. It's no secret how she managed the transition. She was a successful, well-loved actress here in New Zealand, starring in everything from the local soap opera to small budget movies before she took on Hollywood in a highly publicized move. Well, highly-publicized here in our little country at the end of the world. I can't imagine anyone in Hollywood knew who she was before she got there. But that all changed when she landed a role alongside heartthrob Todd Milson in the surprise rom com hit *He's So Not My Type*. They fell in love and married, had a genetically blessed daughter they called Monday for reasons unknown (she was born on a Tuesday), and then promptly divorced before the baby even uttered her first word. All very Hollywood.

With the notoriety gained from her and Todd's hit reality TV show, *Mr. & Mrs. Milson,* she came back to New Zealand and decided to switch up her life running her online business—with me as her long-suffering P.A.

Actually, to be fair to Larissa, I'm only "long-suffering" about twenty percent of the time. Although she works me hard, calling me at all times of the day and night to do things for her, I really do love my job. I mean, how many other jobs out there that allow you to be everything from a personal shopper to an events manager to a counselor, all while hobnobbing with the country's elite?

"I'm happy to give the interview, Darcy. People love to hear my story. They find what I've achieved so inspirational. Small-town girl with big dreams. And look at me now."

"That's true," I reply. "Now, before I go, is there anything you need?"

"My green juice and acai berry granola. Oh, and get Todd on the phone. Monday is being photographed by a magazine this week and I need to get his permission." She puts her hand in the air. "Don't get me started. If there were some way to get rid of exes permanently, to never have to see them again, I would take it in a heartbeat. Believe me."

There is, it's called murder, and I've heard that does the trick nicely. But I won't suggest that to Larissa.

"Do you want your green juice and acai berry granola first, or to speak with Todd?"

"Are you crazy? Definitely the juice and granola first. I can't deal with that man without a good dose of phytonutrients."

I stifle a giggle. Larissa needs phytonutrients while the rest of us crave caffeine. She lives on an entirely different planet to us mere mortals. Celebrity world and the real world have very little overlap.

"I'm on it." I turn to leave.

"Oh. Darcy? I almost forgot. Can you believe it?"

I turn back. "What is it?"

"It's big news. And I'm super, super excited. You know how I'm always talking about synergies between the creative self and the healthful core that we all need to tap into?"

I nod dumbly. Usually, I daydream about what I'm going to sing at karaoke with my friends on Saturday night when she's prattling on about such things.

"Well, I've found the perfect thing."

"What is it?" Finger painting with beet juice? Dresses made from cabbage leaves? Neither of these is beyond the realm of possibility here.

"I'm getting into the art space."

"The art space?"

Her face is aglow as she nods rapidly. "I'm buying this fabulous new space. It's going to be a gallery. Isn't that wonderful?"

I blink at her a few times as I process her news. "Totally wonderful," I enthuse while inside I'm wondering why the heck a former actress turned online self-professed wellness guru is buying a space to make into a gallery. Oh, and how nice it would be to have that kind of money just lying around so you can buy something as expensive as a gallery on a whim.

"Darcy, it's going to be incredible. We'll hold exhibitions there, obviously, but also symposiums and workshops. We'll feed people's minds with art as well as providing them with spiritual and intellectual sustenance. It will be the trifecta. So, so amazing."

I give her an indulgent smile. "I'm really excited for you, Larissa."

"Actually, I'm shocked that I've never thought of this before." Her eyes are wide as she contemplates this. "Of course, I'll need you to organize absolutely everything."

Of course she will. That's what I do, after all. And I should be grateful for small mercies here. I mean, it could be a lot worse. She could have bought a giraffe and asked me to care for it at my apartment. And if she did, I would not be surprised in the least.

"What do you plan on exhibiting?" I ask.

"It can be anything we want it to be. Anything! Isn't that exciting?" She pauses, her features becoming more pensive. "So long as it's black and white photography. For some reason, I'm really feeling black and white photography these days. I want to make the whole place into a space dedicated to the art of taking a really, really good photo."

"Black and white photographs. Okay, I'll get onto it. Can you give me the gallery details?"

"Oh, it's right next to this gorgeous little high tea place. Cozy something. It makes me feel warm and happy just thinking of it."

"Cozy Cottage High Tea? Next to a café of the same name?"

"Yes! That's it."

"My friend Sophie manages High Tea. It's such a wonderful place."

"Hey, maybe I should buy the café and the high tea place, too? I could own all of them in a row." She gives an excited yelp.

Before she embarks on her Monopoly board approach to property ownership and decides to knock all three buildings down and build a hotel, I jam the brakes on. "Great idea, Larissa, but I know for a fact they're not for sale."

She pouts. "What a shame."

"That said, this gallery sure does sound amazing. Black and white photography is . . . the new black, right?"

"Right!" She leans back in her chair. "You see, Darcy? This is why we're such a great team, you and me. You think what I think. We're in sync."

I smile back at her, the band of the same name springing to mind. "Exactly." Only if I thought the way she did and went off buying galleries on a whim, I'd be swimming so deep in debt, not even Aquaman would be able to save me.

"Clear my afternoon," she announces. "I'm taking you to see our new project."

"Awesome. I'll go get your smoothie and granola."

For the rest of the morning, we meet with Therese and hear all about how apparently women can get pregnant by simply looking at the Guatemalan fertility charms (despite the fact they look an awful lot like river stones to me); Jonathan Strangefellow and I manage to get Larissa to sign off on the company's annual tax return without her pouting once; and I manage to wrangle with not one but two celebrities who are surrounded by people who never say no to them, and consequently have no clue about the real world. As a result, Todd agrees to have Monday photographed by the magazine, and both parents are happy. Monday? Maybe not so much, but as every celebrity worth their Beverley Hills mansion will tell you, a beautiful child is the very best accessory.

Cynical much?

In the early afternoon, Larissa's driver pulls the car up outside her newest purchase, the black and white photography gallery, and we climb out into the warm afternoon sun.

"Isn't this place darling?" she says, pointing at Cozy Cottage High Tea with its red and white striped awnings and large glass windows. "Are you sure I shouldn't buy it? Because I would love to own this."

"Absolutely sure. They serve food in there made from not only wheat but dairy products, too."

"But wheat has gluten in it. Don't they know that?" She guffaws, her hand over her mouth.

"I'm sure they do."

"And they use it all the same?"

"Yup."

"Tell me they use coconut oil at the very least. Please."

"You know, Larissa, I'm not sure they do."

"No coconut oil?" Her plump lips form a small "o" at this deeply shocking piece of information.

"And their food has sugar in it," I add to further put her off. Larissa is famously anti-sugar. She's even written a book about it. "Lots and lots of sugar."

"Unrefined, sustainably sourced raw sugar?" she asks hopefully.

I shake my head.

"Agave? Maple? Honey?" she asks hopefully.

Another shake.

Her face is aghast when she asks in a small voice, "Not . . . refined *white* sugar?"

I give a curt nod. "Plain white sugar. It's in all their cakes and cookies. Which, of course, is why they are all so completely delicious."

Larissa's eyes bulge. "But that's . . . that's so *last century*. It's positively caveman behavior."

I might not know my history all that well, but I'm pretty sure that when people used to run around in animal skins with spears, they didn't eat a whole lot of cakes made with refined white sugar. But then I could be wrong.

It's right about now my mouth starts watering and I begin to crave one of the Cozy Cottage cakes filled with gluten, dairy, and sugar. All very good things in my "caveman" mind.

Larissa takes my hand in hers and looks earnestly at me. "Thank you, Darcy. I'm glad you shared that with me."

"I thought you needed to know," I say in a low, serious voice.

She pulls a set of keys from her purse, waves them in the air, and unlocks the door to the gallery. Once inside, we both look around the large, empty, echoing room. With bright white walls and gray, polished concrete floors, it's a blank, personality-free canvas. In other words, it looks exactly like an empty gallery.

"Isn't this place amazing?" Larissa enthuses. "Can you feel it?"

I know better than to reach out and touch a wall. Larissa doesn't mean to feel it literally. "Yes, I can." I search my brain for the right Larissa platitude to use. I've got a bunch of them, all in notes in my trusty notebook with the cute Labrador puppy on the cover, just in case I need one to pull out at short notice. They're airy-fairy clap-trap as far as I'm concerned, but hit the right one and Larissa's super happy. And you know what they say? Happy celebrity, happy life. Or something like that.

"I'm feeling the harmonious interrelationship between textures in this space. It adds to the emotionally satisfying vibe, don't you think?" Pleased with my gobbledygook, I watch her for her reaction.

"You know, I hadn't thought about it that way. But you know what, Darcy darling? You're totally right. The walls and the floor do interrelate."

That's right. I think it's called "construction."

She moves around the room, giving me her "vision for the space," and I scribble in my trusty notebook, the one with the cute Labrador puppy on the cover that I take everywhere with me. I bought a stack of them when I saw them in the stationery store so I wouldn't run out. I'm a sucker for a Labrador puppy. #GoalDog

Some of Larissa's ideas are sane, some less so. But that's the way Larissa rolls. And why not? When you've got oodles and oodles of cash and no one ever telling you not to do what you want, why not indulge your every whim? Although I do draw the line at her suggestion that we have a family of wallabies wandering the room at exhibition openings, dressed as waiters. I don't care how *avant garde* she thinks it will be.

In the end, I've got a list the length of Heidi Klum's legs to organize before we can even open the gallery doors to the public, not to mention having to find a photographer to exhibit their work. This on top of all the other things I do for her every day.

Lucky, lucky me.

As we lock up, Larissa pauses on the sidewalk, her hand on my arm as she gives a furtive glance at Cozy Cottage Café. "Darcy," she begins in a quiet voice, "do you know if they serve anything that's gluten-free in there?"

I bite back a smile. It takes a strong person to resist the aroma of a freshly-baked cake from Cozy Cottage Café. "I know there's a flourless chocolate and raspberry cake that's very good."

She almost licks her lips right in front of me. "Flourless, you say? So, no gluten whatsoever?"

I shake my head. "No gluten whatsoever."

"I follow a strict nutrition regime, which I do entirely for my health, of course."

"Of course." It's got nothing to do with the fact she likes to fit into children's sized clothing.

"But you know, Darcy, lately I've been reading about how occasionally indulging one's self is in fact extremely beneficial for you as a whole."

With my most serious and earnest expression in place, I reply, "I think Cozy Cottage Café's flourless chocolate and raspberry cake is the perfect beneficial indulgence."

Her face transforms into a look of unbridled glee, and I feel a pang of sadness for her. She spends her life drinking ghastly juices and smoothies, starving herself, sticking to a strict exercise regime, and avoiding all the good things in life. The woman has got to live a little.

"A slice of Cozy Cottage Café's flourless chocolate and raspberry cake it is."

I beam back at her. "Come on, then. I'll treat you to a slice."

Chapter 3

Despite the Devan Dating Debacle (the dreaded D.D.D.) this morning, I always feel at home at Cozy Cottage Café. Although I spend more time at High Tea next door these days, thanks to my BFF, Sophie, becoming the manager there recently, I've been coming here for years. I love the comfortable, easy-going, welcoming vibe of the place.

And the cakes. Definitely the cakes.

"Oh, this place is darling!" Larissa exclaims as we step through the door into the café. She's donned her sunglasses so as not to be recognized, although several people turn to gawk at her as she sashays toward the counter, and I know her feeble attempt at a disguise has been foiled. Either that or they're looking at her because it's plain weird to wear sunglasses inside unless you're Bono from U2.

We make our way to the counter where I notice one of the owners, Bailey, is serving. I do a quick scan of the café and feel my shoulders relax. No sign of Alex Walsh. Things are certainly looking up.

At the cabinet, we peruse the assorted cakes. There's the deliciously moist carrot cake with cream cheese frosting, an apple streusel cake, an orange and almond syrup cake, along with the flourless chocolate and raspberry cake that so tempted Larissa before.

"Oh, they all look so good," Larissa exclaims. "But you see, darling, that's how the evils of sugar, dairy, and gluten work. They make you crave them, and you're only ever satisfied by another fix and then another. It's all in my book."

"Yes," I say with a nod. "Yes, it is."

Larissa's book is entitled the very subtle and non-sensational *Sugar is your Nemesis,* subtitle: *How the sugar you eat is slowly killing you and how to destroy its evil grip on your life.* It's rousing stuff if you're into all that. And a lot of people are if Larissa's sales are anything to go by. Although, by the look on her face right now, I'd say the sugar nemesis hasn't entirely lost its evil grip on her life.

"Hey, Darcy," Bailey says over the top of the counter. "Weren't you in here earlier today? Twice in one day. You must truly love us."

I smile through my cringe. The last thing I want to do is think about Devan and his "I'm gay but will you come to my brother's wedding as my date" calamity. "Yes, that's right, and now I'm back to get two slices of your flourless chocolate and raspberry cake. To go, please." I look at Larissa for confirmation, and she nods her assent.

Bailey shoots me her beautiful smile. If she noticed my dodge, she doesn't mention it. "Sure. Two slices of chocolate and raspberry cake coming up."

As Bailey busies herself with the cake, Larissa launches into her ideas for the gallery once more. "Ideally, I want to open the gallery at the same time as we launch the Guatemalan charms. Therese said she can get us some from her next shipment, remember?"

I gasp. "But that's in only a few weeks."

She flicks my concern away with her hand. "Oh, I have faith in you, Darcy darling. You'll totally pull it off. You always do. That's why I love you so much."

It's so easy for her. All she's got to do is come up with the ideas and then show up once all the work's been done. Me? I'm the poor shmuck who's got to do it all.

"Here you are, Darcy." Bailey places two small cardboard cake boxes on the counter in front of me.

"Thanks." I wave my card to pay, and she passes me the receipt. "See you later."

"Are you planning a third visit today?" Bailey asks, her eyes alight.

I shrug. "If you did dinner, then that would be a resounding 'yes.'"

"Come back for the Friday Night Jam."

"I'll do that." I collect the boxes and turn to Larissa. "Shall we go?"

She lets out a light sigh. "I feel like I could stay here all day, even though it's not exactly on-brand for me. It's got the atmosphere of a young child who's free of the restraints of the world, at peace with who she is. Don't you think?"

What? "Sure, yeah. A small child." Personally, I would have gone for "great place," but for Larissa, I go with it. It's easier that way.

As we reach the front door, someone pushes through in front of us, holding a couple of potted hyacinths in her hands.

"Sophie!" I say with delight. I collect my friend in a one-armed embrace as I balance the cakes in the other.

"Hi, Darce." She nods at my cake boxes. "I see you've come in for your sugar fix."

I can feel Larissa bristle at my side at the mention of the "s" word, even though both she and I know that the contents of one of the boxes are for her.

Sophie smiles at Larissa. "Hi, Larissa."

Larissa extends her tiny, fine-boned hand. "Nice to meet you," she says.

"Actually, you've met Sophie a bunch of times," I say.

She crinkles her forehead as she sizes Sophie up. "Of course. How are you . . ."

"Sophie," I say under my breath.

"Sophie," she repeats.

Sophie's face creases into a smile. "I'm great, thanks."

"Soph runs High Tea next door."

"I sure do. You should come by some time," she says to Larissa.

Larissa gives her a tightlipped smile, and I know that despite her declaration Cozy Cottage Café has the "atmosphere of a young child who's free of the restraints of the world," she needs to get out of here, *pronto*. As the face of anti-sugar, anti-gluten, anti-anything worth eating, lingering too long in a café like Cozy Cottage is like flirting with death for Larissa.

"We'd better get going," I say to Sophie.

"Sure." She pulls me in for a hug.

I feel a small hand grip my arm, and I turn to look back at Larissa.

"Oh, my God. Whose work is that?"

I follow Larissa's line of vision to the wall by the window. There's a simple, framed black and white photograph of an ornate building under a dramatically cloudy sky. It's beautiful in its simplicity, and with the frequency with which I'm in this café, I'm surprised I've not noticed it before.

"I don't know," I reply honestly.

"It's got exactly the sort of feel I'm looking for. It evokes a sense of turbulence and beauty as a comment on the fragility of the human spirit. Don't you think?" Larissa bustles over to the wall to get a closer look.

I shoot Sophie a quick look before I follow her. Sophie looks like she's working hard at simultaneously deciphering what the heck Larissa's talking about and suppressing the urge to laugh. It's a state of being I'm all too familiar with.

"I'm sure we can find out who took this photo," I say when I reach Larissa.

"Oh, we've got to!" she exclaims.

"It's by one of the baristas here. Alex," Sophie says at my side.

I snap my attention to her. "Alex? As in *Alex* Alex?"

Alex Walsh, the self-satisfied barista who refused to leave me and Devan alone this morning, is responsible for something that beautiful?

Sophie nods, and I turn to look back at the photo. I knew Alex was a photographer and had disappeared to rove distant lands to indulge his passion for photography, but I've never actually seen his work before. Although I'm not sure I agree with Larissa's interpretation that the photograph comments on the fragility of the human spirit exactly (I mean puh-*lease*), it sure is stunning. And I would never in a gazillion years say it to Alex, but he's got something here. An eye, I guess. An ability to capture something more than just what you see.

"Who's Alex Alex?" Larissa asks. "I adore the name, by the way. Totally unexpected. I think I love him already."

"His name is Alex Walsh. He's my cousin. Darcy and I went to high school with him," Sophie explains. "He's a really talented photographer. Bailey put this one up yesterday, and we've got a bunch over at High Tea."

"Take me to them," Larissa instructs dramatically.

"Sure, I just need to deal with this." Sophie waves the potted hyacinths in the air.

Larissa takes the plants from an astonished Sophie, passes them to me, and says, "Darcy will take care of them."

I struggle to balance the plants and the cake boxes in my hands as Larissa loops her arm through Sophie's and says, "Let's go."

Sophie mouths "sorry" to me as she and Larissa walk out the door.

With a sigh, I make my way back to the counter to ask Bailey what to do with the plants. Instead of Bailey, I find a smirking Alex, looking like he's a cat who drank the cream. All of it. Usually, I give him the cold shoulder or mutter an entirely insincere greeting. But now, having seen how incredible that photograph he took is, I feel . . . what? Impressed? Moved? Like I'm seeing him in a new light? Maybe all those things.

I'm quite sure the feeling will pass. I hate the guy, after all. Alex Walsh and I? Well, let's just say we've got *unfavorable* history.

He quirks an eyebrow. "Are you stealing the plants now, Darcy?"

"Oh, you know me. Always . . . doing stuff."

Doing stuff? What am I talking about? I see one of Alex's photos and I'm reduced to a bumbling, monosyllabic imbecile? This isn't me. I'm Darcy Evans, Personal Assistant to Larissa Monroe. I Get Things Done. I'm not the girl who's so thrown that I lose my inability to form a coherent sentence, even if it is with Alex.

"You're doing stuff," he echoes, a look of amusement written across on his face. His *handsome* face. Dammit.

I suck in a sharp breath as I toss my long hair. "That's right. I'm a very busy person, you know, Alex. I've always got a lot of . . . stuff to do."

Great work, Darcy. That showed him.

He merely keeps his gaze on me, his lips twitching with amusement.

"Now. What should I do with these plants?" I brandish the plants at him as I paste on an "I'm not in the least bit fazed by you" smile. Because I'm not in the least bit fazed by him. Or at least I won't be, just as soon as I manage to pull myself together and get back to normal.

"Let me get this straight. You're asking me what you should do with the plants you're trying to steal? Do you not know how robbery works, Darcy? You try to take stuff without other people noticing."

"Oh, Alex," I say with as patronizing a tone as I can muster while awkwardly balancing cake and plants. It's not an easy thing to achieve. "I don't have time for your games. Sophie asked me to deal with these, so can you please take them so I can get on with my day."

"Why don't you bring them 'round the back. We can find a place to put them out of the way."

"Oh, all right." Begrudgingly, I traipse past the food cabinets and find him holding the counter flap open for me. I plod past him and into the kitchen. I stop, turn, and raise my eyebrows in question.

"How about over here?" He takes one of the plants from me and places it against the back wall.

I follow suit with the second. "Thank you," I say as I turn on my heel to leave.

"Is Papa Smurf waiting for you outside?"

I turn back. What is he talking about? "Papa Smurf?"

"You and your friend. You're both in head-to-toe blue. Or wasn't that planned?"

"Oh, that. It's a thing my boss has. She likes blue."

"I like blue, too, but I tend to limit it to one item of clothing at a time. Not *all* of them."

"Actually, I'll have you know that blue is a very spiritual color."

Another quirk of that darn eyebrow. "Is that so?"

"Yes, Alex, it is. It's very powerful and associated with vision and hearing as well as our sense of smell." I'm spouting a bunch of Larissa-isms like I mean them, but damn him! He's being all superior, and I don't like it one little bit.

"You can *smell* blue?"

I falter, but I'm committed to this now. "Yes, you can. Please don't tell me you haven't smelled the color blue before, Alex, because that would be truly, truly tragic. For you. Blue smells absolutely amazing."

To my surprise, he wanders over and leans in close to me. For a second, I can feel his breath on my neck, making my skin tingle. I clear my throat. "What do you think you're doing?"

He straightens up, his eyes lit with mischief. "You're right. Blue does smell amazing."

"Well, I . . . there you go." I throw him a haughty look, as though what he just did wasn't completely unexpected and… and what? Nice? No, it threw me off guard, that's all. People don't go around smelling other people. It's just plain weird.

He leans back against the counter and crosses his arms across his chest. "I guess I've learned something new today."

"Good. Now, if you'll excuse me, Alex, I need to go."

"Because Papa Smurf is waiting for you."

Exasperated, I roll my eyes. "Yes, Papa Smurf and Smurfette and the whole blue gang. They're all waiting for me outside with Gargamel and Azrael. Happy?"

His smile teases as he replies, "Doesn't Gargamel want to kill the Smurfs?"

"Well, don't you know a lot about them," I quip.

He shrugs. "I watched the movie a couple weeks back with my nephew."

"Right." I refuse to be moved by the fact Alex watched a movie with a kid. People do it all the time. It's normal human behavior. Nothing more.

"He loves the Smurfs. He was sick, and I wanted to do something nice for him."

Seriously?

"Well, that's kind of you," I sniff.

Alex shrugs. "Not really. His mom had to work, and I was at a loose end. He's a good kid."

I point blank refuse to let the fact Alex is a kind uncle to some kid I'll never even meet touch my heart.

"Good. Well. That's that then."

He shoots me a questioning glance. "What's what then?"

"You're an uncle, and I've got to go." I balance the cake boxes in front of me and resume my walk out of the kitchen. Thrown by Alex, I'm not looking where I'm going and I almost walk smack-bang into Sophie. "Oops!" I exclaim as I let go of the boxes.

She catches them with significantly greater dexterity than I could manage right now. "Got 'em," she says with a smile and then hands them back to me.

"Thanks, girl. That could have been a disaster."

"I've got your back," she says to me with a wink. "Alex, can you please go next door? Larissa wants to meet you. Oh, and you need to go, too, Darce."

"Sure," I reply.

"Who is Larissa and why does she want to meet me?" Alex asks.

"Larissa Monroe. You know, the actress," Sophie explains. "She's Darcy's boss and she asked me to come get you."

Alex shakes his head. "Sorry. No can do, even for Darcy's boss." He shoots me one of his looks and I narrow my eyes at him. "Bailey needs me in the café."

Sophie waves his excuse away with a flick of her wrist. "I'll cover you until you're back."

He seems to think for a moment before he says, "I guess."

"Good. Now go!" Sophie instructs.

Alex lifts his hands in surrender. "Okay. But you need to know it wasn't me trying to steal the plants."

"For the last time, Alex, I wasn't stealing plants!" I exclaim in utter exasperation, winning a fresh smile from the guy.

Really, Alex Walsh has got to be the most infuriating person I've met in my entire life. And I work for a celebrity, so that's saying something.

Sophie hustles us both out of the kitchen, and we plod in silence through the café, out onto the street, and into Cozy Cottage High Tea next door.

All tables in the place are full, servers buzzing around, and I find Larissa standing in front of one of Alex's photographs on the far wall above one of the tables.

"Larissa," I say as I arrive at her side, "I've brought the photographer for you to meet. This is Alex Walsh."

She turns and looks up at him, her face aglow. "Alex Walsh." She grabs his arms, pulls him down to her height, and air kisses him. "You are a genius."

I harrumph. "Genius" is going a little far, isn't it? But this is Larissa. When she and Therese discussed the Guatemalan fertility stones this morning, she said they would revolutionize humankind. Hyperbole could be her middle name. (It's not, it's Mabel, but she doesn't want anyone to know that particular gem.)

"Good to meet you, Larissa," Alex says. "I'm glad you like my work."

"Like it? I *adore* it. It's so whimsical yet rooted in the reality of our existence."

"Yes," he replies with a nod. "Absolutely." He shoots me a small smile, and I press my lips together.

I don't want to bond with this man. Sure, Larissa can say some pretty out-there things so I get why he's smirking, but really, I'm not his comrade in all this.

"Alex Walsh, you must exhibit for me. Say you will. I want all of these. All of them." She gestures with her arms, and I notice most of the people in the room are looking at her, recognition dawning if their expressions are anything to go by. She swings her eyes to mine. "Darcy, tell him about my vision."

"Oh, I, ah," I begin uncertainly, "Larissa's opening a gallery next door. She wants all the artwork to be black and white photography, which yours clearly is." I gesture at the handful of photos on the walls. They're landscapes and cityscapes, all with big, dramatic skies. Just like the photo next door in the café, they're absolutely stunning.

"You'd want to sell them?" he asks.

"Of course!" Larissa replies as though he's just asked a preposterous question like "Do birds fly?" or "Are the contestants on *The Bachelor* only in it for the fame?" Preposterous. Of course they're on it for "the right reason," which is true love. *Everyone* knows that.

He shrugs. "Thanks, but I'm happy with them where they are right now. They kind of add to this place. I'm gonna have to pass."

I blink at him. Alex is saying no to Larissa? No one ever says no to Larissa!

She gawks at him, the shock registering on her face.

Part of me wants to fix this, to make Alex agree to what Larissa wants. The other part of me—the morbid part that likes to watch horror movies late at night despite the fact I know they'll give me nightmares—wants to see what will happen next.

With a stunned look on her face, Larissa mutters, "I don't know what to do with that." She turns her gaze to me. "Darcy? Fix this."

My morbid, horror film-watching part slinks back into the shadows as Personal Assistant Fix It kicks in. After all, keeping Larissa happy is my job, remember?

"Alex, why don't we discuss this? Larissa's got a vision for your work. I assure you, it'll be very tastefully and respectfully done."

Larissa nods like she's one of those bobblehead figurines. "I've got a vision," she repeats.

"This could be huge for you, Alex. Right now, you're exhibiting what? Five photographs in a café?"

"Six, actually, if you count the one next door."

Splitting hairs much?

"Six, then." I paste on a smile so fake, I could also be one of those contestants on *The Bachelor*, talking about our "connection." "My point is, Alex, with Larissa's exciting new project, you'll be able to exhibit a large body of work and sell it for a lot of money. It'll be amazing exposure for you."

I watch Alex hopefully, waiting for his reply. If he repeats his initial response, who knows what Larissa will do? *She* won't even know. As I mentioned, she doesn't hear the word "no" a whole lot, unless it's in conjunction with the word "carbs," too, of course. She uses that *a lot.*

He gives a nonchalant shrug, as though this isn't a huge opportunity for him. "Let me think about it."

I reel back from him with a jolt. I always knew Alex Walsh thought a lot of Alex Walsh, but his response to being offered to exhibit his work in a major solo show put on by Larissa Monroe is a noncommittal, unexcited, downright mediocre "let me think about it?"

My eyes dart to Larissa's. Her forehead is creased and she's looking at Alex as though he's speaking in tongues (which he may as well be, as far as she's concerned). "What does that mean?" she asks, looking directly at me.

"Could that become a yes?" I ask him tentatively.

There's a hint of a smile on his face when he replies, "It's a 'persuade me.'"

Persuade him? Is he serious? Who does he think he is, freaking royalty?

"Look, Alex, this is a huge opportunity. Larissa Monroe endorsing your work will put you on the map."

"On the map," Larissa echoes, her eyes wide.

"I get that. It's just, well, I've not exhibited in a while, and I like the photographs where they are right now." He looks up at a nearby photo.

"They do look amazing there," Larissa says.

"But they'd look even better on the walls of your new gallery," I say to her as I shoot her a meaningful look.

"They would. Alex Walsh, say yes," Larissa instructs.

I hold my breath as we both await his response.

His eyes pass from Larissa to me and back again. Finally, he says, "Look, I'm happy to be a part of this on one proviso."

"What's that?" I ask a little too eagerly.

"I get creative control."

Relief washes over me, and my smile turns from brittle to genuine with a puff of air. "That's great. Isn't that great, Larissa?"

"So, so great," she gushes.

And then, my initial euphoria evaporates as his words sink into my brain. "Wait. You want creative control?"

He gives another one of those frustrating shrugs. "It's my work. I get to choose what I exhibit, the theme, placement, that kind of thing."

"But—" My eyes swing to Larissa's. She's got her brows knitted together as though she's thinking hard. She gives a short nod, and I turn back to Alex. "That sounds reasonable."

Larissa totters on her heels over to Alex, takes one of his hands in hers, and pulls him down to air kiss him. "This is going to be amazing. Alex Walsh, I know the synergies that already exist between us will grow transcendentally as we travel on this journey together."

I take in Alex's perplexed expression and have to suppress a giggle. Unless you're in Larissa's world, she can come on a little strong. Or crazy, depending on your point of view.

"Ok*aaay*," he replies uncertainly. "Well, thank you, Larissa. I guess we'll talk some more about this soon. But right now, I'd better go get on with my job." He quietly pulls his hand away from her grasp. "So, ah, thank you," he repeats.

Call me bad, but I quite enjoy seeing him nonplussed by Larissa.

"Oh, no. Thank *you*, Alex Walsh. You are the talent. I am merely your creative springboard, your nurturer, the sunlight to your bud waiting to flower."

Alex's face has gone from perplexed to utterly bewildered as he replies, "Sure. Flowers and . . . all that. It sounds really good."

I bite my lips together so hard to stop a giggle from exploding out of me, I think I can taste blood.

Larissa turns to face everyone in the room, her arms outstretched. "We have our man."

All the people at the tables who have been watching the scene unfold break into applause. Larissa laps it up, smiling and clutching her hands against her chest as though she's won a frigging Oscar—not just simply talked a barista into exhibiting his photos in her new gallery next door.

"Thank you all. We will be opening our little gallery with this rather wonderful man here," she hooks her arm through Alex's, "in only a few weeks' time. It's right next door, and we would love it if you could all come to see it."

A couple of moments later, Larissa is busy having selfies taken with a few of the High Tea patrons, and I find myself standing next to Alex, still holding the cake boxes in my hands.

"Now that I've agreed to do this, how's it gonna work?" he asks.

"Well, I guess to start with, you'll need to get a full catalog of your photographs, so we can begin to work out what to exhibit."

"Sure. Do I get that to Larissa?"

"No. You'll need to get it to—"

And then it hits me, like a heavy blow to the belly. Why the heck didn't this occur to me before? I've just talked Alex into working with me. Not Larissa. *Me.* The guy I can't stand to be near. The guy who makes my blood boil simply by being alive.

The guy I've got history with who I'd really rather forget.

I swallow, my throat tight. "You'll need to get it to . . . me."

"To you, huh?" His grin is wide, his eyes dancing. "Does that mean we'll be working together now, Darcy?"

I open my mouth to reply, then close it again.

Working with Alex Walsh? How fan-freaking-tastic.

Chapter 4

I take a large swig of cheap sparkling wine, followed in short succession by another. Although the bubbles tickle my nose and make me want to sneeze, I need the alcohol to hit my bloodstream. Then I can get on with forgetting my week.

Two more large gulps and I've drained my glass, which I plunk down on the table in front of me with a *clack*.

Seated at the table with me at Jojo's Karaoke Bar, our regular Saturday night hangout, are Sophie, her boyfriend, Jason, and my other BFF, Erin. All three of them are watching me closely.

"Thirsty?" Jason questions, which receives an elbow in the ribs from Sophie. "What did I say? You've got to admit, she drank that real fast."

"Darcy only ever drinks a full glass of bubbles that fast if there's something wrong," Sophie explains before looking back at me. "Darce, is there something wrong?"

I tap my foot against the side of the table. "No. I'm fine."

Erin shakes her head. "No, you're not. We know you too well, Darcy Evans."

"Is it because of that Initial Meeting with that guy Devan? Because that's not your fault," Sophie says.

"What's not her fault?" Jason asks.

Sophie shakes her head. "That's privileged information, Christie. Inner Circle only."

"And I'm not in the Inner Circle?" he asks.

"You're not a girl," Erin explains. "It's us three."

"Oh." He crosses his arms. "It's like that, is it?"

"There are some things us girls need to keep to ourselves," Sophie says to him. "We need to maintain at least some element of mystery."

"How intriguing," Jason replies as he and Sophie gaze at one another with goofy grins on their faces.

I let out a defeated sigh. If there's one thing I can't stand when my own love life is in the pits — okay, buried so deep down in the earth no one could ever find it — is loved-up, sappy, deliriously happy couples flaunting their love in front of me.

Okay, I heard it. I know that's a bit harsh. Sophie and Jason are a great couple and deserve all the happiness they can get. But come on! When is it going to be my turn already?

I can't even find a straight guy to date.

"Hey, guys," a voice says behind me.

Jason leaps out of his seat to go greet the newcomer. "Glad you made it, man."

I turn to see who he's invited, hoping maybe it's a cute, single, potentially dateable doctor friend of his, only to lock eyes with the one person I did not want to see tonight. Or any night for that matter.

Alex freaking Walsh.

The person I stupidly persuaded to work with me just to keep Larissa happy.

The person I least like being around.

"Are you kidding? Miss out on terrible karaoke and fake champagne?" He laughs as Jason shakes his hand.

"Come take a seat," Jason says.

Sophie greets her cousin with a hug, Erin grins at him and says, "Hello," and I give him a brief nod and choose to remain seated — and rue the fact I don't have magic powers that would let me whisk myself back to my apartment and away from Alex in the blink of an eye. With a full bottle of sparkling wine, of course.

Alex sits opposite me, right in my line of sight, and fixes me with his gaze. "Darcy," he says the way he always does, his tone even with a hint of amusement.

Really, what's so amusing about saying my name? Nothing, that's what.

"Alex," I reply coldly, looking him over briefly to show my disdain for him.

But damn him, he looks good. I wish I could say he was ugly, like he has a snaggletooth and frizzy hair and teeth the color of sunflowers. He doesn't. In fact, he's the opposite of ugly, although I don't think I could ever bring myself to call him anything better. "Non-ugly" is about as good as I can manage. Alex Walsh is non-ugly. There. I said it, and it fits him perfectly.

"Have you come to sing?" Sophie asks him eagerly.

"Me?" He shakes his head. "No way. I am the world's worst singer. Believe me, I'll be doing you all a big favor by not singing tonight."

"Oh, it doesn't matter if you're no good at it," Sophie says. "I've been told I sound like a howler monkey up there, but I don't let it stop me from having some fun."

Alex blinks at her in surprise. "Who called you a howler monkey? That's a bit harsh, isn't it?"

"Oh, just some random guy. My point is that it doesn't matter if you sound like a primate. We're all here to have fun. Let off some steam."

"Howler monkeys aren't primates, you know," Alex says, and I roll my eyes. Trust him to get nitpicky. "Primates are gorillas, orangutans, chimps. We humans are primates."

I lift an eyebrow. "You're a biologist now, are you?"

He gives a modest shrug. "I volunteered at an orangutan sanctuary in Borneo a while back. I like animals, I guess."

"I didn't know you did that," Sophie says.

"Volunteering at an orangutan sanctuary sounds so cool, man," Jason says.

I keep my mouth shut. I don't want to hear about Alex doing good deeds.

"Anyway," Sophie says, "whether a howler monkey is a primate or not, my point is that it doesn't matter if you can't sing."

"Well, I can tell you one thing right now," Alex begins with a laugh. "There would have to be a pretty darn good reason for me to get up and sing at a karaoke bar."

"Like you had to do it to save the world from aliens or something, right?" Jason offers.

He is *such* a boy.

"Exactly. Sign me up for karaoke when the little green men turn up." He gives a self-satisfied smirk.

"Yeah, like you could save the world by singing karaoke," I scoff.

"We'll just have to wait and see, won't we?" His eyes are sparkling as he looks at me. "Whatever the reason, it would have to be something super important to get me up there on that stage. That's all I'm saying."

"Well, I guess you'll just have to sit back and enjoy the entertainment, Alex," Sophie says.

"Let me guess, Soph. In another life, you'd be a pop princess," Alex says with a chuckle.

Sophie grins. "How did you know? We all would, right, girls?"

"I'd go back in time and join ABBA," Erin pronounces.

"Yeah, me too," I agree.

Alex crinkles his brow. "Wouldn't you have to marry the guys in the band to join ABBA? And how would it work with the naming thing? Aren't the 'As' and the 'Bs' in the name the band members' first initials?"

I roll my eyes. "Are you always this pedantic?"

Erin is clearly impressed. "Look at you, knowing that level of ABBA trivia. What do you think, Darce? Should we let Alex join our band tonight?"

I open my mouth to say, "Heck no," when Alex beats me to it. "I think ABBA's probably more your thing than mine, Erin."

Taking his comment as the insult I'm certain it's intended to be, I cross my arms and glare at him. "Is ABBA's music not highbrow enough for you, Alex? I suppose you're into cool alternative music that makes you think deeply about the human condition."

His face breaks into one of his irritating smirks. "I'm not sure the Jonas Brothers would consider themselves commentators on the human condition, would you?"

"The Jonas Brothers?" I scoff. Alex "I'm-too-cool-for-school" Walsh is into boy bands? ABBA may be unabashed pop, just like the Jonas Brothers, but at least they're vintage, which lends them a certain edge, in my opinion. "That's not what I was expecting from you."

His eyes are so intense, they feel as though they're boring into me when he replies, "I'm full of surprises, Darcy."

"Is that so?"

He gives a slow nod, his eyes not leaving mine, his smirk stretching across his face. "I guess you could say I'm multi layered."

"Like an onion, right?"

"Sure," he shrugs, falling right into my trap.

"So, you're telling me that like an onion, you smell bad, you're overpowering, and you make people cry?"

I'm more than a little proud of my retort.

He leans closer to me, his laugh low. "Would you like to find out if that's true?" he asks so quietly only I can hear.

I blink at him as his words seep into my brain. Is he *flirting* with me? The guy I hate—and for very good reason, I might add—thinks it's perfectly acceptable to sit in my favorite karaoke bar and flirt with me over a discussion about fresh produce? The gall of the man!

Despite my outrage, my tummy does a weird little zingy thing, and I shift my butt to the very back of my seat. "I have absolutely no interest in finding out anything of the sort, thank you very much," I reply, trying to sound haughty and mildly shocked at his suggestive tone.

"I bet you that's not true."

Discomfited, I swallow, my throat tight. "It is, actually." I turn away from his gaze, pick up my glass and take a swig of my drink, and then another.

"You know, I do remember you and Erin singing an ABBA song a while back at the Cozy Cottage Open Mic Night. You were pretty good, from what I recall," he says. "You had the moves and everything."

I arch an eyebrow as I shoot him another glare. "We were better than just 'pretty good.' The audience loved us."

"I remember." Alex's eyes flash to mine.

I look away immediately. I'm not going to risk anything else that might bring on a return of that zingy feeling in my tummy. The last thing I'm going to do is reignite long-dead feelings for Alex Walsh, that's for sure.

He leans back in his seat. "You're super modest about your singing prowess, clearly."

"Clearly," I echo.

"Darce," Erin says, providing me with a much needed out from this disconcertingly flirtatious interaction with Alex.

I mean, what's up with *that?*

"Do you want to go upbeat with *Does Your Mother Know* or more laid back?"

"*Fernando?*" I suggest.

She beams at me. "*Fernando.*"

"I forgot to ask," Alex says to me. "How was your date with that guy at the café this week?"

"It was fine, thank you. We didn't gel though, and there's not a lot you can do about that." There's no freaking way he needs to know that we didn't gel on a gender-based level.

"We'll have to find someone else for you, babe," Erin says. "Pass me your phone."

"Do I have to?" I ask.

"You do," Sophie confirms as Erin says, "Come on, hand it over."

With more than a touch of reluctance, I pull my phone out of my purse and pass it to Sophie. Who knows? Maybe she'll have better luck finding a guy on there than me. My recent dating track record doesn't inspire any degree of confidence in my man-selection abilities.

Erin's eyes light up. "Oooh, are we going to 'cruise for men' on the Internet?" She shifts closer to Sophie, and they begin to scroll through my dating app.

"You make it all sound so tawdry," I complain. "And don't go swiping right on anyone. Just give me your top three recommendations, and I'll review them myself."

Sophie looks up at me. "So you'll do what? Reject them all?"

I cross my arms. "No," I say, sounding totally unconvincing.

"You three," Erin says as she points at Alex, Jason, and me, "talk amongst yourselves. Soph and I are on a mission here."

With my two girlfriends occupied with fixing my love life, I refill my glass with sparkling wine and ask Jason what it's like to be a full-fledged doctor these days.

"Seriously, the only thing that's really changed is Soph no longer gets to correct me when I call myself Doctor Christie."

"Which you do all the time, I bet," I say with a rueful smile.

"If I were a doctor, I'd claim bragging rights, too," Alex says.

Jason smiles at him. "Thank you."

"You're welcome, *Doctor* Christie."

I roll my eyes. Guys sticking together is so typical.

"I'm gonna go to the bar to order some fries. Does anyone want anything?" Jason asks us.

I shake my head as Alex replies, "No, I'm good, thanks."

"All right. BRB." Jason gets up from the table and heads to the bar.

With Erin and Sophie focused on trolling through potential dates on my phone, that leaves Alex and me sitting at the table in awkward silence.

Alex shifts his position in his chair, his eyes focused on

something across the room. After a moment, he says, "It's a shame it didn't work out with that guy." He turns to look at me. "The one you were drinking Americanos with at the café this week."

"As I said, we didn't gel, that's all."

"No gel, huh?"

"You either do or you don't." I shoot him a "what are you gonna do?" look and turn my attention to a nearby table where a group of older women is having a great time laughing and talking.

"So, you don't think it had anything to do with the fact the guy was gay?"

I whip my head back to gawk at him. "What? No!" My voice is more than a little pitchy. I readjust it and ask, "What makes you say that? Because he was so good looking? Or the fact that he dressed well? Because, you know, Alex, I would have thought a man like you would have been confident enough not to feel threatened by a guy like Devan."

Ha! That'll show him.

"Threatened?" He shakes his head. "No, it wasn't that. I'd say it was more the fact he asked me out."

I blink at him in disbelief. Well, not *total* disbelief. Devan did announce he was gay and ask if Alex was single, and Alex looks, well, the way he does (non-ugly, remember?), so it's not exactly out of the realms of possibility. But really, it's pretty on the nose. "He did?" A surprised giggle tries to burst out.

"After you left, he came back into the café. Told me I was hot and just his type. I've gotta say, it was quite the compliment. You know, from a good-looking guy who dresses well and all."

I put my hand over my mouth to stop from laughing and shake my head at Devan's brazen behavior. "He doesn't hang around, does he?"

"Nope. One minute he's outside on the street kissing you, and next, he's hitting on me."

My throat tightens. Not only is it deeply embarrassing that

kissing me confirmed Devan's suspicions, but also, according to point four on the No More Bad Dates Pact Rules of Engagement, physical contact at an Initial Meeting is strongly discouraged.

And I should know, I wrote the rules.

I twist my wine glass by the stem. "You saw that?"

"Darcy, I see everything that goes on at the café. I guess you could say it's one of my onion layers." He shoots me a smile.

"An onion layer, huh?"

"So someone once told me. Apparently, like an onion, I don't smell good, I can be overpowering, and I make people cry a lot."

I let out a laugh despite myself. "So, Onion Man, are you going to go on a date with him?" I ask.

"Heck yeah. He looks like Aquaman." His gaze locks with mine, and we share an amused smile.

"You'd make a cute couple."

He creases up his face. "Thank you?" We sit in silence for a moment, before he says, "So, this exhibition."

"You know you don't have to do it, even though you agreed to it. Seriously, there's no pressure."

"I got the impression your boss likes my work, what with all those air kisses and telling me how incredibly amazing I am."

"Are you going to tell me someone as beautiful and famous as Larissa Monroe fawning over you doesn't make you feel good?"

He lifts his shoulders in a shrug. "It's nice to get a compliment on your work, but the fame thing I couldn't care less about."

"Larissa will be very distressed to hear that."

"I'm sure she would," he replies with a laugh. "You know what? It'll be good for me to get back into exhibiting. Why don't you come over to my place and you can see what I've got?"

"Are you asking me to come up, and you'll 'show me your etchings,' Alex?"

He chortles. "Take it however you like, Darcy. But I do have a bunch of boxes of my photos at my place."

"Right." I twist my mouth and reiterate, "If you've changed your mind, I'm sure we can find another photographer."

He narrows his gaze. "Are you trying to talk me out of this, Darcy?"

"No, don't be silly," I lie.

Of course I'm trying to talk him out of this! Without Larissa here to keep happy, this is my chance to avoid having to work with the guy.

"Good, because I'm excited about it. I emailed Larissa some ideas this afternoon."

It's not the response I'm looking for. "So, your mind is set?"

"My mind is set."

"Great," I reply through gritted teeth.

So that's it. There's no way out. I'm working with Alex. I drain my glass, and we fall into silence, me churning with trepidation, and Alex? I steal a glance at him. Well, by the looks of him, he's more than happy with his decision.

Typical.

A woman dressed in a veil and a T-shirt that reads "Almost legal" wobbles up onto the stage.

"This should be interesting," he comments.

"Ten bucks says she sings *Like a Virgin*."

"I'm going for *Hopelessly Devoted to You*. She looks like the romantic type."

I examine the woman on the stage. She's swaying from side to side, her makeup is smudged, and a big, goofy grin is plastered across her face. "She looks less like the romantic type and more like the drunk type to me."

"You'll see," Alex replies smugly.

As the opening bars of *Hopelessly Devoted to You* kick in, I reach into my purse and begrudgingly pull out ten dollars. Alex wins again, just like he did back in high school. No surprises there. "Okay. How'd you know?"

He takes the money from me and pockets it. "I told you, she looks the romantic type. And *Hopelessly Devoted to You* is a sappy, romantic, frankly ridiculous song."

"Well, at least that's something we can agree on."

"Oh, my God." Erin shakes my arm, and I turn back to look at my friends. In my exchange with Alex, I'd almost forgotten they have been sitting at the table all this time, searching for a guy for me to date. "We have totally found the guy for you, girl! Look." She spins the phone around, and I'm met with an image of a very good-looking man staring back at me.

I take the phone from her and examine the image more closely. Dark cropped hair, much shorter than I usually go for in a guy, with kind eyes and a small, sexy grin. "He's got potential."

"Potential?" Erin replies. "He's totally hot!"

"Plus, he's smart. He's a dentist," Sophie adds.

Alex's eyebrows ping up. "So, he spends all his time poking around in other people's mouths? I've never got why anyone would want to do that. No offense to dentists, of course."

Sophie shakes her head. "Not all his time. He's got a list of hobbies, too. His name is Seth Heikkinen. I think that's how you pronounce it."

I screw up my nose. "He sounds like a beer."

Sophie ignores me. "He lists his hobbies as being into yachting, which is very cool, as well as horses and show jumping."

"Horses and show jumping? Huh." I've always liked horses. When I was a kid, I pleaded with my parents to get me a pony. When I ended up with a My Little Pony that birthday, and the next, and the next, it eventually dawned on me it would never happen. Although I loved my horse toys, they could never replace the real thing.

"You love horses, Darce," Erin says unnecessarily. "This guy could be so great for you."

"And show jumping is super fancy," Sophie says. "The British royals are into show jumping. There's that big event every year. Full to the brim of classy, rich, horsey people."

"I can see you two riding off into the sunset together, your matching tiaras on top of your heads," Jason says with a smarmy grin.

I bite my lip as I stare at the screen. Sure, he looks fantastic, but after my last date, I'm a little nervous about putting myself out there again.

Erin clearly detects my reluctance. "Nothing ventured, nothing gained, right?"

Before I change my mind, I swipe the app. A little ripple of excitement rolls through my belly. Maybe, just maybe this guy might be one of the good guys. "Okay, done." I place my phone on the table in front of me just as the bride-to-be finishes butchering Olivia Newton-John's seventies hit to loud applause and cheers from her friends at a neighboring table.

"We're up, girl," Erin says, standing up beside me. "Time to get your ABBA on."

I bounce out of my chair and head to the stage with my fellow ABBA-devotee. As the opening chords to *Fernando* play, I can't help but smile to myself. I've got myself a potential new guy.

Maybe things are finally beginning to look up for me?

Chapter 5

There are a few things I know about myself, things that I've known for a long, long time, things I can rely on. Such as (in no particular order):

    1.   I like singing ABBA songs at karaoke, probably a little too much (and lately, I've begun to wonder whether singing at Jojo's every Saturday night with my girlfriends may be contributing to me still being single).

    2.   Even though I'd never admit it to Larissa, I find the color blue totally boring and would much prefer it if we could wear pink every now and then. Barbie pink, to be specific. Ironically, of course.

    3.   I do not like Alex Walsh.

People may not think so if they knew about the whole Barbie pink thing, but I am a sane, normal person who doesn't have any masochistic tendencies. None whatsoever, unless you count Hot Yoga (holding body-contorting poses in three-thousand-degree heat is pretty borderline, I've got to admit). So, as I sit at my desk, researching photographers, I know I need to find someone spectacular to persuade Larissa to drop Alex like a wet, diseased rat. And yes, I am enjoying that image right now.

All I've got to do is find another photographer whose work "speaks" to Larissa to divert her attention away from Alex, and I'll be rid of him forever. I call it my New Shiny Toy Plan, which works with toddlers and celebrities alike. Well, with Larissa, anyway.

And yes, I know, Alex said he wants to do it, and he said he'd already sent some ideas to Larissa. But this is my last chance to be rid of him, and I'm throwing everything at it.

I pull up another website from my search results and begin to scroll through. Some of the photographs on the site are really quite beautiful, and I take some screenshots of the best and send them to the printer. With a small smile, I note the name of the photographer and his contact details in my Labrador puppy notebook.

My eyes flick to my list. After all my trawling of the Internet, I've only come up with three options to replace Alex, but I'm hopeful one of these will do the trick. Then it'll officially be bye-bye, Alex, and hello, happiness.

I collect the screenshots from the printer, grab a (blue) dress I picked up from the cleaners on my way into the office today, and knock on Larissa's door. "It's almost time to go, Larissa," I say.

"Come in, Darcy," comes a small, muffled voice.

I push open the door and walk in to find Larissa on the floor in an advanced yoga pose that makes her look like her limbs are made of rubber bands. Despite punishing myself in Hot Yoga, I can only dream of being able to bend myself into that kind of pose. A croissant-meets-a-human-suitcase kind of thing. My body hurts just looking at her.

She uncrosses her limbs and stretches up toward the ceiling, standing on her tiptoes, then lets out a deep breath of air. "Oh, that feels so much better."

"I've got a couple of things for you before you go to the event this morning," I say as I hang the dress up on a hook and pull the plastic sheath from it.

"What are they?" She slips her shirt off, and I hand her the dress, which she pulls on over her head in one effortless, graceful movement.

"I've been doing some research into options for the gallery."

Her face lights up. "Please tell me you got the wallabies."

"Larissa, we've been over this. Auckland Zoo won't lease wallabies out for events."

"They should! Imagine the possibilities."

Imagine the poop.

"I think it's not considered ethical practice by the animal welfare people."

"Oh, yes. Of course. Animal welfare is an extremely important issue to me."

"I'm talking about the actual photographs for the opening exhibit." I hand her the collection of screenshots and hold my breath. "Here are some examples of some photographers' work. Personally, I really like them, and I'm sure we could find something in there that resonates with you."

Please like them. Please like them.

She leafs through them and then looks back up at me. "Why are you showing me these? We've already got our photographer, and his work is incredible. Although I wish his name was Alex Alex. It's better than Alex Walsh, don't you think?" She stretches her hand out, and I reluctantly take the printouts back.

"But some of these are just as amazing." I pull out an image of a couple of laughing, wizened old women sitting on the steps of a beautiful old church in some place that looks like it could be Greece or Italy. Some country where they have happy, wizened old women and beautiful old churches. "To me, this photograph is all about how age may wither us, but laughter remains . . . particularly with our old friends . . . you know, at churches."

I'm doing my best to channel my inner Larissa here. It's not working.

She takes the photo back and examines it for a moment. "I do like a positive aging message," she says, hope whooshing through me. No Alex Walsh, here I come! "Although, between you and me, these women could do with a spot or two of Botox. Don't you think? The eyelids on this one here seem to have completely eclipsed her eyes. What kind of life can that be? Not being able to see because of your Shar-Pei folds. She must need little sticks to hold them up, like a Salvador Dali painting." She shudders. "Nightmare."

"She looks happy to me, like she's old but happy, so everything is all right with the world," I offer hopefully.

"No." She thrusts the photograph back at me. "I want to stick with what we've got. Alex Walsh's work speaks to me."

I let out a defeated puff of air. When something "speaks to" Larissa, there's no way to talk her out of it. So many things have "spoken" to her since I've been her assistant. Rocks, crystals, ponchos, even a kitten spoke to her once, which made me wonder whether she fancied herself as a bit of a Dr. Doolittle type until I remembered it wasn't *literally* speaking to her. (In my defense, it was meowing a whole lot at the time.)

I always get an image of whatever it is that's currently "speaking" to her with a large mouth, jabbering away. In my lighter moments, I wonder what they say to her? "How's it going?" "You look familiar." "Why are you always in blue?" Whatever it is Alex's photographs have said to her, I'd like to make them shut the heck up, that's for sure.

"The thing is, Darcy, I don't care about those other photographers' work. I care about the work of the photographer that touched me here." She pats her chest. "I need Alex Walsh in this gallery. No one else."

"But—" I give up. My hopes are dashed. My New Shiny Toy Plan has been well and truly foiled, and now I've got no choice but to work with Alex. "Sure. I got it." Knowing when I'm beat, I ball up the images I searched online for hours to find.

"What was the other thing?" she asks me as she sits at her desk.

"I got that info you wanted on wheatgrass supplements. I emailed it to you."

"What would I do without you?"

Have wallabies dressed as waiters wandering around at gallery openings?

"I'm here to help, Larissa. It's my job."

"Remind me to get you some of these mini wheatgrass shots. You simply rip off the lid and drink them in one. They will change your life."

"Wheatgrass shots sound—" Terrible? Horrible? Vomit-inducing? "—really great. Thank you." I paste on a smile.

"While you're reading that info I sent you, I'm going to pop out for half an hour. Is that okay?"

She knots her brows together. "Where are you going? What if I need you?"

"You won't. I'll get your kale smoothie and acai berry granola before I go, and I'll be back before we need to leave to get to the venue for your keynote speech."

"Ooh, while you're out, can you get me something? I want to try skyr. Everyone's talking about it."

"Skyr?" I question.

"It's Icelandic," she replies, completely unhelpfully, and returns her attention to her laptop screen.

Sure, that narrows it down for me.

"How do you spell it?"

She spells it out for me.

"Skyr. Got it. I'll bring you some back."

"What are you scurrying off to do without me, then?"

I allow myself a little smile. The show jumping guy Erin and Darcy found me online has agreed to meet me for an Initial Meeting over coffee today. "I've got a first date."

— ♥ —

60

Okay, I know. Officially, it's an Initial Meeting I'm rushing off to right now, but I didn't want to have to go into the whole No More Bad Dates Pact thing with Larissa. She'd want to know everything about it. Or worse: she might want to join.

The very thought makes me quake in my heels.

I glance at my watch as I push my way through into the busy café. Four minutes late, dammit. Along with being super organized, I take pride in being on time, all the time. Turning up late before you've even met the guy is not exactly a positive message to send a prospective boyfriend, is it?

We're meeting at a café near my work. Not only do I have a short time before I've got to get back to Larissa, but the last thing I want to do is go to the Cozy Cottage Café and have Alex breathing down my neck as I meet another guy. Particularly if that guy ends up hitting on him after I've left.

But lightning doesn't strike in the same place twice, right?

At least, that's what I'm hoping.

I scan the room, searching for Seth Heikkinen. He said he'd be in a white button-up business shirt with no tie, and now that I look around me, half the men in the coffee house are wearing just that.

I bite the inside of my lip as I scan the room. Why did I agree to meet this guy at business person coffee time in downtown Auckland?

"Excuse me? Are you Darcy?" a smooth, cultured-sounding voice says behind me.

I turn around and look up into an open, friendly face, a pair of hazel eyes, and a tentative smile. He's got a hint of Bradley Cooper to him, just like in his photograph. "Seth?"

"That's me. It's great to meet you." He leans down and lightly brushes his lips against my cheek, and I catch the aroma of his aftershave. Subtle, woody, with a hint of vanilla. Nice.

"You, too," I reply with a light blush.

We grin at one another like we're in some kind of daze

before he breaks it with, "Can I buy you a coffee?"

"Oh, sure. Sorry, I was just thinking about how you look a little like Bradley Cooper." Oops. My cheeks heat up another notch with embarrassment. "Did I just say that out loud?"

He lets out a light laugh. "You did, but it's okay. It's not every day I get told I look like a Hollywood heartthrob by a beautiful girl."

Seth-slash-Bradley thinks I'm beautiful?

"Actually, I might have tea," I say as tingles start zinging around inside. "Early Grey, please."

"An Earl Grey tea coming right up." He turns to the server and orders our beverages, and then we find a table.

"These things are always a little awkward, aren't they?" he says across the table.

I push memories of my last date from my mind. "They can be, I guess."

"So, let's break the ice. What are the top three things I need to know about you, Darcy Evans?" he asks.

"Seriously?" I guffaw. "You're putting me on the spot before I've even had my first sip of tea? That's totally not fair."

The corners of his mouth lift. "What would be fair?"

"I don't know. You could start by asking me where I grew up, what I like to do on weekends, whether I'm a cat person or a dog person. Things like that."

"Okay." He leans his elbows on the table, trains his eyes on me, and tilts his head as though he's about to say something super serious. "Tell me, Darcy, where did you grow up, what do you like to do on weekends, and are you a cat person or a dog person?"

"Auckland, karaoke, and dogs." I shoot him a triumphant smile. "You?"

Our server delivers our coffees and we thank her. Once she's gone, he fixes me with his gaze again. "Not Auckland, definitely not karaoke, and I like both cats and dogs equally."

"Oh, no you don't. No one likes cats and dogs equally. You're either more one or the other. So, what is it? Cats or dogs?"

He shrugs. "Both."

"Are you going to be difficult about this?" I tease. "Research shows humans are either cat people or dog people, and their preference says a lot about a person."

"Oh, *research* says it, does it?" His eyes sparkle.

"It does."

Oh, I'm so getting the feels for this guy!

"If I'm a dog person, does that mean I like to run around with a stick in my mouth and sniff other dogs' butts? Because gross." He pulls a face.

A giggle bubbles up inside me. "I think it might be a little subtler than that."

"That's good, because when it comes to animals, I'm more of a horse person, anyway."

"Do you have a horse?"

"I have several, actually. Yoda, Leia, and recently, I acquired Fin."

"Star Wars?" I don't know whether it's cute to name your horses after characters in a sci-fi movie series or just a bit weird. But I'm being open-minded here. It's officially cute — until further notice.

He nods. "Guilty. I've been a Star Warrior for years."

"A Star Warrior?"

"A huge fan of the franchise."

"Got it. Like a Trekkie."

He laughs. "But much better."

I grin at him. "Clearly."

"I, ah, lost one of my horses a while back. Han."

"Han Solo?" I question, taking a stab in the dark at the horse's full name.

Seth nods. "He was a beautiful Thoroughbred with a silky dark coat and a little white mark right here." He draws an invisible line with his finger on his forehead and down his nose.

"I'm sorry. Losing your horse would be hard."

"I've got a picture of him I could show you." He pulls his

phone out and starts to scroll through his images until he finds what he's looking for. "Here." He turns the phone around, and I admire the horse.

"What a gorgeous horse. I'm sorry you lost him. Do you still show jump?"

"Oh, yes. I love it. Although I don't do the same types of shows I did with Han. I couldn't, you know?"

I nod sagely. This guy clearly loved his horse.

"Now, Darcy, tell me why you're a dog person and if it has anything to do with the squeaky chew toys."

I laugh. Wow, this guy is easy to talk to. And cute, too.

We get to know one another over our beverages, joking and laughing together until we get to the tricky end of our Initial Meeting, the point where I need to tell him about the Vetting Process.

"Let me get this straight. You need me to meet your friends and answer a bunch of personal questions before we can go out again?"

"I know it sounds crazy, but, well, I've not exactly had the best dating track record."

"Really?"

"Try terrible, horrible, awful. Take your pick. They all work."

"Will I get quizzed about a bunch of things?"

"You will, but it's just to make sure you're not going to turn into a weirdo or something," I say with a forced laugh. I hold my breath and cross my fingers under the table in the hope he's anything but a weirdo.

"I'm afraid I wouldn't be much of a weirdo. I'm a dentist," he says without a hint of irony — and with a perfect smile.

"I'm sure you'll sail through, no problem."

The skin around his eyes crinkles as his smile grows. "I'd be happy to meet your friends. I think we've got something here."

I beam back at him, Seth Heikkinen, show jumper with the *Star Wars* horses. "Me too."

Chapter 6

The evening of Seth's Vetting arrives, and I'd love to say I'm taking it all in stride, but truth be told, I'm as worried as a Real Housewife when her plastic surgeon runs out of Botox (although not as wrinkly, of course).

All that needs to happen between now and about forty-five minutes from now is for Seth to pass, and then we can sail off into the sunset together for our very first date.

I'm not going to lie; it took me a crazy amount of time to get ready tonight. With Erin perched on my bed, acting as advisor, I tried on at least half my non-blue wardrobe — because I never wear blue anymore when I'm not at work — until I finally settled on a little black dress with a very flattering neckline. It makes me look feminine and cool at the same time. Which is a hard thing to achieve, you know.

The fact that it was the first dress I'd tried on, as Erin very helpfully pointed out, is absolutely irrelevant. It's perfect, and I hope Seth thinks so, too. Because I'm not going to mess around with this. No way. Good guys don't come along that often. Or ever, really, in my depressing recent experience.

Erin and I arrive at O'Reilly's, our favorite Irish pub, and we spot Sophie with her boyfriend, Jason, at the bar. It's early so there's only a smattering of people in the place.

"Hello, hello!" I say brightly when we reach the loved-up couple.

"Hey, babe. You look gorgeous!" Sophie gives me a quick hug. "Don't worry, it'll just be us girls. Jason's not hanging around. Are you, honey?"

"Nope. I've got a date with destiny. Or a mate, to be more specific," he says with a grin.

"Jas is in the throes of a full-force bromance," Sophie explains.

"Sounds like fun," Erin replies with a grin.

"It's not a bromance. We're just a couple of guys who like to hang out, that's all," he protests.

Sophie rolls her eyes and mouths "bromance" to us, and I laugh.

"Not a bromance, and I'm changing the subject now," Jason says in mock irritation. "Erin. You must know Nick Zachary, right? He plays for the Hawks."

Erin throws her eyes to the ceiling. "Don't remind me. Nick Zachary isn't exactly at the top of my list of favorite things."

Erin has worked as a Sponsorship Account Manager for Auckland City Hawks since she graduated, and she doesn't exactly hold its players in high regard. She thinks they're a bunch of egomaniacs, even if many of them are very talented players and the team currently holds the coveted Carter Cup.

"Why not? He's an incredible player. He's super quick and racks up the points for the team. He's one of *my* favorite things," Jason replies.

"Jas, you are rugby mad," Sophie says with a shake of her head. "But I've got to admit, Nick Zachary is very good looking. He does those car ads, right?"

"Ooh, *that's* Nick Zachary? Oh, yeah, he's hot," I say.

Erin shakes her head. "His ego matches the size of the billboards he's on, believe me."

"They're calling him the 'bad boy of rugby' on Twitter today," Jason explains.

"That sounds about right." Erin sniffs then turns to me. "Are you ready for the vetting?"

Sophie lifts an eyebrow. "That's an abrupt change of subject, Erin."

She shrugs. "I get enough of rugby at work. I don't need it when I'm off the clock."

"Fair call, babe." Sophie looks my way. "What's Seth really like? He seemed like your perfect match on the dating app."

"Oh, he's great. I'll be amazed if we spot any red flags," I reply with a broad grin. "Thanks for finding him for me."

"You're welcome," Sophie replies. "It's all part of the No More Bad Dates service."

Jason cocks an eyebrow. "Really? You're matchmaking now?"

"Only for Darce, right, Erin?" Sophie replies.

Erin nods. "Darcy's first two guys weren't up to scratch, so we stepped in to save the day."

"You're both very confident about this," Jason says.

Sophie shrugs. "Maybe this is what we should have been doing all along? I feel like I could be a good matchmaker."

"Yes!" Erin says with glee. "We could hire ourselves out. We could make millions! Well, maybe not millions. I'm not really sure how lucrative matchmaking is."

"How about we start with Darcy and see where it takes us?" Sophie offers.

Erin nods. "Good plan, partner."

Sophie places her hand on Erin's shoulder. "And don't forget, we need to find you a good guy, too."

Erin sighs. "Don't remind me. All of you will be married with six kids between you before I find someone to date."

"Babe, you work with oodles of men every day. You've got a smorgasbord to choose from," I say. Erin's surrounded by hot, buff, sporty guys all day, every day.

"I've told you, I don't want to date a jock," Erin says.

"Because they're all so hot?" Sophie questions.

She pulls a face. "Because they're all so arrogant. Professional sportsmen have women throwing themselves at them all the time. I've got zero interest in competing with them."

"Oh, look. Your new BFF is here, Jas." Sophie elbows her boyfriend in the arm.

I turn to see who this new BFF of Jason's is, only to come face to face with Alex. Again.

Seriously? What is it with this guy? If he's not in the room with me, he's being talked about. It's like he's back here in the city for the sole purpose of infiltrating my world so he can torment me. And I tell you, if that's his plan, he'd succeeding.

I watch as he greets everyone in the group—hugs for Erin and Sophie, a fist bump for Jas—until he gets to me. He does a formal head bow and says, "Darcy," a small smile on his lips. His tone is wry but has that hint of amusement he always seems to add that makes me twist my mouth in frustration.

Oh, he so enjoys tormenting me.

"Alex," I reply, ramping up the frost factor. There's no hint of amusement in my voice, thank you very much, and I definitely do not give him a smile.

I feel my friends' eyes on me, so I toss my hair and plaster on a breezy smile as I announce, "Did you know that Alex is going to be the first-ever exhibitor at Larissa's new gallery?"

Alex narrows his gaze. "So, that's all decided, is it?"

I feel a flicker of hope. "Unless you decided to back out?" I know I'm dicing with death here. Larissa's got her heart set on Alex, but if I tell her he's the one who backed out, well, then there'd be nothing I could do about it. I hold my breath.

One of his irritating smiles teases at the edges of his mouth. "And give up the chance to work with you, Darcy?" He looks up at my friends and says, "I'm excited about being Larissa's first exhibitor, and I'm sure Darcy and I will make a great team." He slides his eyes to mine. "We'll be spending a lot of time together. A *lot* of time."

I throw him daggers as I hold my less than genuine smile in place. He thinks he's so smart, tormenting me like this. Well, he's not. He's a jerk and . . . and . . . oh! He makes my blood boil.

"Well, this is going to be interesting," Jason says as he surveys us both. "I've always had the distinct sense you two don't exactly get on."

"Us?" I say with a forced laugh. "Oh, it'll be fine. I'm a total professional. I can work with anyone."

"Even me?" Alex asks.

I lick my lips and smooth my hair back. "Even you. In fact, as we discussed, I would like to come over to your apartment to look through your catalog of photos, please. We need to move on this project quick smart, you know."

Quick smart? What am I, a P.E. teacher from the '60s now?

Alex's lips lift into a fresh whisper of a smile. "I'd be more than happy to show you my work. Does Sunday suit?"

I extend my hand. "Absolutely. Sunday suits perfectly."

He looks at my hand questioningly for a beat before he takes it in his, and we shake.

I flick my eyes between my friends' faces, smiling pleasantly. "You'll all have to come to the opening. I'm sure Alex and I will put together a wonderful exhibition."

There's a general murmur of "yes" and "we'd love to" among them.

There. That shows them how professional I can be. How I can push my own personal feelings about Alex aside for the common good. (Well, to keep Larissa happy, so it's really more for *my* good. Happy Larissa, happy assistant, remember?) Alex might not be my favorite person, but I can still work with him and be perfectly civil.

"Alex, I'm really happy for you. This is such exciting news," Sophie says, giving her cousin a hug. "Mom said you haven't exhibited for ages."

Alex lets out a puff of air. "New leaf, I guess."

New leaf? What is he talking about? He's a barista who's getting a first big break thanks to Larissa Monroe. That's not a new leaf; that's a dream come true.

"Well, I think it's awesome, man," Jason says, slapping Alex on his back.

"How about some drinks?" Sophie offers, and we place our orders with the barmaid.

"When is Seth due to get here?"

"I told him eight." I glance at my watch. 7:45. "Only fifteen minutes to settle my nerves."

"Have some wine," Erin suggests.

"He's got to be better than the guys Sophie chose before she saw the light and realized she was in love with me." Jason slips an arm around Sophie's shoulders. "Remember? One guy wanted to fatten her up, and another thought he was a merman."

"A merman?" Alex says with a chortle.

"He didn't think he was a merman," Sophie corrects. "He wanted to be one."

"The difference being what, exactly?" Jason asks.

"I'm not sure," Sophie replies, and they share one of their loved-up smiles.

"Can you all please back the bus up a block or ten for me here?" Alex says. "Why are you vetting some poor guy?"

As my friends explain the No More Bad Dates Pact to Alex, I concentrate on quelling my nerves with wine. In record time, I've finished my first glass and am ordering another. It does the trick. I begin to relax.

"OMG. There he is at twelve o'clock." I jerk my head toward the other side of the bar. My nerves kick up a notch, despite the fact they must be doing a backstroke in all that Chardonnay by now.

"Oh, he looks so nice," Erin gushes. "Just like his photo."

"And he's got horses, you said?" Sophie asks as she sizes him up.

"Yup, three of them."

Sophie lets out a whistle. "Cute and loaded. Total score."

"I'm not sure, but he is a successful dentist. He's got his own practice, actually." I feel a burst of pride.

"This is definitely our cue to leave, man. Unless, of course, you want to stick around to torture this guy, too," Jason says to Alex. "But believe me, it's not pretty."

Alex knits his eyebrows together. "I feel kinda sorry for him. Does he know what he's getting himself into here?" He nods at us three girls.

Jason shakes his head. "I hear you."

"Poor shmuck," Alex says.

"Yeah," Jason agrees.

What is this, some sort of brotherhood?

"You should be feeling sorry for *us*," I protest. "We're the ones who've had to date jerks and weirdos. All we're trying to do here is protect ourselves, you know."

Erin says, "Mm-hm," with a nod as Sophie crosses her arms and says, "Exactly."

"See, you two? We don't need you. We are quite capable of doing this on our own," I say with satisfaction.

"We know when we're not wanted," Alex replies, his hands in the air.

"Shall we go? That game of pool isn't going to play itself," Jason says to Alex.

"Sure thing." Alex stands and then turns back to me. "Hey, Darcy? Go easy on the guy, okay?"

Go easy on him? Who does he think he is?

"Thank you *so* much for the advice," I reply, my voice positively oozing sarcasm. "I'm quite certain he'll pass. He's one of the good guys. Unlike some people who don't know how to treat a woman."

Alex's response is to flash me a parting grin before he and Jason say goodbye and leave us girls to it.

Darcy Evans: one. Alex Walsh: minus forty-four-thousand million.

"I'll wave him over," I say as I raise my hand in the air.

Seth sees me, smiles, and makes his way over to our table. After planting a kiss on my cheek, just as he did at our Initial

Meeting, he turns to my friends. "Hi, ladies. I'm Seth Heikkinen. It's great to meet you both."

Erin and Sophie say their hellos, and we all take our seats.

"So, how does this work, exactly? Are there thumbscrews and interrogation lights, or have you got a fold-up rack to torture me on in one of your purses?" His smile is cute and playful, and I can't help but smile back at him.

"No torture weapons," Sophie replies. Her smile drops as she adds, "Unless that's something you're into?" She darts me a concerned look.

He laughs. It's low and gentle and rumbles right through me, making my tummy tingle, just like it did at the café. "No worries there. What's that saying? I'm a lover, not a fighter."

"Good to know. Can I get you a drink?" I offer.

"You're not sticking around for this?" he asks.

I glance at my friends. "I'll let them start without me. It takes the pressure off a little."

"In that case, I'll have a Heineken, thanks."

Sophie nudges me under the table. "A Heineken for Seth Heikkinen. It's got a certain symmetry, don't you think?"

"I guess it does," he replies. "Although technically my last name is Finnish, and Heineken is Dutch."

I spring up from my seat. "A Dutch Heineken coming right up."

As I turn to leave, Sophie begins with, "This won't hurt a bit, Seth. We promise."

"Go easy on me," he laughs.

After ordering his beer, I lean up against the bar and watch Seth and my friends. Erin and Sophie look very serious as they concentrate on something Seth is saying. My insides twist at the possibility it may be something bad. Before I can stop it, my mind begins to run rampant, coming up with a bunch of scenarios.

      1. He could be into weird things.

      2. He could be mean to his girlfriends, ignoring them or not taking them to nice places or even two-timing them.

3. Heck, he could be a total sociopath, pretending to be a nice, normal guy, out to meet innocent girls like me and lure them into a life of crime. We'd have to skip the country and live in Mexico under pseudonyms, riding donkeys everywhere and eating burritos for the rest of our lives.

Yup, I hear it. I've become a drama queen, even though the eating burritos part does sound pretty good. But if you'd had my terrible dating track record, I bet you'd be the same. Married guys pretending they're single, guys who kiss me to confirm they're gay, you name it. (And yes, I know that only happened once, but it was very off-putting.)

I pay the barmaid for the beer and make my way through the pub to Seth and my friends.

As I take my seat, Seth is talking. ". . . because that's the thing with trust: once it's gone, it's very hard to get back."

"You are so right," Erin says, a look of compassion on her pretty face. "We're so sorry you went through that. Aren't we, Soph?"

Sophie nods in agreement.

I'm aching to know what terrible thing Seth has been through. "What were you guys talking about?"

"Seth was telling us about a girlfriend who wasn't at all supportive when his Thoroughbred horse died. She left him, can you believe?" Erin says.

"Seriously?" I ask. "That's horrible."

Seth places his hand on mine. "I have a feeling you get me. And yes, I know that sounds a bit much. I mean, we only just met. But, I hope I'm right."

I do, too.

"I guess we'll have to get to know one another some more and see," I reply, trying to be pragmatic while my heart soars high above the clouds.

"Oh, come on, Darce. Where's the romance in your soul?" Erin, the romantic one of our little trio, demands.

"I'm plenty romantic," I protest. "I'm just cautious, that's all."

Seth raises his hands in the air. "Hey, I get that. I'm exactly the same. You don't want to dive into something before you know the full facts. You're just being rational, thinking things through. It's another thing to like about you."

Happiness bubbles up inside me. This guy is the real deal.

"Okay, now that we've established that you're a decent human being, can you tell us what you do to show a girl you like her?" Sophie asks.

"How about meet her friends to get asked mildly uncomfortable questions over a beer at O'Reilly's?" Seth asks with a glint in his eye.

Erin lets out a laugh. "Great answer."

"How about a girl you're already dating," I ask. "How do you show her you care?"

"Well, let me give you some examples. There was this girl I'd been dating for a while who loved music. Now, I don't have a musical bone in my body, but I really liked her and wanted to impress her. So, I bought a guitar and had secret music lessons. Once I was good enough, I took her on a picnic in a park, pulled out my guitar, and played one of her favorite songs."

We are all on the edge of our seats, listening to his romantic story.

"And?" Erin asks.

"And she seemed to appreciate it," he replies with a self-deprecating shrug. "Not that I think I was any good, of course."

Impossibly romantic and modest. Could this guy get any more perfect?

And the answer to that question turns out to be a big, fat "yes!" when Seth tells us his next story. "Another time, I didn't know this girl very well, but I wanted to ask her out. I found out from her friends that she loved peonies. You know, those flowers that look like oversized roses?"

We nod. We're girls, we know what peonies look like.

"I bought as many as I could find and delivered them personally to her work with a card that said, 'Will you go to dinner with me?'"

Yup, I've swooned. It's official.

"Forget Darcy. Will you date me?" Sophie says to him.

"I think your boyfriend might have a thing or two to say about that, Soph," Erin quips.

"Dammit. I forgot about him," she says with a rueful grin.

"One more thing," I begin. "I never thought I'd need to ask this of a guy, but just to make sure . . . do you think you might be, I don't know . . . gay?"

My friends shoot me startled looks.

Seth almost sprays a mouthful of beer over the table. Lucky for him, he manages to swallow it. "No," he replies with a surprised laugh. He tilts his head. "Why would you ask that? We met on a dating site. For straight people."

"No reason." I avoid my friends' gazes. "Just being thorough."

"Well, now that you've answered Darcy's *unexpected* question," Erin says, "I don't know about you two, but I think I've heard enough."

"Yup," Sophie confirms.

I allow myself a small smile. "Totally."

Seth looks between us. "So, do I get the verdict now or do you make me wait on tenterhooks?"

My eyes dart between my friends, my excitement building inside me as I see the looks on their faces.

I knew it the moment I met him: Seth Heikkinen is one of the good guys. And I'm the lucky girl who found him. With Erin and Sophie's help, of course.

I turn to Seth. "Would you mind if I asked you one more question?" I ask.

"Sure. Why not."

"Would you like to go out with me on a date right now?" I hold my breath, my heart rate picking up a notch.

His wide grin tells me all I need to know.

Chapter 7

We've just finished devouring our delicious pasta dishes at a cute, little romantic Italian place a couple of blocks from O'Reilly's when Seth says, "I'm so glad I passed the interrogation."

I wipe my mouth with my cloth napkin. "I am, too."

"You know, Darcy, you are so easy to talk to." His smile is warm as he gazes across the table at me. He lifts the bottle of white wine out of the ice bucket beside our table and tops up my glass.

I beam at him. "Thank you," I reply with a blush, "for the wine and the compliment."

His smile lights up his handsome face. "You're welcome."

We gaze at one another like a couple of goofy teenagers for a moment. Thoughts bounce around my brain like ping pong balls.

This is so nice.

I made the right choice.

Seth Heikkinen is the guy for me.

"You're a total champ for meeting my friends and letting them quiz you like they did."

"That was nothing. I've had to deal with people questioning me about my choices before, and I always think what it comes down to is that you've got to know who you are. Be confident. Trust in yourself. Do you know what I mean?"

I sip my wine, admiring his confidence. Unlike Alex's overt, in-your-face cockiness, Seth has a quiet self-assurance that isn't at all in-your-face. "I sure do know what you mean."

"I knew it. You and I are totally *sympatico*."

"That sounds like an Italian dessert," I joke.

"I guess it does. Speaking of which, I know you probably won't have any, but would you mind if I order some dessert? The *tiramisu* here is out of this world."

"I love *tiramisu*. Let's order one each."

His eyebrows ping up in surprise. "You eat dessert?"

"Well, yes. Is that weird to you?"

He shakes his head with gusto. "It's awesome. My last girlfriend didn't eat much at all. Mostly just bird seeds and carrots."

"That sounds super delicious," I joke.

"Yeah, if you're a bird or a rabbit." He reaches across the table and takes my hand in his. "I love that you eat dessert."

"Er, thanks." What else can I say? I know if I didn't enjoy my food so much, I'd be a size smaller and could probably contort myself into some of those extreme yoga positions Larissa manages with ease. But in my opinion, life's too short to worry about that kind of crap. And anyway, it would be my own personal hell to watch my date eat *tiramisu* without having some for myself.

"Do you eat birdseed and carrots when you're not on a date?" he asks.

"Carrots, yes, because apparently, they're meant to help me see better at night. Although I've begun to suspect that's just propaganda put out by the carrot farmers because my eyesight is as good at night as it's always been."

"Right?"

"And as for birdseed, that would be a hard no."

"Good to know." He waves at the waitress, who takes our order for two *tiramisu*. "So, on top of all your other qualities, would you say you have an open mind?"

"I guess I do. In what way though?"

"Let me put it this way. If you see a spade, is that all you see?"

I knit my brows together. "Err, I'm not sure what you mean."

"If you're in a gardening shed and you pick up a spade, is a spade all you see, or do you see what it represents: possibilities."

I blink at him. Why are we now talking about gardening tools, and how the heck did our conversation about dessert take this turn for the weird?

I need to think fast. By the eager look on his face, I can tell this is some sort of test of my character or something, and I want to make a good impression on him. I channel my inner Larissa when I reply. "I guess I could see that a spade could help you realize your gardening vision. In that way, a spade is much more than a spade."

He leans back in his seat, shaking his head, a broad smile on his handsome Bradley Cooper face. "You see? You totally get it. A spade is so much more than just a spade."

I beam at him. This must mean I passed! "Exactly."

He leans toward me and takes my hand in his once more. "Do you know what, Darcy?"

"What?"

"I think I want you to meet my horses."

"You do?"

It's not quite meeting the friends or the parents, but it's a great start. And his horses are clearly important to him.

He strokes the back of my hand, which sends tingles shooting up my arm. "I know it's pretty soon, what with tonight being our first official date and all, but there's something really special about you, Darcy Evans. I want to share my passion with you."

My heart expands, warming my chest. *Yes! This is going so well!* "That would be wonderful."

"I've got a show jumping event coming up. Would you like to come see me compete?"

"I would love that. I adore horses."

"And a spade is so much more than just a spade."

I nod. We're back to gardening tools? I thought we'd moved on to less, well, peculiar topics.

"Next Friday at the Windsor Equestrian Centre. I'll get you some tickets so you can bring some friends."

"Ooh, that sounds royal. That would be amazing. Thanks."

"I'm sure I'll have my best event ever, knowing you're there to cheer me on." He lifts my hand to his lips and kisses it like an old-fashioned gentleman.

#Swoon.

"I bet you look fantastic in your equestrian outfit," I say with a flush.

He gives a modest shrug. "I guess I look the part."

I imagine him in a smart black jacket, tan riding pants, and black boots, sitting atop a stallion. He's every inch the dashingly handsome gentleman who can sweep me off my feet. And yes, I know this isn't very modern, independent, I-can-do-it-for-myself-thank-you-very-much of me, but sometimes, a girl simply wants to be swept off her feet by a hot guy on a horse, you know?

"This looks so good," I say as the waitress delivers our desserts, my mouth watering at the sight of the layers of coffee-dipped ladyfingers and mascarpone cream topped with shaved chocolate.

"No birdseed or carrot sticks in sight."

We grin at one another over our plates before Seth says, "Well, what are we waiting for? Dig in."

I take my first mouthful and it's just as delicious as it looks. "Mmm, this is so good."

"I know, right? Did you know *tiramisu* means 'cheer me up' in Italian?"

"I did not know that."

"Not that I need cheering up," he says, his eyes dancing.

"Me neither."

More grinning, more belly tingles, more unadulterated happiness. I must remind myself to kiss Erin and Sophie for finding me Seth.

"Tell me more about what you do. You mentioned you're a personal assistant?"

"I sure am. It's a great job. No two days are the same. I can do everything from helping negotiate a price for Peruvian wind chimes to consulting with my boss over what to wear on a red carpet."

"That doesn't sound like the sorts of things P.A.s do."

"Well, I work for Larissa Monroe."

"Is Larissa Monroe the Kiwi actress who was in that Hollywood movie? Blonde, perky, married to that famous dude."

"Todd Milson?"

"That's the one."

"That's Larissa, only now she's focusing more on her wellness business."

"Her wellness business?" He knits his brows together. It's adorably cute. "As in all that hippy stuff like chia seeds and quinoa?"

I press my lips together at his pronunciation of the word "quinoa." It's totally cute that he doesn't know how to pronounce it, and it makes me like him just that little touch more. I widen my eyes meaningfully. "*Keen-wah* is very good for you, you know," I tease.

He tries the word out. "*Keen-wah.* Is that how you say it? It looks like it should be 'quin-oh-ah.'" He shakes his head. "However you say it, give me a steak and fries any day of the week."

I let out a snort of laughter. "I can't argue with that."

"So she has a business that sells quinoa?"

"Nicely said."

"Why, thank you."

"Actually, she sells a whole lot of stuff as well as consults and runs seminars. She's written a book about the evils of sugar, too."

He loads up his spoon with another mouthful of dessert. "How can this be evil?" he says before taking a bite.

"I know, right?"

We share another grin—this is becoming a habit—and continue to talk through the rest of dessert, an after-dinner drink at a cool bar down the road, and then outside my apartment building. As we stand on the sidewalk, he steps in closer to me and places his hands on my arms. Nervousness whooshes through me. This is it. The Moment. Our first-ever kiss.

"Thank you for tonight," he says.

I look up into his eyes. "I had a really nice time."

"Me, too. I'd really like to do it again sometime soon."

"You're getting me those tickets to your show jumping event, remember?"

"How could I forget?" he says with a shoulder lift. "It'll be wonderful to introduce you to my passion."

"Well, I love horses, and you did mention that you'll be wearing a full equestrian outfit, so . . ." I trail off, a flirty smile on my face.

"So?" he asks with a laugh. "I'll try to look extra good for you."

"I'm not sure you'll have to try that hard."

He loops his arms around my waist and pulls me closer to him. Knowing we're about to share that all-important first kiss, I close my eyes and tilt my head up. A second later, I feel his lips brush against mine, and I inhale his fresh scent. Our kiss is soft and sweet, and it leaves me wanting to kiss him a whole lot more.

He pulls back a little. "Darcy?"

"Mmm?"

"I see you."

"Close your eyes like I'm doing," I suggest helpfully as I pucker up to kiss him once more.

He halts my progress with his hands on my arms, and I pop my eyes open in surprise.

"No, that's not the way I mean it. What I mean is, I *see* you."

I narrow my eyes at him. "You see me."

I'm right in front of you, man. I'm the girl you were kissing moments ago. Speaking of which, I'm kinda hoping we could get back to that part again sometime soon.

"That's right. You're not getting it. I. See. You." When I don't respond, he adds, "You know, as in the 'I get you' kind of way?"

Why didn't he just say that, then? It would have been so much simpler.

"Oh, right. You see me." I give him a knowing nod. "That's, ah, that's good to know."

He waits expectantly. What am I supposed to say? I wrack my brain. This is beginning to feel like a conversation with Larissa—not that we've ever been in this precise position exactly, but you get what I mean.

"I like that you see me, Seth. It makes me feel . . . visible."

Did I really just say that?

"Exactly!" he almost shouts, making me jump back on my heels. "You get it. That's all I want in a woman I date. I want her to know that I see her."

"Well, you got it."

"I hope you can see me, too," he leads.

"Oh. Yes. Absolutely."

His eyes are bright. "Say it."

"Say it?"

"Say it."

"Say 'I see you?'"

"Say 'I see you.'" He looks at me expectantly.

"Sure. Okay." This is weird. Isn't it? But if it's what he needs to get him across the line so we can kiss again like normal people do at the end of a pretty darn fantastic first date, then so be it. I clear my throat. I only want to have to do this once.

"Seth, I see you, too."

He loops his arms around my waist once more and delivers

a knee-weakening kiss, that whole conversation evaporating around us as we get caught up in the moment.

A perfect end to a perfect first date with a perfect, perfect guy.

Chapter 8

Forget about Cloud Nine, right now I'm a whole level up on Cloud Ten, luxuriating in my newfound feelings for Seth. He's sweet, he's fun, he's super smart, and did I mention he's super, *super* hot? Because oh, my, he so is.

Sure, the conversation took a detour down Weird Street a couple of times during the date, but spades and "seeing me" aside, it's clear Seth is one of the good guys. The kind of guy we formed the No More Bad Dates Pact to find.

And now, it's Sunday morning, which means it's time to put on my big girl pants on and go meet Alex. At his place. Just the two of us. None of these things are good.

But I've got to do what I've got to do, so here I stand outside Alex's large, red-brick building. It's in a former industrial area that has clearly undergone serious gentrification. It's smart and trendy as all heck — and *so* Alex.

I take a deep, steadying breath. I can do this. I can put my hatred for him aside and be professional about this. Because that's what I am: a total professional. This is work. All I need to do is get the images and get out of there. Ten minutes ought to do it, fifteen tops. And when I look at it that way, it's only ten minutes of my life. Then I can get on with enjoying my day off doing, well, *anything* but this.

With a clench of my teeth, I press the button for apartment number thirteen. Unlucky thirteen. *Huh.* That's appropriate. I press the button again and wait. And wait. With no response, I press it one more time. Am I early? Late? Do I have the right apartment number? As I pull my phone out to check his address, a voice comes down the crackly line. "Hello?"

"Hey, Alex? It's me, Darcy."

"Oh, Darcy. Right."

I draw my lips into a line. It's as though he's totally forgotten about this super important meeting, the meeting *he* originally suggested. So typical.

Any remnants of Cloud Ten I've been clinging to have now totally evaporated in the morning sun.

"I'll let you in. Third floor. It's a walk-up."

A moment later, the buzzer sounds, and the door pops open. I trudge up the three flights of stairs with as much enthusiasm as someone walking the line to their imminent death. With each step, I roll the thought around in my head. *Hmm.* Electric chair versus Alex Walsh . . . Yup, it's a close race.

I find him waiting beside his opened door. He's dressed in a scruffy pair of jeans and a faded T-shirt with "The Ramones" written across his chest, his hair all messy like he just got out of bed. Which maybe he has? Whatever. I could care less. If he wants to lounge around in bed until all hours of the day and then throw on what clearly look like tattered, old clothes, then that's his business.

"Alex," I say.

"Darcy," he replies in his usual way.

We've got a script, and we're clearly both sticking with it.

He steps to the side, holding his door open. "Come on in."

"Thank you," I reply with as much enthusiasm as a kid invited to sit on the dentist's chair. I step inside and he closes the door behind us. "Cup of coffee? I know I sure need one."

"Oh, no thanks. I'll just take a look at your catalog and then leave you to your day," I say, catching my breath. Stomping up three flights of stairs sure can take it out of a girl.

"An Americano, right?" he says, completely ignoring what I said. "Even *total professionals* deserve a coffee once in a while," he says, quoting the way I referred to myself last night.

I twist my mouth. "Sure. Why not."

"See? That wasn't so hard."

As he busies himself in the kitchen, I take a quick look around. It's a large and spacious loft apartment with hardwood floors and red Persian rugs. The walls are plain white, with no artwork whatsoever. Weird. You'd think someone into photography would have some of it on his walls, even if it's not his own work.

And hang on a second. Isn't this place a bit big and fancy for a barista? I'm sure he gets huge tips from all those adoring females I've spotted smiling and blushing around him at the café—really, some women have no taste—but the rent on this place must be a bomb! How could he possibly afford it?

"Why don't you take a seat?" He gestures at a row of black leather barstools tucked neatly under the kitchen counter.

"Sure."

"Strong black coffee good for you?" He pours coffee into two mugs and slides one across the granite counter to me.

"Actually, do you have any milk?"

"Milk? Sure." He gets some from the refrigerator and pours it into my cup.

"And sugar?"

"Sugar, too?" he questions.

"Yes, but only if you've got sugar cubes, otherwise don't bother."

"No sugar cubes."

"Oh. No sugar cubes," I repeat. I look down at my coffee.

"This will have to do, I guess."

I know I'm being purposefully difficult, but it *is* Alex. He'd expect nothing less. And it's the small victories, right? Even though I don't actually take sugar in my coffee. Or milk, for that matter.

I take a sip. "You're not wrong. This is strong. Late night out with Jason?" It's not that I'm interested in his private life, of course. Just making conversation.

"Something like that."

If he's trying to be mysterious, it's not going to work on me. I could care less about what he got up to last night. I know *I* had a nice time with Seth, a truly wonderful man. That's all I care about.

"How did it go with the guy you had your friends interrogate before you'd go out with him?"

"Not interrogate. We vetted him. It's different."

He sips his coffee, his eyes still locked on mine. "How's it different?"

It's a good question, but I'm hardly going to tell him that. "It just is."

"Good argument, Darcy. Have you considered going into politics someday?" The edges of his mouth curve up into a fully-fledged grin now. Oh, what I would give to be able to wipe that off his face.

Oooh, damn him and his . . . his . . . Alex-ness.

"Very funny, Alex. If I go into politics, you could start your own comedy routine."

"Great idea. Maybe I will."

"So, how about we look through those photos of yours? I'm sure you've got better things to do than sit around talking to me about my date last night."

"Let's finish our coffee first."

Seriously? Why prolong the pain?

I take a swig of my coffee. It's hot and burns my throat. "How long have you had this place?" I ask.

"Oh, about two years, give or take. I was in other countries most of the time, though. This is only the second time I've actually lived here."

Two years? I glance around at the emptiness. In the three years since Erin and I have shared an apartment, we've accumulated so much stuff, we've become like those tragic people who've got to go on decluttering shows just so they can walk down their hallways without bowling over stacks of junk. Marie Kondo could do a major number on our place.

"You haven't got a lot of things, have you?" I say.

"I redecorated not that long ago."

"More like *un*decorated, you mean." I chortle and it comes out like a snort. I clear my throat and paste on an "I totally meant to do that" smile. "Let me guess. You went for the minimalist look."

He shrugs. "I had stuff in here that wasn't me anymore, I guess. You know, things happen, people change."

It seems to me there's more to it than that, but I let it slide. "Sure. Yeah." I take another sip of my coffee. "This is a trendy area. The rent must be steep."

He shrugs. "I bought the place."

He *owns* it? On a barista's salary? I'm itching to ask him how he could possibly have enough money to buy a place like this, but it's rude to ask people questions like that, isn't it? Instead, I simply nod and reply with "Great," as though everyone I know has expensive homes and his is just another one.

"How do you like being back in Auckland?"

"It's good. I needed to move on. Coming home felt like the right option."

"Because — ?" I lead.

He leans up against the counter and cradles his coffee cup in his hands. "You seem to want to know a lot about me today." His eyes are on me, and it makes me want to squirm. Which I won't do. No way. I wouldn't want to give him the satisfaction.

"I'm only making conversation. You were the one who wanted to stop for coffee."

"Is it good coffee?"

"Yes," I reply begrudgingly.

"I'm glad to hear it."

It's time to get down to business, to address the elephant in the room, as they say. "Alex, let's forget the small talk, okay?"

"Sure."

I place my hands on the counter in front of me, ready to launch into the speech I'd recited to myself in front of my mirror only an hour ago. I figured we should put our cards on the table upfront so we both know where we stand before we launch into working together. "Look. You and I both know we're not exactly bosom buddies or anything, but I really think we can—" I taper off as I notice he's arched one of his eyebrows, his lips pressed together. "What?" I say in frustration.

"'Bosom buddies?'"

I pinch my lips together. Is he for real with this? "It's an expression, Alex. It means 'best friends.'"

"I know what 'bosom buddies' means. It's just not an expression I've heard anyone under the age of about sixty use before."

"Well, I use it."

"Often?"

I can't remember the last time I used the term, but I'm not going to mention that. "Yes. All the time."

"Well, I've got to tell you, it creates quite an image."

I throw my eyes to the ceiling at his immaturity as he rolls the term around in his mouth.

"'Bosom buddies,'" he repeats and chuckles to himself.

I shake my head, feeling like I'm suddenly dealing with an eleven-year-old boy. I can use an expression like 'bosom buddies' and not get all stupid about it, which is clearly something Alex can't do. "Try to be mature, Alex, will you, please?"

"Wasn't *Bosom Buddies* the name of a show back in the '80s?"

"How would I know that?"

"It was, I'm sure of it. It was about a couple of guys who

dressed up as women so they could live in a women-only apartment block."

"I don't think so, Alex. You're thinking of *Tootsie* or that other one with Robin Williams who pretends to be his kids' nanny."

"No, not *Mrs. Doubtfire*. It had Tom Hanks in it, I'm sure of it." He picks his phone up off the counter and begins to scroll through it, clearly looking for proof of this nonexistent crossdressing TV show. A moment later, he turns the phone around, and I look at the screen. There's an image of a young Tom Hanks and some other guy, both in dresses and wigs with the words 'Bosom Buddies.'

"See?" he says with one of his self-satisfied grins. It's a grin he sports a lot of the time. Really, they should rename it the "Alex Grin," and people far and wide would know exactly what you meant. He'd be famous, and not in a good way.

I arch an eyebrow. "All that tells me is that you're into shows with drag queens."

"Or that I like shows with bosoms." His shoulders shake as he laughs.

I roll my eyes and shake my head back and forth. "You done amusing yourself there?" I ask.

His face creased in a smile, he replies, "There are no guarantees. And really, that all depends on whether you're going to use any more expressions that make me think of, well, *bosoms*." He draws the last word right out, his eyes dancing.

I push out a puff of air. "When you stop going all *Beavis and Butthead* on me, I'd like to get back to the point I was trying to make."

"Aw, come on. You're going to tell me you're not impressed I knew about some obscure '80s TV show with crossdressers?"

"I don't know how you know this sort of thing. Or even why you'd want to know it in the first place."

He shrugs. "I guess I'm a man of great and mysterious knowledge."

I burst into laughter. "Yeah, sure you are. Be honest. You're just into shows with drag queens, which is actually very interesting too."

"See? I knew you found me interesting." He playfully waggles his eyebrows at me.

Discomfited, I twist my mouth. "You think a lot of yourself, don't you?"

He holds my gaze for a moment then smiles.

"Now, if you're done telling me all about your obsession with crossdressing, I'd like to get back to my point, thank you."

"Be my guest, Darcy."

"Thank you." What was my point? All this talk of bosoms and Tom Hanks and drag queens has totally put me off.

"You've forgotten what you were going to say, haven't you?"

"No. Not at all. I'm simply re-formulating my thoughts so I can communicate them to your succinctly."

His smile spreads. "Succinct points are my preference."

"Well, that's exactly what you're going to get from me: *succinctlyness*."

He screws up his face. "Is that a word?"

"Oh, yes." I gesture at his phone, although I'm pretty sure I added an extra syllable by mistake. Succinctness? Yes, that sounds better. "Look it up if you like. I'm certain you'll find it is a word," I bluff.

"I trust you."

"Good." Thankfully, my brain whirrs back into action, and I manage to return to my prepared speech. "Now, Alex, what I was saying is that I know we don't particularly get on, you and I, but I don't want that in any way to affect our working relationship when it comes to—"

"Why is that, exactly?" he asks, interrupting me mid-speech. Again.

Seriously? This is getting irritating. Why can't he just let me deliver my speech?

"Why is what?" I've only just managed to get back on track,

only to be interrupted by him again. At least I can be happy it's not about bosoms this time, or any other part of human anatomy for that matter.

"Why don't we like each other?" he asks. "Well, to be more specific, why don't *you* like *me*?"

Flustered by the directness of his question, I reply, "You're fine. It's no big deal. We're just not—"

"—bosom buddies," he finishes for me, and I give a reluctant nod. "As you mentioned." He straightens up from his position leaning against the kitchen counter, steps across the floor, and rests his hands on the counter in front of me. "But you know what, Darcy? It's a big enough deal for you to feel like you've got to mention it in that prepared speech of yours."

Dammit! How the heck did he know that it was a prepared speech? I could argue with him, but I've been busted. He knows it and I know it, as much as I hate to admit it.

I cross my legs at my ankles and uncross them again. "Full disclosure?" I ask.

"Even partial disclosure would be good at this point."

I level him with my gaze. "You're cocky."

He lets out a surprised laugh. "Well, you said you were going to be succinct, and that's definitely succinct." He knits his brows. "You think I'm cocky?"

"Yes, I do. You've always been cocky, even back in high school. And I don't like guys like that. It's as simple as that. They're too . . . cocky."

What am I talking about?

"'Cocky guys are too cocky.' Seriously, Darcy, forget politics, you should write a blog. With insights like that, you'd get a massive following." He keeps his bright eyes on me as he takes another sip of his coffee.

"Joke all you like, Alex. You asked a direct question, and I responded. I'm only trying to be honest with you."

"And I appreciate that, really I do."

"Good."

"If I try to lose some of this cockiness that evidently annoys you so much, do you think we could work together on this thing?"

I toss my hair and paste on what I hope is a confident—not in the least bit cocky—smile. "I don't see why not."

"Good. That's settled then. If you've finished your coffee, why don't we have a look at some of my work?"

There's a sudden buzzing sound, and I almost jump off my stool.

"Go ahead and take a seat on the sofa," he says as he walks over to the front door. "I'll be there in a minute."

"Sure." I move into the living area and sit down on one of the large white sofas. It's soft, and I sink into it.

I listen as Alex talks into the intercom. "Hello?"

I can hear a crackly voice say, "It's us."

"Come on up," he replies, opening the door. He walks over to the bookcase, pulls a black folder off one of the shelves, and brings it over to me. "I won't be long. Here. Have a look at some of my work."

"Sure. Thanks." I take the folder in my hands and open it up. There's a sudden bang and a boy of about five dressed as Buzz Lightyear bursts into the room.

"Uncle Alex!" he squeals.

Alex collects him up in a hug and spins him around.

"Wow, is this the real Buzz Lightyear?" Alex says with mock excitement. "From Star Command?"

The boy nods, his face lit up.

"But where's Woody and Jesse and the gang? Don't you know they need you?"

"They're with Mommy, coming up the stairs."

"Because they're not lightning quick like you, right, Buzz?"

"To infinerdy and beyond!" the boy says with his fist in the air.

A woman with hair the color of Alex's, dressed in a cute sundress and pair of sandals, walks through the door. She's holding a ceramic plate covered in foil. "What happened to your elevator?" she puffs.

"I need Buzz here to fix it," he replies. He lifts the boy up into the air and zooms him around. "Buzz Lightyear to the rescue! He can fix elevators. Right, Buzz?"

"No, Uncle Alex! I tricked you! It's me, Nafan!"

I stand up and smile at the boy's inability to pronounce "th." At least that's what I tell myself I'm smiling at and not the easy, fun way his uncle is with him.

"Are you serious? I had no idea," Alex says to an ecstatic Nathan, who he promptly tickles to squeals of delight.

The woman looks over at me, and her face creases into a smile. "Sorry to interrupt. I'm Emily."

I take a few steps closer to her. "Hi, I'm Darcy. It's great to meet you." I smile down at Nathan, who Alex has now put on the floor. "And you, too, Buzz."

Alex squats down next to Nathan and says, "Did you know Darcy works with the Smurfs?"

I shake my head and let out a laugh.

Alex looks up at me, his face aglow. "Right, Darcy?"

"That's right," I reply.

"I like the Smurfs," Nathan replies. "I can sing the song."

"Can you?" I reply. "How does it go?"

"La la la la la la la la la la la," he sings, completely off key.

I join in, and we sing the rest of the tune together. "Wow, you really do know all the words," I say, grinning at him.

"Fat's because the only words is 'la la la,'" he replies, his tone serious.

"That's true," I reply.

"You should sing that at karaoke with Erin," Alex says to me.

I can't help but smile. "We might stick with ABBA."

"I had no idea," Emily says under her breath to Alex as she steals a furtive glance in my direction.

"Darcy's only here to look through my photographs. We're working on that exhibition I told you about," he replies as he straightens up.

"Oh," Emily says. Is it me, or does she sound disappointed?

"Well, we won't hold you up. I just wanted to drop this off for you." She hands him the ceramic plate.

"I told you, I can cook for myself," he protests, but I notice he takes it anyway.

"Mom made it for you. You know how she is about her favorite son."

"She's got the right idea, that woman," he says with a laugh.

"We'll leave you to it. Come on, Nathan," Emily says.

"But Mom," he complains. "I wanna play wif Uncle Arex."

This kid is too cute!

Emily glances at me and smiles back at her son. "They're doing grown-up stuff, honey. We'll come back after lunch."

"I don't wanna," he complains.

"I've got this," Alex says to Emily as he bends down to Nathan's height. "What's this?" He reaches behind Nathan's ear and produces a coin. "What was that doing in your ear, Buzz?"

Nathan rubs his ear and looks at Alex's hand, his eyes almost popping out of his head. "How did you do that?"

"It's magic," Alex replies, as though it's the most obvious thing in the world. "And I'll show you some more when you come back later, 'kay?"

"Really?"

"I promise. But you've gotta do whatever your mom says."

Nathan gives a solemn nod. "I will."

"Come on, honey," Emily says, ushering Nathan through the door. "Thanks," she says to Alex. "Nice to meet you, Darcy."

"Nice to meet you, too," I call out as she follows Nathan out the door.

I press my lips together and do my best to fight off the way seeing Alex as a fun and loving uncle makes my heart do weird things in my chest. There's no way I can go there with him.

Not after what happened when we were in high school.

Chapter 9

"Sorry about that," Alex says as he closes the door.

"No worries. He's a cute kid."

Alex's features soften as he replies, "He's the best." He gestures at the folder I'd left open on the sofa. "Have a look through."

"Sure." I take my seat and open the folder on my lap.

Alex sits down right next to me, close enough to see the photographs in the folder, and instantly, my back stiffens like a rod. First, I've got to witness his softer side with all that cute Nathan stuff, and now he's sitting so close to me, I can smell his intoxicating scent, a combination of vanilla and...grapefruit?

He shoots me a look out of the corner of his eye. "Comfortable?"

"Yes, thank you. Perfectly comfortable." I begin to leaf through the images. They are all landscapes, some including structures, all with the same incredible skies in I saw his work at Cozy Cottage High Tea. "These are awesome," I say, genuinely impressed.

"Thanks. Most of those I took in India and Nepal." He leans back on the sofa next to me, his relaxed posture in stark contrast to my own utterly tense version. Sitting on a sofa this close to Alex has definitely shot into my top ten of things to avoid, along with swimming with sharks and keeping tarantulas as pets.

"It looks incredible there. So many mountains," I say as I study the photos.

"Heard of the Himalayas?"

I scoff. "Of course I've heard of the Himalayas."

"Well . . ." He gestures at the image on my lap of a majestic mountain.

"Wow," I say despite myself. I mean, this is a picture of a Himalayan mountain, a Himalayan mountain Alex has seen in the flesh . . . or in the rock, or whatever that expression should be for a mountain. It's pretty darn impressive.

"The next few I took in Nepal."

I continue to flick through the folder when Alex says, "Tell me something. Why does Larissa always use my full name when she talks about me? She never just calls me 'Alex.' It's always 'Alex Walsh' this and 'Alex Walsh' that. It's kinda weird."

I admit I had noticed that. "She's just quirky, that's all. It could be that she thinks the name 'Alex' is too short, or she likes the way 'Walsh' sounds. Who knows? She thought your name was 'Alex Alex' originally."

"Why?" he asks with a laugh.

I think about how I'd been so shocked that Alex, the guy I'd hated for so long, was the one who took such a gorgeous photo when I first saw it at the Cozy Cottage. "Oh, no reason." I turn the page and see the same image that was at Cozy Cottage High Tea. It's of an ornate building beneath a huge sky. "I love this one. Is this in India or Nepal?"

He shifts a little closer to me on the sofa and a weird, zingy feeling grows in my belly. I flip my hair over my shoulders and do my best to ignore it.

What has gotten into me today?

"I took it in Rajasthan in Northern India. It's so beautiful there. I've got that one and a bunch of others in the same series framed in a box. They were for a show I did some time back. Want to see?"

"Sure."

He gets up, and I let out the breath I'd been holding for the longest time. Why does he have to sit so close to me? I mean, it's a large sofa, so there's plenty of room. He's probably doing it to disconcert me. Yes, that's what! He's trying to make me feel uncomfortable.

Well, Alex, you have succeeded. Well done.

He walks around the back of the sofa and pulls out a file box. He places it with care on the low coffee table and flips the open lid.

I read the side of the box: "Rajasthan landscapes." I lean forward and peer inside. There's a row of black frames, all identical in size, and all neatly stacked against one another. "Can I pull them out?"

"Sure, go ahead."

I randomly select one frame and pull it out of the box.

"That's **Taj Lake Palace** in Udaipur. They filmed a James Bond movie there years ago, and restaurants in the town show the movie most nights of the week."

I examine the image in my hands. It's of a beautiful, ornate building in the middle of a lake. "It's gorgeous." I place it carefully on the coffee table and reach into the box for the next one. This feels like Christmas Day, waiting to find out what each wrapped present is.

I pull another framed photograph out. This one has a group of men standing in front of a fortress-like building, turbulent clouds swirling above their heads.

He takes his seat on the sofa again, sitting just as close as he did before, and I can't help but catch another hint of his scent. Combined with the closeness of his warm bulk, that zingy feeling starts up inside once more. It's more than a little unnerving. I move to the very edge of the sofa, as far away from Alex as I can be without slipping down onto the floor—I'm literally holding on by a butt cheek here.

He doesn't comment this time. Instead, he says, "That's the Brahma temple in a town called Pushkar. The temple is actually really brightly painted in blues and reds, which you can't see in this shot. I met those men, and they allowed me to take a few shots of them. That guy here," he points at one of the men in a long white shirt over white pants, "he had only three teeth. He was super proud of them, though." He's so close to me now, I can almost feel his warm breath on my cheek. What is it *with* him today?

"How did he eat?" I ask, focusing on the photo.

"I don't know, but I'd say carefully and slowly. Wouldn't you?"

"Yes. Totally." I give a light laugh. It helps release some of the weirdness I'm feeling. "You know what?" I say as I hop up onto my feet. "I'm going to start two piles. A 'yes' pile and a 'no' pile. I'm going to add this to the 'yes' pile." I place the framed photograph on top of the original image on the coffee table.

"Sounds like a good idea to me. Whatever you choose, you can take with you now to show Larissa, and I'll send you the electronic files."

"Sure." I reach into the box and pull out another photograph. It has another big sky, this time with a man walking away from the camera through a field of knee-high grass. "This one is gorgeous."

Even though I turn it around so he can see, he comes over to stand beside me. Seriously? He's like a tracking beacon, homing in on me wherever I go. Doesn't he know behaving like this only makes people feel awkward?

"That's Three Tooth Guy again. He took me to that field. Said the light was really good there. I think he was right."

"Another 'yes.'" I lean down and place the framed photo on top of the other two. I reach into the box and pull out the next one, and the next, and the next. Alex tells me about each one, still standing uncomfortably close, still smelling ridiculously good, his low voice rumbling through me with each explanation, each compelling anecdote. By the time I've finished the box, every image is in the 'yes' pile, and the 'no' pile has yet to receive its first entry.

I do a quick count. "That's ten images. With the six from Cozy Cottage, I only need another twenty, thirty tops, and we've got ourselves an exhibition."

He leans back on his heels and laughs. "As I said, I'm not sure I have enough of what Larissa's looking for, but let's check." He wanders back around the sofa.

As he begins to rummage through things, I give my butt a discrete rub—it's not worked that hard since my last Hot Yoga session—and sit back down on the plump sofa.

He lifts another box out and places it on the table. He removes the lid and pulls out the first framed photograph. "I took this in a place called Manali, in the province of Himachal Pradesh. Manali is a really special place. It's the mountainous region in the north of India, so all the mountains you see are the Himalayan foothills. This whole box is from there, so expect a lot of mountains."

"Makes sense."

Much to my annoyance, he sits back next to me, and I've got to work hard at being relaxed, which of course means I'm once again about as relaxed as a cat in a room full of plump mice. We work our way through the box, and by the end, I've not added a single photograph to the "no" pile.

"You know, Alex, you're a really good photographer."

"Coming from you, that's a real compliment."

I shoot him a look. "You may not be my favorite person, as we discussed earlier—"

"Ah, yes. The bosom buddies conversation. That was fun."

I roll my eyes. "As I was saying, you're not my favorite person, but I know talent when I see it."

"Well, thank you." He hands me the folder from the coffee table. "Have a look through this to see if there's anything else you like the look of." He stands up, and I swear my butt lets out a groan of relief as I relax a notch or ten. "Want another coffee? Personally, I could do with some more caffeine."

"Because of your late night?" I lead.

He raises his eyebrows at me. "Sure."

"Another coffee would be great."

As he wanders over to the kitchen, I begin to look through the images. I select eight of them, including one of a little girl, sitting in a field of daisies, a majestic mountain behind her. "There are so many great photos in here, Alex. Larissa is going to be deliriously happy," I call out.

He walks back over to the sofa. "Keeping Larissa happy seems to be the biggest part of your job."

I look up at him and shrug. "I guess."

"Is she the reason you wear head-to-toe blue at work?"

I raise my chin, feeling weirdly protective of Larissa. "I like blue."

"Sure, but you've got to wear it every day, right?"

I think of my closet, full to the brim with blue clothes. There's this one small section, reserved for the weekends, that's filled with every other color in the rainbow. Including my preferred shade of pink.

I open my mouth to respond when I hear a phone chime. Alex walks over to the kitchen counter and picks his phone up. "I've gotta take this," he says as he walks past me toward a door at the end of the room. "I'll be back in five." He says "hello" as he closes the door behind him.

Once I finish looking through the images in the folder, I stand up and stretch. I arch my back and give my butt another rub to ease the now persistent ache. It's Alex's fault for sitting so darn close to me. It's like he enjoys bugging me. Like he knew sitting that close would make me super uncomfortable.

See? Cocky.

I wander around the room. I know I should be waiting quietly for him to return, but I can't resist a quick snoop. Don't judge me. I'm only human. And anyway, isn't it good

NO MORE TERRIBLE DATES

to get to know the person you're working with? Larissa is taking a huge punt on him, and I need to make sure there's nothing lurking in any closet that might leap out and bite us. Well, that's my excuse, anyway.

I walk over to the large bookshelf and peruse the shelves. There's some fiction — typical boy books like thrillers — and a bunch of coffee table books, some on photography, some on different countries, including India. I pull one out and flick through it. I've not been to India, but from what I've seen today, it looks like a spectacular country. I slot the book back in its spot.

I can hear Alex's muffled voice echoing through the closed door. I let out a puff of air, my hands on my hips as I wait. I know Larissa is going to be thrilled with these photos. I also know I need about ten more to have enough for her to choose from for the exhibition. Are there more boxes behind that sofa?

Curiosity gets the better of me, and I step around to the back of the sofa. There I see another five boxes, all labeled in the same handwriting. Only ten or fifteen photographs my ass. There must be fifty here, at least!

Feeling a little like a naughty child opening the presents under the tree before Christmas Day, I pull the nearest box out and remove the top. I'm met with another row of black frames, stacked neatly, just as in the other boxes.

I pull the first picture out and turn it over in my hands. It's a profile shot of a beautiful woman, her head thrown back as she laughs. Her long dark hair pools on the mat behind her as she sits in a field of daisies. She looks happy, free. I examine the image closer. That field looks familiar. I lean the photograph against the back cushion of the sofa and rifle through the images in my 'yes' pile until I find the one of Three Tooth Guy. I place the images side by side and look from one to the other. Yup, that's the same field for sure.

I return my attention to the box and pull out another photo. I hold it in my hands and study it. It's of the same woman, only this time, it's a close-up of her face, her eyes wide and beautiful. She's looking directly out at me, her lips curved into a Mona Lisa smile. It's an arresting image, and it gets me wondering who she is to Alex that he'd take a photo like this. And then keep it in a box.

"What do you think you're doing?"

With a jolt of surprise, I look from the image up to Alex. Gone is his habitual smirk, now replaced by a look of pure thunder, his features tense, his hands balled into fists at his sides.

"I found some more boxes. I wanted more images for Larissa, and I didn't think you'd mind."

"Well, I do mind." His voice is cold, uncompromising.

"Okay." I shove the image back into the box and pat the neat row of pictures. I have no clue why. Nerves, probably. I've never seen Alex like this before.

He reaches across me and collects the photo of the woman's profile from where I'd placed it on the sofa, slots it back into the box, and replaces the lid. Without looking back at me, he picks the box up and stalks out of the room with it.

I'm left alone, wondering what I've inadvertently stumbled across. Who is that girl? It's obvious it's someone who means something to Alex. I feel a twinge. Of what, though, I'm not quite sure. Embarrassment? Guilt? Envy? I capture a lock of my hair in my finger and twist it.

Envious of what? *Her?*

No. It's got to be guilt. I snooped and got busted.

I hear his footsteps returning to the room. I turn to face him as he walks through the doorway. His shoulders are taut, his lips drawn into a thin line. The look on his face makes my heart thud hard.

I've really upset him. I need to fix this. We've got to work together, and this is not a great start.

"Alex, I'm really sorry. I assumed they were just more scenic images. I didn't think they'd be anything . . . personal."

"I didn't tell you to look in any other boxes," he says evenly, his voice low. If I'm to be completely honest, it sounds a little threatening.

"I know, and I'm sorry. I didn't think you'd mind, and you were making coffee, and then you were on the phone and I—" I pause in my rambling as I notice his expression hasn't changed. "Look, all I can say is I'm sorry. Again."

"Put the ones you want back in the boxes ,and I'll help take them to your car. As I said, once you've chosen what you want, I'll send you the files."

Is he completely ignoring my apology? It was an honest mistake!

"Sure," I reply uncertainly. I chew on my lip. How do I fix this? How do I undo what I've done?

In my defense, it really was an accident. I didn't mean to stumble across those pictures. But even so, I don't like the feeling that I've somehow hurt him, even if I don't like him. Which is weird, isn't it?

We pack the "yes" pile into the boxes, the silence anything but comfortable. Once we're done, he tucks one box under each arm, and I pick the final box up myself. He leads me toward his front door.

"I'll, ah, get the door for you," I say.

"That would be helpful."

I follow him down the three flights of stairs. Out on the street, he carefully places all three boxes into my car.

I close the door and turn to him. "Really, Alex. I am so sorry."

His steely gaze is averted. "Yeah, you said that. Quite a few times." He looks back at me, his features still taut. "Don't worry about it."

"Right. Well," I say with forced brightness, "thanks for these. Can I arrange a time to swing by and collect the others from Cozy Cottage?"

"Give Sophie a call."

Taken aback, I reply, "Sophie. Yes, of course."

"See you later," he mutters as he turns away from me and begins to walk back toward his building.

"Okay, Alex. Thanks again!" I trill and then instantly cringe at the over-the-top sing-song-y tone of my voice.

I climb into my car and close the door behind myself. Wow, I've really rattled his cage. As I start the car, I wonder about that woman in the photos? Who is she?
And more importantly, what the heck did she do to Alex?

Chapter 10

I'm sitting in the only room at the office that isn't blue. In fact, it's red. Bright red. The room is — somewhat unimaginatively — called the Red Room, so you get what you read on the label. Apparently, red isn't just the color of sexy dresses and the shade my skin goes if I stay in the sun too long. Oh, no. The color red is, apparently, so much more than that. According to Larissa, research shows that red stimulates vitality and helps one's creative juices flow. Even though, sitting in this room right now, I imagine this is exactly what it's like to be stuck inside a giant tomato.

I let out a sigh. I wish I were reclining on a sun lounger on a beach in Fiji (wearing sun lotion, so I don't end up looking like the room I'm currently in), a piña colada in one hand and a good book in the other as a cute guy massages my feet. Instead, I'm listening to some guy who smells of incense and mud — and looks like he last washed sometime in the twentieth century — espouse the power of the Ethiopian "charms" he's brought for Larissa to "have a life-changing experience" with. Apparently, when it comes to what look suspiciously like twigs wrapped in twine, you can't just look at them or pick them up to examine them. According to Aleron, a.k.a. Mr. Smelly, you've got to "experience" them.

My cynical eyebrow is on perma-salute in this room, and today is no exception.

Larissa's? Not so much.

"Can you feel the way everything inside of you is more alert, more in tune, more *incredible* than it was before you placed your hand here?" the guy, Aleron, says to a riveted Larissa.

"That could be this room, you know. It's optimized for creativity," Larissa replies.

"Of course. Red is the color of vitality, of excitement," he pauses, his eyes intense as he adds, "of human sexuality."

I raise my eyebrows at him. Is this guy *hitting* on Larissa now?

She nods, totally and blissfully oblivious to anything that may or may not be going on. "You're so right, Aleron."

He cups her hand, holding the "charm" in his own, and says, "Close your eyes and concentrate. Feel the charm working. Feel the way your blood pulses through your body."

Well, I had hoped her blood had already been doing that all by itself, for her sake.

Larissa's eyes pop open. "Oh, my goodness. Yes! I totally felt that."

Aleron gives a knowing nod. "That is the power of the *unanyo*. It's working at a deep level to improve your circulation. What it does is strengthen your body's internal connectivity."

I clamp my lips shut to stifle a giggle. Strengthening your body's connectivity has got to be a good thing. You wouldn't want to be walking down the street and have limbs and things just fall off, would you? Maybe your internal organs drop out of your butt? A messy experience for sure.

Aleron turns his head to glare at me momentarily before he returns his attention to Larissa.

I'm not always so cynical about the things people peddle to Larissa. Sometimes I actually believe in them, or *want* to believe in them, I guess. Like the time I wore a rock pendant that was supposed to attract love. Well, it attracted love all right, only not the human kind. The day I wore the pendant, Erin and I found a family of mice living in our oven, and despite the fact they're super cute with those long whiskers and twitchy noses, we had to get someone in to get rid of them. They were eating our food and leaving little deposits all over the kitchen, which was pretty gross. Of course, we asked the guy to trap them and release them into a pretty field somewhere for them to play in, which he agreed to do, but I'm not sure how honest he was about their fate.

My phone vibrates, and I flip it over. It gives me a break from all this connectivity strengthening babble. I smile as I read a new message from Seth.

Did I tell today you how beautiful you are? I'd love to see you again soon.

Aww. He's so sweet! Maybe a little corny, but I'm not going to think anything but positive thoughts about this one. After two dating disasters, I know Seth is one of the good guys. Three's a charm and all that.

I tap out a message.

Dinner tomorrow night?

His response is immediate.

Perfect.

It's a date.

I add two kisses at the end of my message and turn my phone face down on the table. I return my attention to the conversation in the room.

"Does it work on a cellular level?" Larissa asks, her hand still gripping the Ethiopian "charm."

"Deeper. Much, much deeper."

"Deeper than your cells?" I can't help but question.

"Yes. Picture this, if you will. If your cells had cells, it would be working at *their* cellular level."

Wait, what?

Larissa's face is bright when she tilts her head to look at me. "Darcy, this is an amazing feeling. You have got to try it." She turns back to Aleron. "How many charms do you have?"

My ears prick up.

"Oh, I've got a large supply, although they are in high demand, as you can well imagine."

Larissa gives a knowing nod. "Yes, I can imagine. They're so powerful. We'll take a thousand, to begin with."

"A good start, Larissa, but I need to warn you that there isn't a limitless supply," Aleron replies, if "Aleron" is even his real name. I bet it's really something like Nigel or Derek. Colin maybe. Yes, he looks like a Colin under all those beads and hemp clothing.

Larissa's face creases in distress. "What are you saying? My followers could miss out on these?"

It's blindingly obvious she's been sucked in by Aleron-slash-Colin's super-powered vacuum. I need to do something about this fast.

"Larissa? I don't think we should rush into this, do you?" I say.

"I think rushing in is exactly what she should do," Aleron says. "The *unanyo* have proven very popular in the wellness arena. Larissa, your followers need these. No, they *deserve* them."

Larissa nods emphatically. "Yes, yes, you're so right, Aleron."

Uh-oh. Not a good sign.

Quietly, trying my best not to be noticed, I pick up my phone and send a quick message with the number *104*. It's a secret code between me and my coworkers. The whole company is in on it, unbeknownst to our boss. We had a meeting and everything, which is where the *104* code was decided (although one time, when I briefly dated a cop, he told me 104 was actually the official police code for "stupid cat stuck up tree," but I think he was joking). Right now, I need the code to work.

109

The thing with Larissa is, she's what she calls "open," which is New Age speak for "pretty darn gullible," as far as I can see. She readily believes in all this mumbo jumbo nonsense, lapping it up. People like Aleron know it all too well. She once bought an entire container of rubber ducks because she was told they were imbued with the spirit of a former Dalai Lama. Rubber ducks, people! I'm not so sure Dalai Lamas go in for little plastic things that float in the bath. That's much more Ernie and Bert's scene.

"You wouldn't want your loyal followers to miss out on the incredible strength of the *unanyo*. They would miss out on experiencing the deep, deep healing power of body connectedness, the power you, yourself, have been privileged to experience with me here today. And you wouldn't want that, would you?"

Larissa shakes her head. "No, I wouldn't."

I message *104* again, this time followed by a series of "!!!!!!" to show just how urgent this situation has become.

"Might I be so bold as to suggest closer to ten thousand units, Larissa?" Aleron continues. "You have a massive international following, after all, and I'm absolutely certain you'd want everyone to experience the life-changing benefits of the *unanyo*."

Even though I'm fully expecting it, when the door bangs open, I jump right out of my seat. Maureen O'Connell's imposing figure virtually fills the space where the red door was closed only moments before. She pauses to survey the room before she strides in, a determined look on her face.

"Maureen," I say, widening my eyes in mock surprise at the head of our Accounts Payable team. "What are *you* doing here?"

Of all the brave people who respond to the *104* distress messages, Maureen's my absolute favorite. She brings a touch of the theatrical, and, if I'm honest, it doesn't hurt that she's almost six feet tall and wears a men's size ten shoe. When dealing with pushy salespeople, sometimes size does matter.

"I had a sudden need to be in this room," Maureen replies as she pulls out a seat at the table and drops down. "I can't explain it. It was like I had a . . . a calling."

Or a message on her phone.

"Well, if you had a calling, you must be in the right place," I say with a wise nod of my head.

You see, this is one of the benefits of working for Larissa. You can use any kind of excuse you want, like "my chi made me take an extra-long lunch break today," or "my soul told me to stay in bed way past my alarm." She simply accepts it, so long as it has the required New Agedness to it, and so long as you do it with the right attitude. Maureen knows it, I know it. We all know it.

"Maureen, this is Aleron Whitehead. He's showing us these amazing Ethiopian charms that help work on the cellular levels of your cells' cells," I explain to her, my eyes wide with mock amazement. "Isn't that unbelievable?"

"Wow, they *do* sound unbelievable, Darcy," Maureen replies, her face serene.

Gosh, she's good. That's why I use her for these sorts of situations. She's only getting started right now, but I know she's tough and uncompromising. One time, she was on my bowling team when Larissa decided the whole company needed to "get back to basics" by playing the game of the "common person," and she smashed the opposition. Literally. I won't go into details. All I'll say is it wasn't pretty.

Maureen picks one of the "charms" up in her hand and Aleron eyes her suspiciously. I'm quite certain that right about now, he's wishing both Maureen and I would have a "calling" to leave the room entirely so he could manipulate Larissa into purchasing even more of his little bundles of twigs.

Maureen holds the "charm" up in the air and says, "This must be why I was called in here."

"It could well be. The *unanyo* is very powerful," Aleron says.

"*Unanyo*," Maureen says. "Interesting. Tell me more about

them."

Aleron launches into his speech once more about circulation and the cellular level of our cells' cells.

Maureen nods along, looking as though this is the most interesting thing she's heard in her entire life, although I know better. She's sitting there, working out when to pounce.

His spiel done, Maureen sits back in her seat. "How much are they?"

Aleron throws her a look of irritation. "For Larissa, and only Larissa," he turns back to her, "I could be persuaded to let them go for $45 apiece."

$45? For literally a pile of twigs that are probably from his garden down the road? This guy is gooood. But not good enough. Not when Maureen's in the room.

"You could sell them upwards of $150," Aleron adds hopefully. "That's a huge profit margin for your business."

Larissa bites her lip. "Okay. I think ten thousand at that price sounds reasonable."

Aleron works hard to suppress a smile.

This has gone on waaay too long. I shoot Maureen a look, and she leaps into action.

"Listen, Al. Can I call you that?" she says.

"It's Aleron."

"Great. The thing is, Al, we already have something very similar in our warehouse right now."

"We do?" Larissa asks.

"Yes. They're the," she looks around the room until her eyes land on a bottle of water on the side table by the window, "the Evian-ilors."

The Evian-ilors. *Brilliant, Maureen. Brilliant.* I almost break into applause.

"Yes, that's right," she continues. "I saw them on an inventory list I was reviewing only last week. The Evian-ilors. They're from French Polynesia. Remember, Larissa?"

Larissa's brow is as furrowed as her Botox will allow. "It does sound familiar. . ."

"From memory, the power of the Evian-ilors is that they work on the cells of your cells' cells' cells. So, you know, one better than these." Maureen picks up one of the *unanyo* once more and then drops it carelessly on the table.

Now I want to give her a standing ovation, she's so good.

Aleron-slash-Colin opens his mouth to speak, but before he gets the chance, I jump out of my seat and say, "Thank you, Maureen. We had completely forgotten about the Evian-y things."

"Evian-ilors," Maureen corrects with a satisfied smirk.

"Yes. Those." I turn to Larissa. "Larissa? You've got that ten o'clock, remember?" I tap my wrist and raise my eyebrows.

"Oh, of course. My ten o'clock," she says, looking as confused as a Kardashian in a camping store. She stands up. "Aleron, can we pick this up some other time?"

Colin—sorry, *Aleron*—narrows his eyes at me, and I smile back at him.

As I hustle Larissa out of the room, I hear Maureen say, "Thank you for your time today, Aleron. It's been so enlightening. Would you like to take a bottle of Evian with you when you leave?"

Later that day, Larissa is back in her office going over product descriptions for the online store with one of the guys from marketing. She looks up at me as I walk in the room.

"The *unanyo* really was very potent," she says.

"Yes, but the Evian thingies are even more so, Larissa."

"You know, I really don't remember those."

"I'll get you one." I roll one of the spare Swiss balls over to her desk and sit down on it. "Hey. Joseph, right?" I say to the marketing guy. He only started here in the last week, I think.

"That's right," he says with a smile. "Larissa, if you're happy with these, I'll get them uploaded on the site."

"They look amazing. Thank you for all you do for us." She reaches out and takes him by the hand. "You are truly a valued member of our family. Here." She presses a *unanyo* into his hand.

He looks down at it, clearly unsure how to respond to being given a clump of twigs. "Err, thanks for the, ah, gift. I'll go get on with these." Joseph's eyes dart around the room. He'll work out how these things go. You accept whatever thing Larissa gives you and act grateful. Then she's happy.

"See you soon, Joseph. Enjoy your twigs," I say to him with a warm smile. There's no need to spook the horses. Or the product marketers, as the case may be.

Once he's beaten his hasty escape, I say to Larissa, "I want you to see what I've got for the new gallery."

She beams at her. "Oh, goody! Show me, show me."

I got in early this morning and hung the photos Alex gave me on the hallway walls. I take Larissa to see them. As she oohs and ahhs over them, I tell her, "I'm collecting the ones you saw at Cozy Cottage High Tea later this morning."

After "The Incident" at Alex's place on Sunday, I did what he suggested and contacted Sophie to collect the photographs from Cozy Cottage. Not having to see Alex after I upset him so much is simply a side benefit of the arrangement.

Larissa pauses in front of the photo of the little girl in the field. Instantly, I think of the other photos in that collection, of the beautiful woman Alex didn't want me to see. "Oh, this one speaks to me. You know, I didn't think I wanted people to be the focus in my pictures, but this changes my mind."

"It is gorgeous."

"Oh, it's more than gorgeous. It's transcendental. Alex Walsh has such an eye." We both look at the photo until she says, "Darcy, darling, write this down."

I flip open my trusty notebook, my pen poised. In some ways, I like to think of myself as the anti-millennial. I still know how to use pencil and paper. It's one of my superpowers.

"I need to know how Alex Walsh thinks, how he feels, how he taps into his higher state of consciousness."

I write down "how A.W. thinks, feels, higher state of consciousness." I look back up at Larissa. "How many more of his photographs do you need to answer these questions?"

"Oh, I need to talk to him. Face to face. I need to search his soul for these answers. Darcy, I want you to bring me Alex Walsh," she says with a flutter.

My throat tightens.

"Couldn't you just call him, instead?" I suggest. "I've got his number," I add feebly, thinking of the name he tapped into my phone: "Alex the photographic genius."

She shakes her head. "I want him here, in the Red Room with me. I want to know everything there is to know about Alex Walsh. I want him totally exposed. Naked."

She wants Alex Walsh here, totally exposed and naked? Nope. I cannot have that image in my head. Not after seeing his amazing, creative side in his photographs. Not after seeing the sweet way he is with his nephew.

"And anyway, you've got to collect the photos from the café, don't you?"

She's got a point. "I'll, ah, see what I can do."

"I feel very strongly that this is something important. So, Darcy? Just do it." She stands up straighter. "Hey, that's a great, motivational line: just do it."

"That's what Nike thought."

"Oh. Shame. I liked the sound of that."

An alarm sounds on my phone, signaling that it's time for Larissa's kale fix. "I'll go get your juice." As I leave her standing in the hallway, gazing at Alex's work, my insides tighten at the thought of having to see Alex again.

And after what happened at his apartment, I'm pretty sure I'm the last person he wants to hear from right now, too.

Chapter 11

The weather turned cool and blustery while I was in the office, so I'm grateful for the warmth of Cozy Cottage High Tea. Sophie's at the podium, talking with some customers. I look around as I wait patiently for her to finish. There's no sign of Alex or his photographs. They must have been removed, ready for me to collect.

"Hey, Darce!" Sophie greets me with a quick hug. "I've got the photos out back, boxed up and ready to go. They looked so good here, though. I hope you don't sell any of them at the opening because I really want them back."

"I hope we do! Larissa will not be happy otherwise. A large part of her 'vision' is always to make stack loads of money, you know."

She chuckles. "I bet. Come with me. I'll get you the box."

"Actually," I say as I put my hand on her arm, "I need to talk to Alex first." I look nervously around the room once more, trying to appear casual—and not like I inadvertently invaded his personal space and made him all angry about it. "Is he here today?"

"He's working at the café." She narrows her eyes at me. "Darcy? Why do you look weird?"

"Weird?"

"You know, nervous or worried or something."

"Who? Me?" I wave my hand in the air. "Why would Alex make me nervous or worried?"

She raises her eyebrows in question. "I don't know."

"Exactly. There's no reason." I arrange my limbs into a relaxed pose but probably look nothing but.

She twists her mouth. "You are acting strangely, though. Did something happen with him?"

"What?" My voice sounds a lot like a guinea pig's squeal. "Of course nothing's happened with him. Don't be silly, Soph. I've just got a lot on my mind, that's all."

She eyes me up. "All right. Well, come back to get the photos when you're done."

"Will do. Now I'll, ah, go find him next door," I say.

"You do that," Sophie replies. Her eyes are narrowed as though she's trying to work something out.

I push my way through the door out into the street, round the topiary at the entrance to High Tea, and then in through the door to the café. The place is full, and as the tempting aroma of coffee and freshly baked cakes reaches my nose, my tummy rumbles, right on cue.

I scan the room quickly, looking for Alex. No sign. Well, since I'm here, I may as well get something yummy. A girl's gotta eat, right? And kale juices and acai berry granola really don't count as food in my book. I'll wait in line until Alex turns up. I know I'll need a major sugar boost for that conversation.

As I wait in line, my mouth waters as I work out which of the Cozy Cottage cakes I'm going to indulge in this morning. The cakes here are so good, all moist and tasty with ample frosting. If I worked close by, I'd be in here so often that I'm certain I'd be a prime candidate for obesity or diabetes.

Probably both.

"Hi, Darcy," Bailey says with a smile when I reach the front of the line. "What can I get you?"

"Hey, Bailey. A cup of Earl Grey and a slice of carrot cake, please."

"Earl Grey. Nice. Coming right up. Oh, did you get Alex's photographs? I think Sophie's got them all ready for you next door."

"Yes, thanks." I shoot her a smile, and add, "Is, ah, he around?"

"Our soon-to-be-famous photographer is out back having a break right now."

"Oh. I guess I'll wait for him. I need to talk to him about some things to do with the gallery."

She leans closer to me, and says, "How about I let you go back to see him while I fix your tea and cake?"

My heart rate kicks up—from nerves and something else I can't quite name. Or don't want to. I push my confused feelings away. "It's fine. I'll wait here. I don't want to interrupt him." And there's safety in numbers out here in the café.

"Oh, don't be silly. Come on. I'll let you in.

"Thanks, that would be awesome."

Awesome and completely terrifying, that is.

I walk with trepidation past the cabinet and around through the counter flap, which Bailey holds up for me. The last time I came through here was with Alex to find a place to put the hyacinths. Back then, my feelings about him were simple and straightforward. I hated him, end of story. Now, the hate is mixed with guilt, and both emotions churn around inside.

"I'll bring your tea and cake out to you if you like?"

"Oh, this won't take long. I'll take them to go, thanks."

She smiles. "Sure. They'll be here at the counter when you're ready."

I make my way past her and into the kitchen. Alex is sitting on a stool at one of the stainless steel counters, his head down, concentrating on something on his phone.

"Alex," I say, my voice suddenly croaky. At least I no longer sound like a guinea pig. I clear my throat and try again. "Alex," I say more firmly, hoping my tone is bright and breezy.

He looks up directly into my eyes, and my belly twists. As recognition registers, his features grow dark. "Darcy," he says, only unlike before, there's not a hint of amusement in his voice, nor a smile on his face.

As irritating as I found those things before, right now, I miss them.

I squeeze my hands at my sides and step further into the room. "Can I talk to you?"

He puts his phone down on the counter. "What about?"

"I wanted to thank you for the photos you gave me on Sunday. Larissa absolutely loves them." I think of the way she ooh-ed and aah-ed when I showed them to her. She sounded like she was in the throes of utter ecstasy when she saw his photo of the little girl in the field.

"Okay."

"Larissa thinks . . . we *both* think you're really talented."

"Good."

He's really not giving me anything here.

Like the fool I am, I press on, regardless. "I also wanted to say that I'm sorry. Again. I-I know I've said it already, a few times, actually. But I want you to know I mean it. I should never have looked at the photos in that box. It was private, and it was wrong of me. So, so wrong." I pause, hoping he'll say something.

All he does is sit and watch me.

It's obvious to me I need to say more. "If they were my private photos and you accidentally looked at them, I would feel just as angry as I'm sure you do right now. Even though it would be an honest mistake, and we would both know that. Nevertheless, I would feel aggrieved. Like you do. Right now. Totally and utterly aggrieved. So—"

I know what I'm doing. By babbling on, I'm filling in the

silence, the one thing I know I shouldn't be doing. But I'm feeling so freaking thrown by this guy. It's like he's got some kind of weird hold on me, and I'm trying desperately to talk my way out of it. It might not the best thought-out strategy, but I'm running with it now.

"—and even though the photographs are exquisite, I know they're your personal items and not—"

As I continue to waffle on, I wonder why he's not saying anything. All he's doing is arcing an eyebrow as he watches me carry on with (un)happy abandon. It's like he's enjoying this. Yes! That's what this is. He's enjoying me waffling on about how I was in the wrong and he was in the right.

I clamp my mouth shut, mid-sentence. Two can play this game (and yes, I know I'm the one in the wrong, but it wasn't that wrong, and it was an accident, and I've apologized *a lot*).

After a beat, he finally opens his mouth to speak. "Are you done?"

"Yes. I am."

"Well, then, thank you for that." The corners of his mouth twitch. "*All* of it."

He's mocking me, even though I'm giving him a heartfelt apology. Even though I mean every word I'm saying and I really, truly do feel bad.

I give a curt nod. "You're welcome," I reply solemnly, as though I've done him some kind of favor.

"You're right. They're my personal items, as you referred to them, but I'm happy to forget it happened. So, if you're looking for it, I forgive you. Let's forget about it and move on."

Relief washes through me. "Moving on sounds good to me."

Silence falls once more. Alex is still looking at me intently, and I'm still wishing this was over and I was back in the office. Being in the Red Room with Aleron and his bundles of twigs is preferable to this level of tension, believe me.

"Is there something else?" he asks.

"Oh, yes. Actually, there is."

"Another prepared speech?" he asks, and his lips quirk into a small smile.

Something stirs inside me. Something I don't want to think about.

"It's from Larissa, actually."

"A prepared speech from Larissa. That's new."

I shake my head. "It's not a speech."

"That's a shame. I quite enjoy your speeches."

I regard him in surprise. "You do?"

"Yeah. You get all serious, like you've really thought about what you've got to say. It's . . . charming."

Alex thinks I'm charming?

I press my lips together, ignoring the way his smile makes me tingle. It's only due to my relief that he's forgiven me. It's nothing more than that. And saying I'm charming? Well, that's his way of putting me off my stride, of getting back at me for looking at those photos.

I refocus on my message. "Larissa wants you to come to a meeting with her. She wants to talk to you about some things, specifically," I pull my Labrador puppy notebook out of my purse, flip to the page where I'd written down her questions, and quote her word-for-word. "She wants to know how you think, how you feel, and to ask you about your higher state of consciousness." I flip the cover of my notebook over and await his reaction.

His brow is furrowed. "She wants to ask about my higher state of consciousness?"

"Yes." I give a solemn nod.

The corners of his mouth twitch again in that all-too-familiar way before blooming into a smile.

Relief washes through me. He may be laughing at me right now (is he laughing at me right now? I think he is laughing at me right now.), but this sure beats the frostiness of before — and my guilt over finding the photos of that girl. Whoever she is.

Slowly, he gets up from his stool and walks around the counter until he's standing closer to me. His smile now firmly in place, his eyes boring into me. "You know, I can't say I've ever thought about my 'higher state of consciousness.'"

"You haven't?" I ask, shocked to hear how breathless my voice has become.

It's only Alex Walsh. I hate him, remember?

"What is a 'higher state of consciousness' exactly?" His voice is low and sexy, and it rumbles right through me.

Uh-oh.

My heart begins to thud in my chest. Why does he have to stand so darn close to me? First at his place and now here. Doesn't he know it makes me incredibly uncomfortable? Doesn't he know I can catch a hint of his scent (fresh, woody, with a hint of lime)? Doesn't he know I could reach out and touch him? That he's close enough for me to take one small step toward him and . . . and kiss him?

Wait, *what?!*

What the heck am I thinking? This is Alex Walsh. *Alex Walsh.* He's not someone I think about kissing. He's . . . he's a cocky, arrogant jerk who did what he did to me back in high school. I hate him. I *hate* him.

But oh, my. My conviction is melting with every second he's standing here, smirking that sexy smirk at me. I bet he's acutely aware of the effect his proximity is having on me, and he's enjoying making me squirm.

Well, I'm determined not to let that happen. With a dry mouth, I back away from him, only for my butt to smoosh up against the counter behind me.

I'm trapped.

I toss my hair and shoot him a breezy smile. Well, breezy is the aim, anyway.

When I still haven't responded to his question (I've had other things on my mind), he says, "Darcy? Are you okay? You look a little flushed."

"Oh, um, I was just thinking about how to explain what a higher state of consciousness is," I reply. "But you know what? I wouldn't worry about it. That's just Larissa-speak.

All you've got to do is prattle on about your creative vision or something. She'll be more than happy with that."

He rakes his fingers through his hair, messing it up. It makes him look even hotter. "You know, I'm not much of a prattler," he says.

He moves closer to me, his eyes still locked on mine.

Thud thud goes my heart.

Zing zing goes my belly.

What the heck is happening right now? goes my brain.

My hands grab the counter at my sides, the cool touch of stainless steel capturing my attention. But it's only a temporary reprieve from the new and confusing things I'm feeling inside.

"Well, not prattle then. Talk, I guess," I say.

"Sure, I can talk to her. But I quite like talking to you." He pauses before he adds, "Darcy."

The way he says my name has my eyes drifting from his eyes down to his mouth. His lips are parted, ready to be . . . what? Kissed?

No no no no no! What has gotten into me? *Pull yourself together, Darcy!*

He still hasn't moved away, and he's still got his eyes trained on me, boring holes the size of moon craters into my skull. His gaze drifts to my white-knuckled hands and back up to my face. Immediately, I let go of the counter and cross my arms over my chest. I couldn't look any more uncomfortable if I were wearing a ski suit in hundred-degree heat.

"I've been thinking about you today. A lot, actually."

"About how much you don't like me?"

"I never said that. It was you who said you didn't like me. Although secretly, I think you do like me, even if you won't admit it."

"No, I don't," I reply, but it's so lacking in conviction, no court in the land would believe me.

"No you don't like me, or no you won't admit you do?"

I'm too thrown to respond because now he's reaching his

hand out and lightly touching my cheek, making my whole body tingle.

He's going to kiss me. Alex Walsh is going to kiss me.

My mind turns to Seth, the nice guy I've only just begun dating. I think of Alex, and how much I've despised him for so, so long. And then, I push the litany of reasons not to let it happen from my brain as I uncross my arms and drop my hands to my sides. I inch closer to him. We stand as though in limbo, not quite taking the next, inevitable step.

And then, in one fluid motion, his arms circle around me, pulling me into him, and his lips crash against mine. Before I even have time to think, I'm wrapping my arms around him as I kiss him back, and everything—*everything*—around us fades to nothing.

It's just him and me.

Us.

And oh, my, what a kiss! It's the kind that sucks the air from your lungs, makes your legs turn to jelly, makes you completely dizzy. The kind you never want to stop.

My mind whirs with conflicting thoughts. *I'm kissing Alex! But I can't be because I hate him. But oh, my, this feels so good. But it's Alex Walsh! What am I thinking? God, I hope this never stops.*

Eventually, after I swear I begin to see stars, I pull back as my heart bangs like a drum. My confused feelings are strewn across the linoleum floor.

What. Just. Happened?

One second, I'm setting up a meeting, and the next, we're kissing like . . . like *that?*

I have got to get out of here.

I pull my eyes from his and step back, once again smooshing my butt against that darn counter. I begin to slide along the side away from him. I must look totally ridiculous, but what just happened cannot happen again. Kissing Alex? Have I gone *insane?*

"Darcy," he says, reaching out his hand.

I duck away from him. "I, ah, I need to go."

"Do you?" he asks softly.

I nod rapidly. "I came here to—" What did I come here for? My mind's gone blank.

"You wanted to set up a meeting with Larissa."

That's right! "Yes, a meeting," I reply breathlessly.

"I'm out of here at two today. Would that work for Larissa?"

"I'll make two o'clock work for her."

"Will you be there?"

"Yes."

"Okay."

I inch away. "I'll, ah, see you then, then."

Then then?

A fresh smile spreads across his face. "I'm looking forward to it it," he teases.

I slink back from him until I'm far enough away to break the spell. Only, the spell isn't broken, and all I can think about is that kiss.

On legs as wobbly as jelly, I somehow manage to put one foot in front of the other. "And thanks for—" the kiss? "— the photos."

"No problem." He smiles at me, and something new and unexpected moves inside my chest. "See you, Darcy."

I turn away from him and scrunch my eyes shut, clasping my trusty notebook in my hands. I throw my head high and put one foot in front of the other, leaving Alex and that confusing, incredible, so very wrong kiss behind.

Chapter 12

Only, I don't leave it behind. Far, far from it. In fact, it's all I can think about. The way he smiled at me, the touch of his hand on my cheek, the way his lips felt pressed against mine. He's sparked something inside me. New, scary feelings. Feelings I never thought I'd have for him. And now, back in the office, I can't concentrate. I can't do anything but sit at my desk—and think of him.

Work? *Gone.* Seth? *Who?*

Well, not entirely "Seth Who?" I mean, I can't go that far, and certainly not for a guy like Alex. That would be insanity at its most extreme. I'm dating Seth, and I'm very happy about it, too. Extremely happy. Deliriously happy, in fact. Seth is a good guy, the kind of guy I agreed to have the No More Bad Dates Pact find. And I want to be with him I really, really do.

But then Alex kissed me and turned my whole world on its head.

Guilt stabs me in the side. I can't go kissing Alex when I'm dating Seth. Sure. We're not exclusive or anything yet, but that's where we're heading. That's the whole point of the No More Bad Dates Pact.

I bury my head in my hands. What am I *doing?*

I glance at the clock on the wall every couple of minutes. And I know it's every couple of minutes because I'm looking at a freaking clock. I'm totally on edge, waiting, waiting.

Two o'clock comes and goes.

He said he'd be here after finishing work at two. I tap my pencil on my desk. I guess he needs to get across town, so that would mean if he left at exactly two, he would get here by about two-thirty, traffic allowing. But then, does he have a car? Would he get the bus? Walk? There are so many options. Why the heck didn't I pin him down on these details?

And then, when I'm in fear of my pencil shattering from my endless *tap tap tap-ing*, it dawns on me. I've worked it out. I know exactly what's going on here! I know why he kissed me. I slump back in my chair, my mind suddenly clear. If I lived in a cartoon, there would be a big, illuminated lightbulb above my head right now.

Alex is the kind of person who delights in other people's discomfort. Yeah, that's it. He delights in other people's discomfort, mine in particular, and he uses whatever tools at his disposal to achieve his goal.

Jerk.

I can just picture him smirking to himself after I stumbled out of the café kitchen. I bet he sat back down at the counter and congratulated himself on making me squirm. Who knows? Perhaps kissing me was his way to get payback for me looking at that box of photographs he didn't want me to see? Oh, my God. That's it! He lured me in with his smiling and flirting and sexiness until I was powerless to resist him, until kissing him was really the only option open to me. He used his lips as a weapon! I should be able to report this, call the police or something. I need to warn the female population of Auckland that there's an evil mastermind on the loose, using his masculine wiles (is that a thing?) as an extremely effective weapon.

The cheek of him! Well, if that was his plan, then I'm not falling for it again. No way. That kiss will never be repeated. It was a misunderstanding, an accidental meeting of the lips. I'm onto you, Alex Walsh.

Now that I've worked him out, I'm resolved. I'm not going to let him take up another second of my time. I've got a job to do and a celebrity to keep happy in our lovely blue world. I am an extremely busy and important person, and Alex can go stand too close to other girls and kiss them for all I care.

And if he tries to kiss me once more, I will definitely rebuff him. I mean, *puh-lease*. Kiss Alex Walsh? On what planet could *that* ever happen again?

I'm busy undertaking the vital job of sharpening the pencil I've been endlessly tapping against my desk, calm in my resolve, when I get a call from the lobby.

"Hi, Darcy. I've got Alex Walsh here for Larissa," Juliet, the receptionist says.

He's here. My belly does a flip. I glance at the clock. Two thirty on the button. He must have driven. "Right. Yes. I'll be right down."

"Take your time," she replies.

I detect a distinct note of girlishness in her voice that's not usually there.

Typical. Alex will be charming the pants off her, I bet. Maybe standing too close to her, too, making out like he's going to kiss her. Really, I should warn her about him. Sisterhood and all that. Sisters before misters, chicks before d— Oh, I forget that one.

It's like I've been sitting on a spring that's suddenly released. I bounce out of my chair and rush to the ladies' where I do a quick check of my lipstick, pull my long hair over one shoulder, and smooth down my skirt. Just to look professional, of course, nothing more. Whether my legs look good in my black pencil skirt or not is completely irrelevant (they do, in case you were wondering).

I pull my shoulders back and walk through our offices, catch the elevator down, and stride out into the lobby. I spot him straight away. Dressed the way he was when that thing I'm no longer going to think about happened, he has one elbow resting on the reception desk as he talks to Juliet. She's so busy blushing and giggling that she doesn't even notice my arrival.

I clear my throat, and they both turn to look at me. "Thank you, Juliet," I say in clipped tones.

Juliet has the good sense to look abashed. "Oh, hi, Darcy. We were just . . . talking. You know."

She's right. I do know. She was flirting her little hiney off with him. I want to tell her not to waste her time. Sisterhood, remember? I make a mental note to come back down and tell her after Alex has gone.

I turn to Alex and use my smooth, professional voice when I say, "Alex, good to see you again. Shall we?" I gesture toward the elevator and raise my eyebrows in expectation at him.

"We shall," he replies, totally mocking me.

Jerk.

Gone are my feelings of guilt and regret that made me into that bumbling idiot back at the café. Gone are my confusing feelings for him that have been churning inside me all day after our kiss. He said we should move on, and that's exactly what I'm doing, right back into "I hate Alex Walsh" territory. The status quo, where I know what's what and how I feel.

"Good. Excellent," I say to Alex. I turn to Juliet. "Thank you, Juliet." Oops. I already said that. Dammit. I shoot her an embarrassed smile.

"No problem," she replies, although she's not even looking at me. Instead, she's gazing up at Alex as though he's some sort of god, here visiting us mere mortals on Earth.

I turn on my heel and stomp across the lobby toward the elevator. As I walk, I give myself a stern talking to. So what if Alex was flirting with Juliet? What does it matter to me? He can flirt with whomever he wants. It's absolutely none of my business.

And anyway, I hate him. Totally and utterly hate him. And I would do well to remember that at all times, particularly if I ever find myself in the position I was in in the café kitchen this morning.

"You like to walk fast, huh?" Alex says as he catches up with me.

I glance at him out of the corner of my eye. "That's right. I'm a very busy person, you know. I've got lots and lots to do."

Hmmm, yes. Like tap my pencil incessantly against my desk.

"Good to know," he replies.

We reach the elevator and I press the "up" button. I wait, tapping my heeled foot against the marble floor. When the elevator doesn't arrive within about two and a half seconds, I press the "up" button again.

Alex throws me a concerned look. "You okay? You seem a little stressed."

"Yes, thank you," I reply as I press the button for the third time. Where the heck is an elevator when you need one?

"Look, Darcy," he begins, but I refuse to look at him. "If you're feeling weird because of what happened between us this morning—"

"I'm fine," I snap. Talking about kissing him has got to be almost as dangerous as doing the actual kissing.

"Are you positive you're fine? You don't seem it."

"I am. I'm perfectly fine. Thank you, Alex*ander*." I risk a furtive glance at him only to see a smile growing on his face. I turn away immediately. Smile equals weapon, remember?

"Alexander?" he questions.

"That's your name, isn't it?"

"I guess." His eyes skim over me before he adds, "Darce-ette? Darce-arina?"

A bubble of laughter rises in my throat, and I work hard to hold it in. It's the nerves and the absurdity of the situation.

Me, here with Alex, post-kiss. "You sound ridiculous," I scoff. "What exactly are you trying to say?"

He shrugs. "Darcy's got to be short for something, right? If it's not those first two, maybe it's Darc-ence?"

I bite my lips together to stop the giggle bubble from popping out. It's getting harder to contain. "My name is Darcy." I press the button again.

"Come on. Darce-end. You've got to admit that's a little bit funny."

I give him a condescending look. "Go flirt with Juliet. I'm sure she appreciates your humor a lot more than I ever will."

"Oh, I see."

I whip my head to look at him. "What does that mean?"

"Nothing. It makes sense, that's all." He turns his attention to the elevator door.

"No, it doesn't."

"Oh, I think it does."

"Alex, you don't know me, so don't go assuming things about me. Got it?" Even though he's completely right. Seeing him flirt with Juliet did something to me, something I'm not ready to admit.

I tap my foot some more. Where the heck is this freaking elevator?

"Sure," he replies with a shrug. "But, for what it's worth, that thing that happened between us before was, well, I liked it."

I glare at him. "Well, that's good because it's not going to happen again. Ever."

With his eyes intensely concentrated on me, he replies, "Pity." He's got that condescending smirk back on his face, and I wonder why I've been obsessing about this guy for the last three hours. I mean, what was I thinking? A total waste of my precious time. He's the same old Alex Walsh: a self-centered, cocky jerk.

I return his condescending smirk with additional volume. "No, it's not a pity."

He turns up the dial up on his own darn smirk. "I think it

is," he pauses before he adds, "Darce-onia."

I roll my eyes. "I told you it's Darcy. Plain and simple."

"Oh, believe me," he says with a chortle, "there's nothing plain or simple about you."

My hands fly to my hips. "What does that mean?"

He shrugs. "It means what it says."

The elevator pings and the doors slide open. *Hallelujah.*

"After you." He gives a sweeping gesture with his arm as though he's doing me some big favor by allowing me to enter the elevator before him.

"No, after you," I reply. "You're the visitor."

"Ladies first."

I clench my teeth. "Fine." I walk into the elevator, followed by Fake Gentleman Alex and all his comments and shrugs and superior smiles. I press the button for my floor then turn and face the doors. As they begin to close, it occurs to me that we're now alone for the second time today.

Well, even though it's a total cliché for two people to make out in an elevator, particularly when those two people have already made out in the kitchen of a café on the same day, there's no way that is going to happen.

I stand rigid, facing the doors, willing the elevator to reach my floor in record time.

He clears his throat.

I don't look at him.

"Darcy?"

Without turning, I say, "What?"

"You've got something stuck to your shoe."

I roll my eyes. There's nothing stuck to my shoe. What is he talking about? I'm certain it's some sort of ploy, but I look down at my feet regardless, only to see a trail of toilet paper attached to the heel of one of my shoes. Oh, no. It must have got caught on my shoe when I visited the ladies'. Of all the times for something like this to happen! Icy mortification creeps up my neck. I scuff my heel against the elevator floor to loosen the paper. It takes some effort and several attempts, and my cheeks begin to burn. "Thank you," I mutter as I bend down to collect the offending paper in my hand.

"No problem." There's more than a simple note of amusement in his voice. In fact, it's a virtual symphony. "I know you're a really busy person with work and all, but sometimes it's good to stop and smell the roses. Or stop and remove the toilet paper from your heel. You know, whichever one crops up."

I shoot him a fake smile while I fume inside. Hot lava bubbles up, ready to burst out of me and burn him to cinders.

The doors slide open, and I give a silent prayer of thanks. With only a scrap of dignity left, I stride out of the elevator. I ball the offending paper, put my hand behind my back (as though that's going to make this situation any less embarrassing), and turn to face Alex.

"Welcome to Cinnamon, Larissa Monroe's wellness platform," I parrot, delivering the message Larissa wants every person who visits her company to hear.

"And here I was thinking this was Smurf headquarters. Nathan would love it here." He looks around the office. "Seriously, is everything in this place blue?"

I press my lips together and ignore his jibe. "You used that weak joke already," I point out. And yes, it's not that I haven't wondered about the insane amount of blue in here before. But I'm not about to share that with Alex "kiss me in the kitchen" Walsh.

"Have a seat." I indicate the two-seater sofas. "I'll go see if Larissa is ready for you."

He surveys the seating area. "Which one is Papa's favorite? I wouldn't want to sit there. I bet that guy has got a real temper on him."

"You're hilarious," I deadpan.

He shrugs. "I'm a barista-slash-photographer-slash-comedian. Don't you remember? In fact, I believe it was you who suggested I pursue a career in comedy. When you were at my apartment. Or was it when you were alone with me in the kitchen earlier today?"

Is he trying to put me off? Well, it's not going to work. I put on my best motherly voice and say, "Alex, might I offer you a suggestion? Drop the Smurfs thing before you meet with Larissa. She takes the whole color therapy thing very seriously."

"Good advice. I'll go with an Avatar approach, shall I? More up her alley? Or maybe Cookie Monster?" He laughs at his own joke. "Oh, yeah, definitely Cookie Monster. That guy has got 'Larissa Monroe' written all over him."

I shake my head in frustration. Okay, and a touch of amusement. But there's no way I'm telling him that.

The balled piece of paper is beginning to burn a hole in my hand now. "Wait here," I instruct. I beat a hasty retreat to the ladies', where I dispose of the paper and wash my hands several times over (because *euw, toilet paper*). I look up at my reflection in the mirror above the basin.

You can do this. He's just a guy.

Yeah, a guy I had the most incredible kiss of my life with a mere handful of hours ago.

I suck in a breath and then blow it out. It'll be fine. We'll be with Larissa, talking about his work.

I smooth down my hair and square my shoulders.

I can do this.

Fully psyched, I walk back out into the offices only to find the sofa where I left him empty of one Alex Walsh. I tap on Larissa's door. When there's no response, I swing it open. Empty.

He's got to be here somewhere.

I walk down the hallway and pause at Maureen's desk. "Have you seen a guy come through here in the last few minutes?"

"You mean the one who looked like he could have stepped out of an aftershave commercial?" she asks with a grin, and I nod. "He came through here with Larissa. They're in the Red Room."

The Red Room. Of course. Larissa wants answers to her

questions about his "higher state of consciousness." I suppress a smile. Watching how he deals with Larissa's questioning is going to be fun.

"Thanks," I say to Maureen.

"Let me know if you need a *104*. It was fun this morning, although the guy who just went past didn't look the type to me."

"You never know, Maureen. Wolves in sheep's clothing and all that." She nods her agreement then I make my way through the office to the Red Room. I knock and then push the door open to see Alex and Larissa huddled over his portfolio. Alex is pointing at something, saying, "—and they're considered the foothills of the Himalayas," just as he had to me at his apartment.

"Fascinating," Larissa says, clearly hanging on his every word.

Huh. Another woman falling for Alex's charms. *So* predictable.

His eyes meet mine. "Oh, there you are, Darcy. Did you get the shoe emergency sorted out?"

"Shoe emergency?" Larissa questions in alarm.

"I dealt with it. It was nothing." I give a wave of my hand while I throw Alex a series of sharpened daggers with my eyes. I turn to Larissa. "What have you got up to?"

"Oh, Alex Walsh was just telling me about the mountainous region of northern India. I feel such a connection to it, even though I've never been there." She crinkles her forehead. "Why haven't I been there, Darcy?" She tilts her head to look at me as though I have the answer.

I'm ready with my response. "Because the time hasn't been right, Larissa. Perhaps you'd like me to schedule you a trip?"

"Yes. Yes, do that. Alex Walsh told me the Dalai Lama lives there. Did you know that, Darcy? The Dalai Lama."

"No, I didn't."

"I need to visit this place. It's calling me." She raises her hand to her ear. "Can you hear it?"

Larissa "hearing" something call to her is all par for the

course in my job, but I swear I spot Alex straining to listen.

I flip open my Labrador puppy notebook. "Absolutely. What I'm going to do is take a note, and we can organize a trip for you when your calendar allows."

"Wonderful. Now," she says as she loops her hands around Alex's arm, "I was just telling this incredibly talented man here that I want this exhibition to open when I launch my new line of herbal tinctures."

My eyebrows ping right up. She'd already given me a tight timeframe, but this is insane. "Your herbal tinctures? But that's soon, Larissa."

"It's in two weeks," Alex says, and I snap my head up to gawk at him. He raises his own eyebrows in silent communication. He knows it's an insanely short period of time to organize a gallery opening, too.

"Two weeks?" I say breathlessly.

Alex's eyes lock onto mine. "Well, one week and five days, to be precise."

"But . . . but that's hardly any time at all. We need to work out what to exhibit, hanging it, catering, the guest list, the—"

"Darcy, darling, everything will fall into place, just as it always does. Trust me on this."

I harrumph. Everything will fall into place because of all the hard work I put in.

Larissa's hands fly to her chest, and she lets out a satisfied sigh. "I have such faith in you. Really, I do." She reaches for Alex's and my hands. "In both of you."

"Err, thanks," Alex says awkwardly.

If it wasn't for the fact I'm freaking out about this significantly shortened timeline right now, I might have laughed.

Larissa walks toward the door. "I'll relieve you of your other tasks, Darcy. I want you all over this one hundred percent."

I try to swallow. My throat feels like it's shriveled right up. "I'll, ah, I'll get it done."

"We'll get it done," Alex corrects me.

"I know you will. I have such faith." Larissa looks from Alex to me. "You two have a truly beautiful synergy. Did you know that?"

Yeah, a beautiful synergy that got us playing an extended game of tonsil hockey in a café kitchen only this morning.

Alex raises his eyebrows at me, his mouth lifting into a smile. "A beautiful synergy, huh?"

Larissa looks between Alex and me, her face bright. "Yes! A strong, incredible synergy that the two of you must capitalize on. I can feel it. Can you feel it?"

"Oh, I can definitely feel something," Alex replies, his eyes not leaving my face. "Can you feel it, Darcy?"

I shoot him a withering look. Synergy or no synergy, I know one thing for absolute certain: the next week and five days working with Alex is going to be nothing short of sheer, unadulterated hell.

Chapter 13

"What the heck am I going to do?"

I take another slug of sparkling wine, willing the alcohol to hit my bloodstream and somehow miraculously make Alex disappear. I let out a defeated sigh. Alcohol may be good, but it's not that good.

Erin has dragged me to Cozy Cottage High Tea to help me eat and drink away my bad feelings about Alex. Of course, I made her check to ensure he wasn't working here today first. Twice. You can't be too sure when the person you're trying to avoid seems to crop up wherever you go.

"Come on, Darcy. Is it really that bad?" Erin asks as she chooses another sandwich from the tiered cake stand.

"Yes, Erin. It is that bad."

"I don't get it. Why does he get under your skin so much?" She pops something into her mouth. "Oh, yum. You have got to try this, Darce. It's passionfruit, I think. No, wait, it's feijoa." She raises her eyes to the ceiling as she chews.

"Whatever it is, it's delicious. Here." She picks one up in her fingers and holds it out for me.

With a distinct lack of enthusiasm, I lift my plate, and she places in on it.

"Try it. Go on. It's so good, I'm sure it'll pull you right out of your Alex-induced grump."

I blow out a puff of air and then put it in my mouth and chew.

"Well?"

"It's delicious," I say, my enthusiasm level at about a minus ten.

Erin laughs. "Say it like you mean it, babe."

My posture sags as I slump back in my chair. "You see? That's what Alex has done to me. He's sucked all the pleasure out of eating delicious, sugary treats. And you know how much I love eating delicious, sugary treats."

Erin pulls a face. "I do."

"I was forced to work with Alex all day on Friday. All day! It was a nightmare."

"Darce, it's only Saturday."

"You see? One day of working with the guy and I'm already off sugar. It's a bad sign, Erin, a very bad sign."

She twists her mouth as she studies me. "Has something happened with him?"

I move my glass of sparkling wine to my lips and drain it. Placing it carefully back on the table, I lift my eyes to hers. She's looking at me questioningly, waiting for my reply.

I could really do with getting this whole Alex thing off my chest. You know what they say: a problem shared is a problem halved. I chew on my lip for a moment. "Okay. I'll tell you. But you need to know that I'm working on it and it's not going to be a problem."

"Sure. Working on it, not a problem. Got it," she replies with a business-like nod.

I glance around the room on the off chance Alex is about to jump out from behind the curtains and yell, "Surprise!" Which is crazy, I know, because a) Sophie's told Erin twice that he's not working here today, and b) that would be totally weird. But, as I said before, when avoiding someone who seems to crop up unexpectedly everywhere, you can't be too careful.

With no sign of the man in question, I begin. "I needed to get the photos from him that were here at High Tea, so I went to see him at the café. He was in the kitchen. Bailey said I could go back there, which I did."

"And?" I'm clearly not getting to the interesting part fast enough for her.

"Actually, I need to back up a bit."

She lets out an exasperated sigh. "If you've got to."

"At his apartment, I looked at something I shouldn't have looked at."

Her eyes bulge. "It was him, naked!"

"No! I'm not a Peeping Tom, or whatever the female equivalent of that is. A Peeping Thomasina, perhaps? Or a Peeping—"

"Just get on with it!" she exclaims in irritation. "I want to know what you saw."

"Okay. So, I saw these photographs, totally by accident, and he got pretty angry with me."

"What were the photos of?"

"A beautiful woman. Like, next-level beautiful."

"Oh."

"So, the next day, I went to the café to apologize to him."

"And?" she leads.

"I apologized, and something else happened."

"What? You're killing me here, Darce. Talk about dragging a story out."

I press my lips together for a moment. "We kissed."

"You kissed?!" Erin shrieks.

People at the neighboring tables turn to look at us.

"Erin," I protest through clenched teeth.

"Sorry, sorry. My friend kissed a hot guy, that's all," she explains to the room, much to my mortification.

"I cannot believe you did that."

"Don't worry about it. They've all gone back to eating their high tea. So, I want details. Did you kiss him or did he kiss you?"

"He was the one who came over and stood right in front of me, and he made it pretty clear he was leading up to it. But when it came to the actual kiss? It was mutual."

A smile spreads across her pretty face. "How was it?"

"Oh, Erin, I wish I could tell you it was terrible, but it wasn't. It was the opposite of terrible."

"The opposite of terrible?" Erin repeats with a laugh. "You have got to get better ways to describe kissing hot guys."

"Well, I can tell you one thing right now: it's never happening again. And I told him that."

"You did?"

"Of course I did. There's no point letting him think I want to go there again with him."

Her face creases into a smile. "But you do, don't you?"

"No!" I protest. Heat blooms in my cheeks.

"I think the lady doth protest too much."

"You sound like Sophie's brother." Sean, Sophie's brother, loves to quote Shakespeare because he thinks it makes him cultured or super smart or something. It doesn't. It's just a bit irritating for everyone else.

"But I'm right, aren't I?" Erin is persistent. "You'd like to kiss Alex again. Probably more than once."

I clench my teeth and draw my lips into a thin line. After a moment, I give a deeply unenthusiastic nod.

"Interesting."

"It's not interesting. It's terrible. I'm supposed to be dating Seth. He's the guy I decided to go out with. He's the one you and Sophie vetted. And more than that, he's the good guy here. Alex is . . . well, Alex is not a good guy."

She creases her forehead. "Why do you say that? He seems like a great guy to me."

I harrumph. A great guy? Alex? I don't think so. "He's not."

"But—" she begins.

"Can we leave it at that, please?"

Erin lets out a puff of air. "Okay, but one of these days you're going to have to tell me about what happened back then."

"Sure." Like when hell freezes over. "The problem is, we've got to work together, and there's this constant tension between us."

She fans her face with her hand. "Oh, I bet there is, girl."

"Erin!"

"Look, you've either got to just go for it with the guy and get over the whole high school thing," Erin says.

"Or?" I add hopefully.

"Or you'll have to set some clear boundaries."

I leap on her second idea. The first one is *so* not an option. "Boundaries sound like an awesome plan. Like what?" I reach down to my purse and pull out my trusty notebook and a pencil, open to a fresh page, and write "Alex: Boundaries" at the top of the page. I underline it twice.

"What is it about him that makes you want to kiss him again?"

An image of Alex's eyes looking at me intensely flashed into my mind. "It's the way he looks at me."

"Oooh, he *smolders*."

I smile. "Yeah, he does."

"In that case, tell him he can't smolder at you anymore."

"I can't say that!" I balk. "It would seem completely weird."

She bites her lip. "Good point. You'll just have to look away at the first sign of one of his smolders coming on."

"I guess I can do that." I write "No smoldering" down as number one. "Good start. What next?"

"No more kissing. That's a given."

"Definitely." I write "2. No more kissing" down. "Anything else?"

"Talk to him about how much you like Seth. The power of positive thinking is proven, you know."

I write it down under number three before I look back up at her. "You're saying I should try and think my way out of my feelings for Alex by talking about Seth?"

"Exactly. And make sure Alex knows you're really into Seth. That way, if he tries to kiss you again, you can throw it in his face with the whole 'I can't be unfaithful to my man' kind of thing. If he doesn't feel bad about that, then he's not a decent person."

"This is good stuff, Erin. I've got three points now. What else have you got?"

She taps her chin for a while before her face creases into a smile. "I guess there's only one other thing you can do."

"What's that?" I ask, my pencil poised.

"Pray."

I write "4. Pr—" before I stop and look up at her. "Pray? That's all you've got for number four?"

She crosses her arms. "Tell me again how terrible kissing Alex was."

My heart sinks to my shoes. "The opposite of terrible."

Erin gives a sage nod. "Pray, honey. A lot. Because from what you've told me, I think you're going to need it."

Chapter 14

I spend the rest of the afternoon and into the evening preparing myself for my date with Seth. Both mentally and physically. As I style my hair into loose waves, apply a second coat of mascara, and slip on my favorite date dress — a halter dress with an A-line skirt in (ironic) Barbie pink — I remind myself of all the things I like about Seth. He's sweet, honest, and straight-up, plus he's very good looking. What more can a girl want in a date?

Really, I've blown this whole Alex thing out of proportion. All I need is some space from him, spent with a cute, uncomplicated guy. And Seth is the man for the job. And anyway, thanks to my discussion with Erin at High Tea today, I've got my four-point manifesto for dealing with Alex. I have totally got this.

The buzzer sounds and Erin calls out, "I'll get it," as I smooth my lipstick on and take one final check in the mirror. Date-ready, I reach the living room as Erin is leaving the front door ajar for Seth.

"Remember," she stage whispers as though he's within earshot, "no thinking about kissing anyone but Seth."

"Got it," I say with a nod, although my mind betrays me with a traitorous memory before I can even think the word "boundaries."

"Knock, knock," Seth calls out at the front door.

Erin shoots me an encouraging smile. "Good luck, girl."

"Thanks." I collect my purse from the kitchen table. "Coming, Seth," I call out as head out to meet him.

"Wow, you look incredible, Darcy," he says as he plants a soft kiss on my cheek.

I take in his sports jacket over a white polo and pressed jeans. Although he's only twenty-nine, he dresses a lot like my dad. I push the thought away. "You do, too."

"I've got an Uber waiting for us downstairs."

"Great."

"Bye, you two," Erin says behind me. "Have fun."

"We will," Seth says as he slips his arm around my waist.

Down at street level, we slide into the car, and he takes my hand in his. "Do you like sushi?" he asks.

"Of course. Who doesn't?"

It's a rhetorical question, but he takes it literally. "My mom. And my cousin Dale. They don't eat fish or shellfish. Weird, huh?"

"Weird."

"I mean, what would they do if they were stranded on a desert island? Starve to death?"

"I bet there wouldn't be a whole lot of sushi on a deserted island."

He snorts with laughter. "Beautiful *and* funny. You're the real deal, aren't you, Darcy?" He squeezes my hand, and I smile at him. Seth's sweet and generous. I'm lucky to be dating him.

We pull up outside a restaurant in the swanky Britomart area of downtown Auckland city.

"Do you want to have a drink before we eat?" he asks.

"Sure, sounds great."

We cross the street and enter a busy bar with people chatting and a live band playing loudly.

"What would you like to drink?" he yells into my ear.

"A glass of Chardonnay, please."

With our drinks in hands, he yells, "Shall we try upstairs? It might be quieter."

I give him the thumbs-up, and he takes me by the hand. We walk up a flight of stairs into another part of the bar. The place is still busy, but a whole lot quieter than downstairs. I spy an empty table and two chairs on a balcony, which we sit down at.

"To us," he says raising his glass.

"To us," I reply as we clink glasses. I take a sip. The cool wine slips down my throat and warms my belly.

"How was your week?" I ask him.

"I was busy, as usual," he begins.

As he tells me about his work dramas, I listen intently. It's clear he cares about what he does and enjoys success. Both very attractive things in a man. So, that's two big ticks for Seth. Not that I'm running a tally on him or anything. It's simply useful to focus on the positives. Glass half full and all that.

"Tell me something, Darcy. Is this our second or third date? I get confused."

"Well, according to the No More Bad Dates Pact, this is date number two," I say.

"You're so cute with your pact."

"Thanks," I reply uncertainly. "Do you mean that or are you being sarcastic?"

"Oh, I mean it. You're taking control, taking the horse by the reins."

"Exactly," I reply with a nod. "Looking for guys like you."

"I'm glad to hear it. So our third date will be my show jumping event."

"I'm really looking forward to it. That would be amazing. I love horses."

"*Eventing* is one of my passions, and I'm so excited I get to share it with you. Although I do need to warn you, this is eventing with a difference."

I beam at him. "I'm sure I'll love it."

"I really hope you do."

"Do you wear the whole equestrian outfit? You know, the black jacket, the knee-high boots, the tan pants that pouf out?"

He smiles. "They're called 'jodhpurs,' and of course I do. You've got to look the part, you know."

I beam at him as I imagine Seth in his equestrian clothes, looking completely dashing. He must look like Mr. Darcy out for his morning ride. Formal, dapper, and oh-so cute. I'm more than a little excited when my belly does a little flip at the thought. Yes! This is exactly what I need! Forget about Alex, Seth is an equestrian hottie, and I'm the lucky girl who gets to be out on a date with him.

"I bet you look good," I say shyly.

"I'm far too modest to say that," he replies with a cheeky grin.

Fortified by our growing bond, I decide to tackle this Alex thing head-on.

"Seth, can I ask you something?"

"Anything?"

"Are you any good at smoldering?"

His eyebrows ping up in surprise. "Excuse me?"

"You know, *smoldering*." I draw the word out for emphasis. "All sexy and whatnot."

"Oh, ah, I'm not sure." He pulls a face that makes him look like he's either got trapped wind or eaten a dodgy curry.

"Are you okay?" I ask.

The expression disappears. "That was my attempt at a smolder."

It was? Oh, dear sweet Lord.

"It was really good, Seth. You've got a talent there. A smolder talent."

Damn Alex and his expert smoldering! I felt sure Seth — who

I might add is just as good looking as Alex, if not more so — would be able to produce an equally knee-weakening smolder.

He grins at me, clearly chuffed with his efforts. "I must remember to smolder more often, then."

I paste on a smile. "Absolutely."

Oh, please no.

He pulls the weird face once more, and I titter nervously before I take a large gulp of wine. I need to focus on the equestrian thing. That worked a treat before. Seth on a horse. Seth looking like Mr. Darcy. Seth whisking me off my feet and carrying me to his castle. Okay, I may be getting a little carried away, but it's working.

Just as long as he doesn't try to smolder again.

We finish our drinks and, flush with the wine and my renewed sense of attraction for Seth, continue to the restaurant where we enjoy a tasty meal. Conversation flows, and by the end of the evening, we are standing by the entrance to my building, and I know we're about to have our second kiss.

He takes a step closer to me, and my nerves kick up a notch. "I had a really good time tonight."

"Me too. That new sushi place is really good."

"Who knew sushi could be fused with Thai and Mexican food at the same time?" he replies with a smile.

"It sure sounds like it should be a total disaster."

"Exactly." He slides a hand around my waist. This is it. Seth and I are going to kiss for the second time, and it's going to be amazing. So amazing, in fact, it'll knock me sideways and dispel any memories of Alex. I'm absolutely sure of it.

He angles his head down, and I tilt mine up. As his lips brush mine, I let out an expectant sigh. It's a nice kiss. Soft, tentative at first, careful. Pleasant. Really, there's nothing wrong with it. Not too soft, not too hard. But . . . but what? He's sweet, he's cute, he's into me, and I've even had a couple of belly flips tonight. This *should* work.

I know what! All I need to do is think of sexy things. That's it. If I think of sexy things while I'm kissing Seth, I'll feel all the things I'm supposed to be feeling.

Here goes nothing. Seth on a horse. Seth looking like Mr. Darcy.

I kiss him again and . . . nothing. Well, not nothing, exactly. But nothing in comparison with locking lips with He Who Shall Not Be Named. (Not Voldemort, by the way. Alex.)

I pull away and muster a smile from somewhere. "Thanks, I'd, ah, better get inside."

"Shall I come up?"

"No," I reply hurriedly. "No, my, ah, roommate's sick," I lie and instantly feel bad about it. "I would hate for you to catch it."

His forehead creases in concern or confusion, I don't quite know which. "Erin's sick? She looked all right before we went out."

A brainwave hits. "She messaged me. That's what she did. She messaged me during our dinner to say she was sick. Terribly, terribly sick. Vomit and mucous and all that nasty stuff."

Lies, lies, lies. Gah! I'm a truly horrible person.

"Vomit *and* mucous? Wow, that sounds serious. Should we take her to see a doctor?"

Wy does he have to be so sweet? And why can't I enjoy kissing him more?

"Oh, I'm sure she'll be okay," I say with a wave of my hand. "But I'd hate for you to catch it, you know, before your big show jumping event."

He stands up taller. "That's very thoughtful of you, Darcy. Thank you. I guess I'll be going then." He leans in for another kiss, and I quickly peck him on the lips, like he's my aged aunt with upper lip whiskers and the last thing I want to do is kiss her crinkled, hairy skin.

"Goodnight," I trill as I turn and bolt up the steps to my building. As I swing the door open, I catch a glimpse of his confused face before I dash up the stairs.

Once in my apartment, the door safely closed, I lean up

against it and drop my purse to the floor. I scrunch my eyes shut and try not to think it, but there's no use. No matter how much I will myself not to, all I can think about is how kissing Seth felt absolutely nothing like kissing Alex.

Chapter 15

"More tea?" Erin asks as she holds the pretty china teapot in her hands.

"More tea would be simply wonderful," I reply with a bright smile.

We're back at High Tea. I know, I know. Twice in a matter of a mere handful of days does seem a little indulgent. What can I say? There are a lot of things going on for me right now. Alex has me twisted up into an emotional pretzel, I've been working myself ragged on getting this gallery ready for its opening in just over a week, and I've got to visualize Seth dressed as Mr. Darcy just so I can kiss him.

All in all, it's amazing I can even function. Bring on the sugary treats.

Of course, it helps that Larissa is out of town for the day, and if you catch Erin in the right mood, she's easily persuaded to skip out on her job for a couple of hours. She said she's always in dire need of some estrogen to balance out all the testosterone she's got to deal with in her job at Auckland City Club. Really, my heart bleeds for the poor girl being surrounded by hot rugby players. Some people have it so tough, right?

So here we both sit—a three-tiered cake stand on our table, crammed full of delicious treats—as we chat, listen to the relaxing music, and sip our tea. It's perfect girl time. Well, it would be if it weren't for the current state of my life polluting my brain.

I hold my teacup up for Erin. "Don't you love the way these Cozy Cottage High Tea cups are so elegant and cute? This is no regular beverage. They make you feel like you're sipping something really special."

She pours tea into my china cup with a little giggle.

"What?" I ask.

"Nothing. It's just you're in a bit of a manic mood today."

My mind darts instantly to Alex. If I'm manic, it's only because I have so many confusing feelings about him. I want to murder him slowly, but I want to kiss him again, too. Seriously, this situation is not good for my mental wellbeing. I delay my response by taking a sip my hot tea. I place my cup on its matching saucer and calmly state, "I'm not manic. I'm perfectly fine, as you can see."

Erin gives me a knowing look. "Oh, you so are manic, girl. And I know exactly why."

I shake my head and implore her with my gaze. "Don't say it. Don't say it."

"Look, you should at least talk about it, babe." Her eyes light up when she leans in closer to me. "Has he kissed you again?"

I lift my eyebrows and feign innocence. "Who?"

"Don't pretend you don't know who I'm talking about. We're at High Tea again, in the middle of the workweek no less, and you've skipped all the savory treats and gone straight for the sugar. I know you too well, Darcy Evans."

I let out a puff of air. "There's been no more kissing."

Erin's face drops. "I was sure there had been."

I slowly shake my head from side to side. "I've been deploying my four-point manifesto of boundaries, remember? Any time he's smoldered at me or stood too close, I've maneuvered myself away."

"It's working?" Erin asks, surprised.

"Either that or he got the message."

"Maybe his attraction to you was a fleeting thing for him. Maybe he felt something for you in the moment, and now that moment has gone. Poof, in a cloud of smoke."

"That would be ideal." My heart sinks, and my shoulders slump as I think of Alex not having any feelings for me. Even though I know it would be so much simpler, I feel a little empty inside.

"Say it like you mean it, babe," Erin replies.

"I do mean it. Kissing Alex was a momentary lapse of reason on my part. And anyway, I'm dating someone else, and he's just the kind of guy we set up the No More Bad Dates Pact to find."

"Exactly. Do you know how few genuinely nice guys there are out there?"

"Sadly, I do."

"I found you your great guy, now I need to find one for myself."

"Maybe Seth has a brother?" I offer.

She laughs. "Maybe. Now, have you tried this?" She points at one of the little pastries on the cake stand.

"Oh, you've got to," Sophie says, materializing at our table. "They're new. Bailey came up with the recipe, and I swear they'll add ten pounds a week to my thighs, they're that good."

I pick one of the little slices up in my fingers and pop it into my mouth. "Mmm."

"See?"

"*So* good," I murmur as I relish the flavor.

"They should be. They're made of sugar and butter, with added sugar butter. Topped with more sugar and butter," Sophie says.

"You can't go wrong with sugar butter," Erin says. "Can you take a quick break to chat, Soph?"

Sophie looks around the room. "Sure. The customers look happy enough, and I need to know how your boundaries thing is working with Alex."

I'd told Sophie about what had happened with Alex when she dropped 'round Erin's and my apartment on Sunday. She agreed the four-point manifesto was the right choice, and she's been checking in with me through messages ever since.

"Is he working today?" Erin asks as her eyes flash to mine.

"Oh, please don't say he is," I moan. Did I just say that out loud? The look on both Erin's and Sophie's faces tells me I did. "What I meant to say is I see him all the time right now since we're working together on his exhibition, that's all."

"There hasn't been any more kissing," Erin tells Sophie.

"Oh." She looks at Erin before adding, "That's a good thing, right?"

"Oh, yes. Definitely," I confirm. "I hate him, remember? People don't kiss people they hate. Or at least they shouldn't. It's bad for their health."

Erin and Sophie share a look.

Sophie pulls a chair over from an empty table beside us and sits down. "I've got to tell you Alex is working for a few hours, Darce. He just arrived." She jerks her head in the direction of the front door, where I spot the man himself.

My chest tightens. He's pushing open the door and taking his long-legged stride across the floor. He turns his head toward us, and our eyes lock for a moment before I give a curt nod and turn away.

Why did I choose High Tea to bury my concerns in sugar?

Sophie asks, "How's it going working with him?"

"Fine," I reply as I take another morsel from the cake stand and pop it in my mouth.

"Do you know how to put an exhibition together?" Erin asks.

I give a shrug. "Alex seems to think he knows what he's

doing."

"He does. He's exhibited before. Lots, I think," Sophie says.

I give a tight-lipped smile. "Good to know."

I notice Sophie and Erin share another look, and I furrow my brow as I look between them. "What is going on with you two?"

Sophie places her elbows on the table. "Tell me something, Darce. How long have we been friends?"

That's an odd question. "Sophie, you know how long."

"Humor me," she replies.

"Ever since Mrs. Matthews put as all in detention on the same day when we were fourteen."

"It was like we were our own little *Breakfast Club*. Only, no Judd Nelson wearing a single, black fingerless glove," Erin adds.

"Yeah. What was up with the single glove? And that weird foot bandana?" Sophie asks with a laugh.

"It was an '80s thing." I shrug because everyone knows they made some pretty suspicious fashion choices back then. Frizzy hair, leg warmers, and oversized shoulder pads, anyone?

"So," Sophie says, clearly wanting to get back to her point, "that means we've been BFFs for over eleven years now."

"You know your math. Mrs. Matthews would be proud," I reply.

"Eleven years is a long time. A very long time," Erin says with a philosophical nod. "I bet you could know someone inside and out in that amount of time. Right, Darce?"

I shoot Sophie a sideways glance. "True."

"And everyone knows BFFs tell each other everything. *E-ver-y-thing*." Erin carefully sounds out each syllable of the word.

Sophie nods as she stares at me. "Yup. Everything."

I narrow my eyes at my friends. It's like they've rehearsed this conversation, decided who's going to say what, and are now delivering it to me. It's beyond strange. "You girls are acting weird. What's this all about?"

"Nothing *specific*. Not unless there's something you think

you might have missed telling us about yourself? Something that might bear some relevance to certain people now?" Erin says in a suspiciously leading way, and they both look at me intently, waiting for my response.

"Like, say, back in high school, to choose a timeframe. Totally randomly, of course." This from Sophie.

"I have no clue what you two are going on about," I say in utter exasperation. "Can't a girl enjoy her sneaky high tea in peace when she should be at work?"

"Of course you can, Darcy," Erin says kindly.

Sophie has another stab at whatever the heck they're trying to get at. "Is there any piece of information we should know about . . . you?" she asks.

They both continue to stare at me in expectation. And then it dawns on me. They *have* rehearsed this conversation, they *have* decided who's going to say what, and they *are* now delivering it to me.

I place my cup on its saucer once more, cross my arms, and lean back in my seat. "Okay, you two. What's this little show of yours really all about?"

"Nothing *specific*," Erin repeats with that meaningful look on her face.

This is getting silly now.

"Erin Andrews, you have always been the worst liar on the face of the planet. Will one of you *please* spill the beans?" I glare at them both.

I can be quite direct and bossy when I want to be. Although I don't pull it out very often, I impress even myself at times. It can really come in handy with Larissa, like when she thought we could increase our sense of spiritual calm by dying our hair blue to match our blue office. I had to explain to her that blue hair is for pop divas and the elderly, and since we are neither of those, we should all stick with our current natural looks. (Well, some are more natural than others, but that's all I'll say on the subject of Larissa's completely "born with it" blonde locks.)

Sophie lays her hands on the table, palms down. "All right.

We were hoping you would volunteer the info, but since you're clearly playing dumb, I guess we'll cut to the chase."

"What happened with Alex back in high school?" Erin asks.

My heart begins to race as a sudden coldness worms its way around inside my core. "Nothing in particular," I respond with faux confidence.

"Nothing in particular?" Sophie questions. "Really? Because we think something in particular *did* happen. Something that you're not telling us about. And it's clearly still an issue for you now."

I wave my hand in the air. "High school was a long time ago. Move on, girls. I have."

"Aha!" Erin points a finger at me. "You've moved on from the thing that happened between you and Alex." Her eyes are bright because she thinks she's caught me out. Which she kind of has.

The truth is, Erin's totally right. Something did happen between Alex and me in high school, and it's something I'd really rather forget about.

I throw my eyes skyward. "There's nothing to tell. Alex is . . . fine."

"Wow. What every guy wants to be called: 'fine,'" a distinctly male voice says at my side.

I don't need to turn around to know exactly who it is. Besides the fact about ninety percent of High Tea's clientele is female, it's just my luck to encounter *him* once again. Because Alex is everywhere in my life right now, and it's beginning to drive me slowly (and probably deliberately on his part) insane.

With my lips drawn in a line, I tilt my head up to look at him. "Alex."

He's smirking at me with a knowing look on his face.

Knowing? What does he know? Nothing, that's what. *Jerk.*

"Darcy," he replies in that irritating tone of his.

He's everywhere. *Everywhere.* With that smug smirk on his face, I half expect him to jump out of the pantry when I get my morning granola. He might even try to kiss me up against my own kitchen counter, too.

"Thanks for coming in on short notice, Alex," Sophie says to him.

"No worries," he replies. "I'll handle things if you want to stay here for a while. You know, to finish talking about *whatever it was* you were talking about." He shoots me another knowing smile.

Ooh, I bet he's loving this. He knows full well we were talking about him. This is just the type of arrogant, self-absorbed thing that's so typical of him. But then, I guess he did hear me mention his name, so maybe I'm overreacting? I look up again at his smugly smirking face gazing back at me. Nope, definitely not overreacting.

"That'd be great, thanks, Alex. You're awesome," Sophie replies.

"I'm not sure I'd go that far," he replies.

Neither am I.

"I'll see you at the gallery, Darcy," he says to me, my cheeks instantly heating up. "Four o'clock still suit you? It's when I finish up here."

With my friends' gazes fixed firmly on my face, I reply, "Sure. I'm looking forward to it."

He shoots us all his dazzling (read: cocky) smile before he turns and leaves.

"Darcy Evans, I do believe you are blushing," Erin says, which of course only makes me blush so much more. Because that's what happens when people are told they're blushing. Your cheeks turn positively nuclear. So *not* helpful.

I glance at Alex's retreating figure and turn back to my friends. "For the record, I'm only blushing because he busted us talking about him."

"Sure," Sophie replies as Erin says, "Totally." Neither of them looks the least bit convinced.

"So?" Sophie leads. "Tell us about high school."

They're not giving up on this. I twist my mouth. "It's not a big deal. It was nothing, really."

"It was clearly something or you wouldn't hate him as much

as you do now," Sophie observes.

"He's not my kind of person, that's all," I reply.

Erin's eyes light up. "Talented, fun, smart, and handsome guys aren't your type, huh?"

I let out an exasperated sigh. "Okay. I give in. You're obviously going to pester me about this."

"Because we're your BFFs and we care about you," Erin says.

I roll my eyes. "Sure. Something like that."

I can tell both of my friends are working hard at restraining their excitement as they lean in closer to me. I steel myself, ready to tell the story I've never told.

Chapter 16

"Well?" Erin says from across the table.

I take a sip of my tea and let out a breath. "Back in high school, Alex . . . well, he humiliated me."

"What happened?" Sophie asks, her voice soft.

"When I first met him, I thought he was cute. You know, in an older guy kind of way. I was fourteen, he was sixteen. He was much worldlier than me."

"Two years does make a big difference when you're a teenager," Erin says.

"Exactly. Anyway, I got a bit of a crush on him. A huge one, really." I remember the feeling as if it all happened yesterday. The way I'd get a thrill just to hear someone mention his name, the way I'd see him with his friends across from me at lunch, hoping, praying he'd look my way. I was totally at his mercy, and all I wanted was his attention on me, even just for a split second.

"I told Erin just last week that I thought you must have had a thing for him back then!" Sophie says in excitement. "Didn't I say that, Erin?"

"To be fair, it's not exactly a giant leap, Soph," Erin says. "Darcy's a girl, Alex is a guy, both at the same high school together. You do the math. What I want to know is how we didn't know about this crush at the time."

I shrug. "I guess I was embarrassed. He was Sophie's cousin, and it was all so overwhelming. Teenage crushes always are."

"Remember that crush I had on Brandon Richardson?" Erin says. "I thought he was amazing. I would have taken a bullet for him."

"You would?" I question.

"Well, in the leg maybe," she replies.

"You got to date him when you were sixteen, Erin, so your crush wasn't unrequited," Sophie explains. "Not like yours, Darcy, right?" Her features change. "Unless you're going to tell us you secretly dated him or something?"

"My crush was definitely unrequited. At least I thought it was until I saw him at the mall one Saturday afternoon. I was with my mom, and he was there hanging out with a bunch of friends, kids I recognized from school. I remember what he was wearing like it was yesterday: a light blue open shirt over a white T and a necklace." I smile at the memory. That whole look he was sporting was so hot back then. "He was leaning up against a pillar down by the fountain, like he was James Dean or something."

"I can imagine," Sophie says with a chortle. "He was super cool back in the day."

"Mom had to go buy something, so I told her I'd grab an ice cream and meet her later. That's when I saw him again, at the ice cream parlor, only this time he was alone." I remember the feeling of standing near him, closer than I'd ever been. It was nerve-wracking and utterly exciting at the same time. "I decided to be brave and move so he'd see me, and when he did, I smiled at him, and he smiled back. Then, he came over and asked me my name, and he asked me where I went to school. I told him, and he said he recognized me, but even the dumb fourteen-year-old version of myself knew he wasn't telling the truth.

"He told me I was pretty, and I thought I would die from happiness right there in the ice cream parlor. I remember looking up at him and thinking he was the absolute perfect guy. I was so freaking nervous, but I knew this was my shot with him."

Both of my friends are sitting on the edges of their seats.

"What happened?" Sophie asks.

"He kissed me," I state simply.

"He did?" Erin says in surprise. "Alex kissed you at an ice cream parlor."

"Yup," I reply. " I never did get that ice cream."

Sophie shakes her head, her eyes wide. "How did we not know this?" she says to Erin. "You're our BFF, and he's my cousin."

"You kept that secret well, girl," Erin says.

I cast my eyes down. "The thing is, right afterwards, Cora Huntington turned up, and he left me standing there, looking like a total idiot. I remember him saying an extremely un-heartfelt sorry and whisking her and her perfect ten body and gorgeous curly hair away." My insides twist at the memory of the feeling of utter humiliation.

"Oh, no," Erin winces. "Bad form, Alex."

"What a dick," Sophie says, not beating about the bush. She holds her hands up in the stop sign. "I can say it because he's my cousin."

"So, now you know," I say with a shrug. "The secret I've kept from you all this time."

"Oh, honey. We all had crushes back then, but he did not treat you well," Erin says. "On the plus side, at least you got to kiss an older, more experienced guy. That counted for a lot when we were that age."

I shake my head. "You're looking for the silver lining here, and I'm not sure there is one."

Erin shrugs. "I guess I am. Was it a good kiss?"

The memory of it fills my brain. When he reached out and gently cupped my face in his hands, leaned down, and brushed his lips against mine. I knew beyond a whisper of a doubt it was love. Big love. And here he was, finally noticing me, finally showing me that he felt the same way, too.

Idiot, right? Complete and utter idiot. He was just a teenage boy who happened to know how to give a girl a kiss. And I was the silly, romantic girl who lapped it all up.

My cheeks heat up. "It was a good kiss. You know, for a kiss with a teenage boy." Instantly, my mind flashes to the kiss we shared at the café kitchen. But I can't go there. I'm *not* going there.

Erin prods me in the arm. "OMG, girl. You're blushing about a kiss from years ago!"

"It was my first kiss." I twist my hands in my lap.

Erin's eyes grow huge. "Alex Walsh gave you your first-ever kiss?"

I bite on the inside of my lip and nod. That big moment in a girl's life, when she gets her first ever romantic kiss, and mine had to be with a guy like Alex.

Sophie knits her brows together. "But you always told us that your first was with Gavin the Tongue."

"OMG, Gavin the Tongue! I forgot about that guy," Erin says. "What was with that guy and his tongue?"

I shudder at the memory. "I think someone told him the way to kiss a girl is to ram it in as far as it can go and say a little prayer she'll like it."

Sophie lets out a light laugh and groans. "*Euw.*"

Erin places her hand on my arm. "I always felt bad for you that Gavin the Tongue was the first guy you ever kissed. Now I don't have to."

"I guess," I reply.

"What happened after that?" Erin asks.

I look down at my hands in my lap as my familiar friend Mortification alights inside. "I found him by that burger place by the supermarket and asked him why he kissed me if he was with Cora Huntington. He told me I was a nice kid but that he wanted to be with 'a woman.'" I use air quotes.

Erin's eyes are like saucers. "He seriously said that?" she asks, and I nod.

Sophie shakes her head as she repeats, "What a dick."

I toss my hair and paste on a smile. "So, now you both know. My deepest darkest secret is that my first kiss was with a guy who treated me like I was nothing."

"Babe, I'm so sorry," Erin says. "What a jerk. No wonder you've hated him all this time."

Sophie is clearly angry. "Wait until I get my hands on him. I'll tell Auntie Margie, that's what I'll do. She'll deal with him, believe me. Us Irish can be tough when we need to be."

"No!" I cry at the outlandish notion of Sophie sharing my high school story with Alex's mother. "Can't you see how much worse that would make it? And anyway, it was such a long time ago."

"Okay. But I'll do it if you change your mind. Auntie Margie takes no prisoners, believe me," she replies.

"This puts a totally new spin on what's happened between you two in the last few weeks," Erin says.

I hang my head. "Not for me it doesn't."

Erin holds a mini scone with jam and cream up. "Here. Eat sugar. It'll help."

I do as I'm told and pop the scone into my mouth. Although it tastes delicious, Erin is wrong. It doesn't help.

She picks up the teapot and pours more tea. "I bet he regrets what he did back then."

"I doubt it," I harrumph. I think of that smug look on his face every time I see him. He knows what he did. He *knows*. And he finds it funny.

"He's probably reminded of it every time he sees you, and wants to make things right," Erin continues.

"Don't forget that we live among unicorns and slide down rainbows with big, happy smiles on our faces every day, too." I sulk and then pull my lips into a line. "I know, I'm being sarcastic. Trust me on this, he doesn't want to make things right."

"Just kiss you," Sophie adds with a grin.

I let out a heavy sigh. "I should never have let that happen."

"Which time?" Sophie asks.

"Either of them!" I snap and instantly regret it. "Sorry," I mutter.

"No worries. We get it." Sophie stands up and pushes her chair into the table. "I need to go greet those people who've just arrived." She nods at the podium where a group of middle-aged women is talking happily among themselves. "I'm sorry that happened to you, Darce. But you know what? You've got to work with the grown-up version of Alex now. Do whatever you can to put that high school stuff behind you. Otherwise, it'll be a nightmare for you until the gallery opens."

"Sophie's totally right. Move on dot com," Erin adds.

I cross my arms. I feel like I'm being told to pull my socks up by my mom. Whatever that meant. (I'm in a cute pair of silver sandals today, anyway, my small rebellion against the head-to-toe blue regime.) "I guess you're both right."

Sophie gives my shoulder a quick squeeze. "We are right, Darce. Now, enjoy the rest of your high tea. This one's on me."

We both thank Sophie, and she leaves to go greet the newly arrived gaggle of women at the podium.

"You know, this whole high school past thing changes that kiss you two had in the kitchen."

"No, it doesn't. All it says is that I've been an idiot when it comes to Alex for far too long."

"Maybe? Or maybe you're meant to be together."

What is she talking about? I'm meant to be with Alex? How absurd. "Erin, that's insane," I scoff.

She shoots me a sly grin. "Is it?"

"It is," I reply firmly.

She turns her head, and I follow her gaze to see Alex standing at a nearby table. He's concentrating on listening to one of the customers, his pink High Tea apron tied around his waist. He should look ridiculous in that apron, but somehow, he doesn't. Somehow, he still manages to look incredibly hot.

He lifts his eyes, and they flash to mine. Immediately, I look away. You don't know where you stand with a guy like Alex. He's the type who could let you down in a flash, and undoubtedly would. Guys like him are the reason why I agreed to the No More Bad Dates Pact in the first place.

I'm done with guys like Alex.

Chapter 17

The problem with feelings is that they can be pretty tricky to control. Sure, there are things like deep breathing to combat worry, and deep breathing to deal with too much excitement. Oh, and there's deep breathing to relax you and help you sleep better.

There's one thing I know for sure. Deep breathing does not help with feelings about Alex.

I've been trying it, and so far, it's had zero effect. Sometimes, it even makes the feelings that much stronger, which is the last thing I want to happen. He's still right there, stuck inside my head, the memory of both kisses lingering on my lips.

Sure, the glass or two of Chardonnay I had with Erin last night while watching *Gilmore Girls* at our apartment helped for a while, but even then, I had to remind myself about my four-point manifesto again before I left for work today.

So, with what amounts to only a tenuous hold on my totally inconvenient and evidently uncontrollable feelings for Alex,

I arrive at the gallery on Friday afternoon with more than a dash of trepidation.

In fact, I'm straight-up terrified.

Through a series of short and to the point (me) and cheeky and even sometimes flirty (him) emails, we have arranged to meet today to begin the process of unpacking boxes of photographs I've had printed, framed, and delivered to the gallery. Between Alex, Larissa, and myself, we've agreed on a hanging plan, and I've got the notes on what goes where in my notebook, ready to get on with the job. Well, until Larissa arrives and rearranges everything, of course.

I've had all the images Larissa chose delivered to the gallery ready to be hung. So, when I unlock the gallery door and push it open, the only thing in the room is a stack of boxes, labeled "Darcy Evans." I shrug my jacket off, pull a Stanley knife out of the new toolbox I got with a bunch of hardware store-type things on my way over here from the office, and begin the process of opening each box. As I pull each one out and unwrap it from its bubble wrap, I distract myself from looking closely at each image. There's no way on this sweet Earth I'm going to let Alex get to me through his photography. I've let that happen once before, and look at where that got me. In a completely ill-advised passionate embrace in a café kitchen with a man I hate, that's where.

Instead, I force myself to think about anything but the images in my hands. My mind roves around such important topics as: what I'm going to sing at karaoke with the girls on Saturday night; whether I should I sing that cute Taylor Swift song, or stick with the ABBA classics Erin is obsessed with (okay, me too); and whether I should pair my new white pants with my black high heel sandals or my favorite silver ones. You know, important things in my life that require deep thought and analysis.

When my phone beeps, I pick it up and find a message from Seth.

I can't wait to see you again tonight.

I smile. Seth is such a great guy, and what's more, I'm going to watch him show jump tonight. I fully expect to swoon when I see him in his equestrian outfit, sitting atop his horse. Seth's the one, the guy I should be focusing on. I tap out a reply.

Me too! I'm excited to meet your horses.

I add some kisses and hit send.

A reply pings back immediately.

Remember what I said about the spade xoxo

I crinkle my forehead. The spade? Is he still carrying on about that? And what has a spade got to do with a horse, anyway? I shrug and type *I will xoxo* and press send then get back to work.

I'm about ten percent of the way through my unpacking task, humming a song I heard on the radio in my car on my way to the gallery when the door swings open. Despite knowing exactly who it is going to be, when I notice Alex's bulk filling the doorway, my belly does a flip-flop.

I return my attention to unpacking boxes and continue to hum, acting as though I don't know he's here. As irritating as it is that he has this effect on me, I know it's only because of that inappropriate kiss stirring things up for me. Nothing more. The weirdness between us is only temporary. It'll pass, a lot like gas does. Yes, that's it! My feelings for Alex are nothing but an inconvenient build-up of methane.

I smirk to myself as I stall for time by peeling off the bubble wrap from another photo. With my back still to him, I walk over to one of the walls and lean the photo up against it. All the while, I recite my four-point manifesto:

1. No smoldering.
2. No kissing.
3. Mention Seth a lot.
4. Pray.

I know I have zero control over number one (how *do* you stop someone from smoldering at you?), but I sure can control numbers two through four, and that's exactly what I intend to do again today. After all, it's been working up to now, so there's no reason for it not to work today—even if we're alone together for the first time since the day we kissed.

He clears his throat behind me, and I know I've got to turn around. Time's up. I need to face the music. Or Alex Walsh, which is infinitely trickier for me than facing music could ever be.

I steel myself and turn. "Oh, hi, Alex. I didn't see you there," I say brightly.

He's in jeans and a white T-shirt, that typical smile on his face. I do my best to ignore the way the sight of him makes things zing around inside me. I don't want zings. *Four-point manifesto. 1. No smoldering. 2. No kissing. 3. Talk about —*

"Darcy Evans with a knife," he says, punctuating my thoughts. "This could end really, really badly."

I glance at the Stanley knife I'm holding firmly in my hand. "It could." I toss my hair and try out a different tack. "Do as I say, and the blonde goes free."

His shoulders shake as he lets out a laugh, and the sound makes me smile, despite myself. "You're funny. I never knew that about you."

"Oh, I am very funny." I give another indignant toss of my hair. "My friends tell me that all the time." They don't, but he doesn't need to know that. "In fact, I'm a lot of things you don't know about."

"I bet you are."

I ignore his suggestive lilt. "Yes, I am." And I've got a four-point manifesto that's going to stop you in your tracks. Take that, Alex, with your distracting smolders and impossibly good kisses!

He stands, watching me for an uncomfortable moment before I tear my eyes away, breaking the weirdness between us.

"We've got a lot to get through today," I warn.

"Where do you want me to start?"

"There are still a bunch more boxes to unpack, as you can see," I keep my tone even and professional as I gesture at the stack in the middle of the room. "I figure once we've got all the photographs out, we can begin to arrange them per the plan." I walk over to my purse and pull out my Labrador puppy notebook, flipping over to the relevant page. "The photographs are numbered on the back, so all we've got to do is put them in this sequence, hang them, and our work here will be done."

"You make it sound so easy." He comes to stand next to me and peers over my shoulder at my notebook. He's standing far too close. Of course he is. It's his thing. Maybe he's got a personal space issue? Maybe someone should point that out to him? I bet he makes a lot of people uncomfortable with his closeness. Really, it's a personal fault that could be easily rectified.

"Good thing you're so organized. Organized *and* funny," he says, his voice low with an amused edge to it. I can feel his breath on my neck, catapulting those darn zingy feelings into overdrive.

"Yes, it is," I say briskly as I move away from him. I place my notebook on top of one of the boxes and begin to slit open another one with my knife. "I'll open these boxes, and we can then both pull out all the photographs and put them in order."

"Sure." He rubs his hands together. "Let's get this beautiful synergy of ours going, shall we?" he says, quoting Larissa's comment about the two of us.

I shoot him a patronizing smile. "Yeah, let's." The only beautiful synergy I want with Alex Walsh involves him moving permanently back in India and me getting on with my life in peace.

I set about opening boxes, and we work surprisingly well together as a team, removing bubble wrap, consulting my number plan on where to put each photograph, then leaning them in their respective groupings up against walls. When we talk, it's about the task at hand. But, despite the perfunctory nature of our communication, there's an unspoken tension between us. Larissa would no doubt call it our "synergy." Whatever it is, it fills all the spaces in the room like an oversized balloon, and when he's close to me, the balloon presses against me, making it hard to breathe.

I run through my four-point manifesto in my head. Frequently. I can avoid seeing his smolder if I concentrate on working and avoid looking at him when he speaks. Easy. As for point number two (No kissing), well, not seeing Alex smolder should take care of that. Number three is talk about Seth a lot. That I can do, no problem.

I straighten up and carry out an exaggerated movement to look at my watch. I hold my pose, arm in the air, as I look at my wrist and wait for him to notice. Finally, he looks my way and I say, "I can only stay until six. I've got an important event tonight."

He only glances briefly at me before he returns his attention to the work. "Sure," he replies.

No, Alex, that's not the plan here. He's meant to ask me why I can only stay until six, not simply accept it with a noncommittal and frankly disappointing "sure."

I try again. This time I throw my hands in the air. "Gosh, we have so much to get through. I really hope an hour and a half will be enough time. It's already after four-thirty," I tap my watch, "and I need to leave at six for an *important event*, you know."

He straightens up, placing his hands on the small of his back and stretching. "Don't stress out. What we don't do today, we can do tomorrow. Sophie's given me the weekend off."

I grind my teeth. Why won't he take the bait? I'm blatantly dangling it in front of him, after all.

He returns to his work.

I've had enough. "Come on, Alex. Aren't you even a little bit curious?"

"About what?"

Seriously?

Exasperated, I reply, "Don't you want to know what this important event is that I've got to leave at six for?"

He places one of the photographs against the wall and turns back to face me. "I've got a feeling you're about to tell me."

"I don't have to," I huff. "I'm just making conversation. That's all."

"Okay, I'll bite. Please, tell me, Darcy, what is the important event you've got to leave to go to at six?"

I narrow my eyes at him. His tone doesn't sound in the least bit like he actually wants to hear why I've got to leave at six. But since it means I get to create a boundary from my four-point manifesto with him, I leap on it.

"Funny you should ask, Alex." I give him a sly, triumphant grin. "I'm going to see Seth compete in a show jumping event," I say proudly. "Seth's the guy I'm dating, in case you forgot," I add for good measure. No point being subtle about it now. That ship has well and truly sailed, crossed several oceans, and docked in a foreign land by now.

I search his face for a reaction, fully expecting him to show he's impressed. Who wouldn't be impressed by a show jumping event? Horses, people dressed in equestrian fashion, tricky, daredevil leaps over high things. *Royalty.* Not that there's going to be any royalty at Seth's event tonight, of course, but they do attend these sorts of things. Really, you never know who might turn up (the fact they all live on the other side of the world is totally irrelevant right now).

He raises his eyebrows, and I can tell he's secretly impressed. "Show jumping, huh?"

"Yes. Seth owns three horses, you know. He's *eventing* tonight with one of them," I reply, using the term Seth himself used. "I'm taking some of my friends along to watch."

"Are you into horses?"

"Well, yes. But most importantly, I'm into *Seth.*"

Why is he not getting this?

He studies my face for a beat, then two, before he replies, "You're acting weird again."

"No, I'm not," I snap. "And what do you mean I'm acting weird again? When have I ever acted weird?"

"All week, and I know why."

My heart rate kicks up a notch. *Don't mention the kiss, don't mention the kiss.* "Oh, do you, now?"

"Oh, yeah. It's because of what happened between us in the café kitchen."

He mentioned the kiss. *Dammit!*

He licks his lips as though priming them to be kissed once more, his eyes beginning to smolder.

I take a step back from him. At all costs, I must avoid the smolder! Instead of looking at him, I concentrate on a spot on the wall just to the left of his face. "*That* should never have happened. And I only kissed you because I felt guilty about opening that box of photographs."

He quirks an eyebrow. "You kissed me because you felt guilty?"

I raise my chin defiantly. "Yes."

"That's a new one for me. I'm not sure I'd kiss someone out of guilt." He pauses before he adds, "Not like *that*, anyway."

My eyes dart to his face. Yup, full-force smolder.

I clear my throat as I push away the memory. "As I told you, it's not going to happen again. I'm dating Seth."

"The show jumper."

I toss my hair and arrange my features into a confident smile. "Yes, the show jumper. Which is why I need to leave here soon, so I can watch him riding his horse."

He nods slowly, and I can almost feel his eyes boring into me. "Well, I hope you have a good time."

"I'm positive I will." I give a brief nod and return my attention to the work. As I unwrap another photograph, I press on with point three in my four-point manifesto: mention Seth a lot. "Seth is a really great guy. I think you'd like him."

"Sure."

"He's so sweet. Very thoughtful. So unlike other guys our age."

"Good for him." He crosses the floor to where I'm standing.

"Actually, I'd say it's good for *me*. I'm the lucky one to have a guy like Seth." I watch him for his reaction.

His eyes flick to mine as he places his hand on the

photograph I'm holding. "I'm really happy for you."

"I am, too." I muster my most confident, breezy smile—as though him standing this close to me doesn't throw me totally off my game. Which it so does.

Seth who?

My hands still gripping the photograph, Alex says, "Shall I take this one?"

Immediately, I let go of the frame. "Sure, yes. Good idea." Heat rushes to my face. I turn away quickly, hoping he doesn't see, and busy myself with the next box. It's the final one, and as I pull out the first photograph I read the number on the back and say, "Could you grab my notebook and check where number forty-three should go? It's there, on the stack of empty boxes."

He picks it up and flips it over to look at the cover. "You're into puppies, huh?" He holds the notebook up and flashes the image of the cute Labrador puppy at me.

I flush slightly. Sure, it's a little embarrassing to carry around the sort of notebook I might have had when I was nine, but it's not a crime. "I've always wanted one, actually. A golden Lab and a horse."

"Well, you should make sure you get both someday."

"I'm working on it."

"Where's your plan again?" he asks as he begins to flip through the pages.

"It's the last entry, so right at the back." I hold up a photo of an elderly man with a wizened face standing by an old, crumbling, orate building. "You know what? Looking at this right now, we might need to rethink the plan. This one should definitely be enlarged. I mean, I know we've already made the call to go with the one of the temple with the tree for this group, but this one could really pop." I turn around to see him studying my notebook. "Don't you think?" When he doesn't reply, I snap, "Alex? Are you listening to me?"

Slowly, he looks up, his lips doing that sexy twitching that they do. Uh-oh. This can't be good.

"What's this?" He holds the page titled "Alex: Boundaries"

up in his hand.

My heart begins to thud. He's seen it. He's seen my list.

The look on his face tells me he knows. He knows I've got feelings for him. He knows I've been struggling to contain them. What was I thinking. writing them down on the same notebook with the gallery plan? *Epic fail, Darcy, epic fail.*

I dash across the floor to grab the notebook from him, but he holds it up in the air. He's got a good four or five inches on me, so I can't reach it, even when I stand on my tippy toes. "Alex, give me my notebook."

"'No smoldering,'" he reads, then looks down at me, his eyes shining. Oh, he is so enjoying this. "Is that me doing the smoldering or is it you? It's not clear from this boundaries list."

I clamp my teeth together, my insides twisting. My face feels so hot, I know my cheeks must be the color of a ripe tomato by now. I reach for the notebook once more, but he's still holding it too high. "My notebook, please."

"And what's this?" he says, completely ignoring my polite request. "'Mention Seth a lot.' Did you think I'd be especially interested in Seth? Because I can tell you right now, I'm not."

Humiliation floods every part of me. I reach up once more to try to grab the notebook from him, but he moves it to his other hand, and instead, I look like I'm trying in vain to swat flies. "Alex!" I say, shocked my voice comes out wobbly. "That's enough."

His eyes land on mine, and his expression instantly changes. He lowers the notebook, closes it, and holds it out for me. I try to take it from him, but he doesn't let go. "Shame about number two."

Number two on the list flashes before my eyes. *No kissing.*

I pull the notebook from his grasp and clutch it to my chest. All I can manage is a nod, my heart thudding like a cannon, my cheeks so hot with embarrassment, you could scramble eggs on them. I swallow and tear my eyes from his. "You weren't meant to see that."

"I'm glad I did," he replies, his voice soft. "You see, what it tells me is that I've been on your mind. So much so, you've had to write a list of ways to avoid how you feel about me. You see, the thing is, Darcy, I've been thinking about you a lot, too. That kiss —"

With a burst of bravery, I stand tall. "I don't want it to happen again."

He nods at the notebook in my hands. "Is that why you've got a list of boundaries? Because you *don't* want to kiss me again?"

I lift my chin. "Because I'm seeing someone else."

His lips curve into a small smile. "Someone called Seth. Point three on the list."

"Yes. Seth is sweet and kind and not a jerk. All the things you are not." I think of the girl in the photo I saw at his place, and of his poor, broken heart, and add, "To me, anyway."

He scrunches up his face. "I'm *not* not a jerk?"

I raise my head and give him a superior look. "Yes. A double negative makes a positive."

He has the audacity to laugh. "That's all very well, Ms. English Teacher, but does that make me a jerk or not a jerk. I'm still unclear."

"Are you always this frustrating?" I ask in exasperation.

"Only with you."

The memory of our kiss rushes at me like a charging bull. No. I won't go there. Boundaries! Boundaries!

The amused look on his face tells me he's fully aware of my internal struggle right now. "Darcy? Can I ask you something?" I give a reluctant nod, my notebook still clasped to my chest as though I need to keep it warm for fear it could die. "Why do you think I'm a jerk?"

"Are you serious?"

"Yeah. It's a genuine question." He places his hand over his chest. "From the heart."

"But . . . but you know why."

He shakes his head. "I don't."

I blink at him. Seriously? He can't remember what he did?

Did I mean that little to him that I could be completely forgotten? I drop my notebook from my chest and turn away from him. My mind is bumbling around like a puppy on caffeine. I've been carrying around this hurt for all these years, hating him for it, and he doesn't even remember doing it?

I feel his hand reach out and touch my shoulder and I instantly tense. "Darcy, if there's something I've done, or not done, just tell me. I've been trying to work it out ever since I got back to this country."

My anger flares as I round on him. "You really don't remember?" I ask in disbelief.

"Look, if you tell me what it is, who knows? Maybe I can fix it."

I lock my jaw and stare at him. "High school. I was fourteen. You kissed me at that ice cream parlor and then took off with Cora Huntington. Any of that ring a bell for you?"

Realization dawns on his face. "That? You hate me because of *that*? Darcy, it was one kiss a million years ago."

I cross my arms and glare at him. "I wanted to I mean something to you, and you . . . you hurt me." I'm mortified to feel tears sting my eyes. I hurriedly blink them away as I raise my chin boldly.

He lets out a puff of air. "Darcy, I am so sorry. I didn't realize it was such a big deal to you. If I'd known it would hurt you this much, I wouldn't have kissed you, even if you did look as pretty as you did that day."

"It was more that you told me after you wanted a woman, not some girl."

He scrunches his eyes closed. "Geez, I was such a dick."

"Yes, you were."

He studies me for a moment. "Darcy, I get that it upset you, and for that I am truly sorry. You've got to believe me that I had no clue I'd hurt you like this. I was a dumb teenage kid. I'm not that person anymore."

I chew on my lip. "You know what? Nothing you say can ever undo it." I turn my back to him as I struggle to control

the emotions swirling around inside. He may have
apologized, but I've carried this thing around for so long
now, I'm not sure I'm ready to let go of my hatred for him.
Without it, what have I got?

A voice inside of me tells me what I've got left is a guy I'm
crazy about.

But I'm not ready to admit that to anyone.

Especially not Alex.

Chapter 18

We've been working hard, and there is only a handful of boxes left to unpack. It's been a weird afternoon. I've gone from trying to hold a brick wall up around myself, to baring my deepest hurt to the guy who caused it, to hearing him say he's sorry.

Since then, we've been working side by side in an almost companionable way. Sure, I still need those boundaries in my four-point manifesto—the guy's smolder is like a lethal weapon, I tell you—but that feeling of anger, of hatred for him, has all but left the room. And now, it's easier. Nice, even.

"Last box," I announce.

He smiles at me from across the room. "Great."

I push back the flaps on one of the boxes and pull out a photograph. I unwrap it and turn it over to check it and my heart squeezes as I take in the image of a beautiful woman, her head back, her hair pooled on the mat behind her. How did this get in here?

"Oh, no," I mutter before I can stop myself.

"What is it?" Alex wanders over to me, and I hastily stuff the photograph back into its bubble wrap.

"Oh, it's a damaged frame. So annoying." I roll my eyes to show just how annoying that would be. "I'll take it and get it re-framed by the supplier."

His hand is extended, palm up. "Come on, hand it over."

I put the offending photograph behind my back and shake my head. "No. I . . . I can't."

He takes a step closer to me. "I'm sure whatever it is it's not a big deal," he says lightly.

I shake my head as I press my lips together. Once again, he's getting too close for comfort, but this time it's different. This time, when he sees the photograph in my hands, the easy, relaxed vibe we've finally been able to achieve will be completely shattered.

The edges of his lips curve into an easy smile. "If you don't hand it over, I'll have to do something drastic."

My heart thuds as I ask breathlessly, "What would you have to do?"

"I'd have to tickle you," he says in a matter-of-fact way, as though it's the only logical choice.

Tickle me? I blink at him. How old does he think I am? *Five?* I shake my head again, although I'm not at all committed to it.

He takes another step closer to me, and I make a snap decision: get tickled (read: get well and truly kissed and all boundaries demolished) or hand over the photograph.

Sanity wins.

Although I know he's not going to like what he sees, I pull the photo from behind my back and pass it to him. I hold my breath.

"Thank you," he says with a smile as he takes it from me. "Although, I had kinda hoped you'd go for the tickle." He flips it over in his hands and pulls off the bubble wrap then studies the photograph.

I watch his expression drop. My insides twist. "I don't know how it got in there, Alex. I'm so sorry," I say in a rush. "If you give it back to me, I'll deal with it."

He doesn't reply. Instead, all he does is stand still, looking down at the photograph for what feels like an absolute eternity.

I fill the tense silence. "It must have been on the file you sent to us." I chew on my lip and wait for him to say something. I reach my hand out to take the photograph. "Alex, I'll get it sorted out."

"Here." He thrusts it at me, and I take it with both hands. He turns away, taking a few short strides to the door. He pauses, his hand on the door handle.

I don't say a word. My heart is breaking for him. Whoever the girl is in the photograph, she did a real number on the poor guy.

His shoulders slump. He turns to look at me and gestures at a spot by the wall with no photographs leaning up against it. "Wanna sit for a while?"

"Sure."

We lower ourselves onto the hard, cool polished concrete floor. Sitting side by side, feeling about as comfortable as a hippo in Spandex, I wait for him to talk.

Eventually, he begins as he stares ahead of himself, his head resting against the wall behind him. "She's the reason I'm back here in New Zealand."

"The girl in the photo?" I ask softly.

He nods. "I knew her when I was in India. I took that photo and probably thousands more of her where she lived in Jaipur."

"Jaipur's a city in Rajasthan."

His eyes flick to mine, and a brief smile passes across his face. "You've been paying attention."

As we've worked, Alex has told me a lot about his time in India, from the temples to the food to the majestic mountains. He's never mentioned her.

I smile back at him, but it's too late. His own whisper of a smile is gone. "I try. What's her name?" I ask.

KATE O'KEEFFE

He presses his lips together. "Chetana."

"That's a beautiful name."

"Yeah. It means 'to be perceptive and conscious.'"

"Chetana. I'll have to tell Larissa. She'll love that."

He harrumphs, but I can tell it's kindly.

When he doesn't volunteer any more about her, I ask, "What happened?" Then I add, "If you want to tell me, that is. No pressure."

He rubs his eyes with the heels of his hands and then says, "It's fine. I can tell you. We've been busting through boundaries lately, right?" His eyes sweep to mine and hold my gaze for a beat.

"True," I reply with a small smile. "Was Chetana your girlfriend?" I ask, not sure I want to know the answer.

He lets out a short, sharp laugh that takes me totally by surprise, and I nearly jump back up onto my feet. Luckily, I don't because that would be very inappropriate right now.

"Should I take that as a no?"

He lets out a puff of air. "I worked for her father, Adarsh."

"Is he a photographer, too?"

"He's a businessman. Very successful. He owns half of Rajasthan—and made sure I knew it, too."

"Is that how you met her, through her dad?"

He nods. "He saw some of my work in a gallery and asked to meet me. He wanted some family portraits done. I don't usually do that kind of work, but Adarsh was the kind of man you didn't say no to." He pauses and then adds, "With Chetana, it was an instant thing, you know? Like, somehow, we both knew the moment we laid eyes on one another."

Love at first sight.

He shakes his head and looks down at his hands. "When her dad found out about us, he fired me and told me he never wanted to lay eyes on me again. I wanted to stay, to fight for her, but . . . she told me to leave."

He told her he was going to fight for her and she told him not to? My heart has well and truly broken for him now.

"Oh, Alex. That sounds so awful." Tentatively, I place my

183

hand on his arm.

He gives a shrug and turns to look at me, his eyes intense. "What can I do? It is what it is."

"That's very philosophical of you."

"Yeah." He rubs his eyes and pinches the bridge of his nose.

"Did you love her?" I know it's a deeply personal question, but he asked me to sit with him. And besides, I'm intrigued.

"Whatever I did or didn't feel for her, it's over. Done."

Well, that clears that up.

I look down at my hand, which is still on his arm. Suddenly feeling awkward, I remove it. "I'm sorry, Alex. It sounds terrible," I say. It sounds woefully inadequate, considering his tragic story, but I don't know what else to say.

"It was terrible. You're totally right. But you know what?" He turns to look at me. "It's in the past now, and even if I wanted to, there's nothing I could do about it. And anyway, I'm back here in Auckland, and I've got an exhibition to prepare for."

"Onwards and upwards?" I offer tentatively.

He nods, his face still grim, although I can tell he's trying to be brave about it all. "Onwards and upwards." He hops onto his feet and offers me his hand. I take it, and we stand together for a moment in silence, our hands clasped. "I guess we've both bared a little piece of our souls to one another today, haven't we, Darcy?"

I nod, and we share a small smile.

Something has shifted between us. It feels more, well, comfortable to be with him, like we're a couple of friends, working on a project together, sharing our stories, creating a relationship. The thought is nothing short of staggering.

Me? Friends with Alex?

"Alex?" I ask. "Are you doing okay?"

He loosens his jaw for the first time since we sat down together. "Yeah. I am." He gives my hand a squeeze. "Thanks, Darcy."

"Hey, what are friends for?" I reply breezily.

"Is that what we are?"

My heart hammers as I breathe, "If you want us to be."

He squeezes my hand once more before he drops it. "I do."

"Well, I guess that's settled then."

As he returns his attention to the photographs, I stand and watch him for a moment. Friends. That's what he wants us to be. Friends. Because although he liked our kiss, he's still in love with someone else.

I twist my mouth as I watch him hold a photograph up against the wall. It turns out I didn't need my four-point manifesto after all. Just like our first kiss all those years ago, the only person truly invested in us, with any real feelings, is me.

I guess, when it comes to Alex, I'm still that eager, stupid fourteen-year-old girl with a desperate crush. And he's still the guy who's barely even noticed me.

Chapter 19

"Are we there yet?" Jason says for about the millionth time since we left the city, right before he, Sophie, and Erin break into a fresh wave of laughter. Again.

"Very funny, guys. That's not getting old in the slightest," I say from the driver's seat. I shoot them a stern look in the rearview mirror. It has zero effect.

"I'm glad to hear it, Darce, because you know what?" Erin says, barely keeping the laughter from her voice. "I've got a question for you."

"Let me guess. Could it be 'are we there yet?' by any chance?" I deadpan.

"How'd you know?" Erin replies, and they all laugh at their silly joke once more.

"Seriously, you guys kill me," I reply. "And I still don't get why you're all sitting in the back. It makes me feel like a chauffeur."

"Oh, you need the hat to be a proper chauffeur, babe,"

Sophie says.

"Ooooh, Darcy would look good in the hat," Erin chirps.

"True," Sophie confirms with a nod. "You would totally rock that look, Darce."

Jason leans forward. "Don't listen to them, Darce. You know you'd get really bad hat hair."

"Jason!" Sophie and Erin both shriek.

Although I'm not looking in the rearview mirror at them (drivers really do need to keep their eyes on the road, you know, particularly when they've left the familiarity of the city behind and are in unchartered rural territory), I'm certain he gets a good slap on the arm from his girlfriend.

"What?" he says. "Girls are weird about that kind of stuff."

"So are guys," Sophie replies.

"No, we're not," he huffs.

"Oh, I know. You're too busy thinking about how to solve global warming and lower the rate of youth unemployment to bother with such things as hat hair, right?" Sophie says. I can hear her hands placed firmly on her hips by the tone of her voice.

Erin chortles. "Let's see how you look with flat hair, Jas."

"Hey, leave the hair alone!" he protests.

I glance in the rearview mirror to see Erin slap her hand down on top of his head, his locks instantly plastered to his head.

"Settle down, you three." I feel like a mom telling off her naughty kids.

"Yeah, Jas," Sophie says.

"What?" he protests.

I turn onto a gravel road and pass under a semi-circular sign that reads "Windsor Equestrian" in gold lettering against a dark green background. The sign matches the grandeur of the place, and I feel a thrill of excitement at the prospect of seeing Seth on his horse, looking every bit the dashing gentleman.

The gravel crunches beneath the tires, but I don't think my bickering "children" have even noticed we've turned off the main road yet. "You guys, we're here," I announce.

"We are?" Sophie says in surprise as she peers out the window.

"Where are all the horse floats?" Erin asks. "I thought there would be loads of things like floats and horses—"

"And cute guys in riding boots, right, Erin?" Sophie says as I pull on the handbrake and turn off the ignition.

"I'm not the one into horsey guys," Erin protests. "That's Darcy's *thang*."

"Excuse me. I don't have a *thang*," I sniff. "And if I did, I wouldn't call it that."

"Oh, you so do, babe," Erin says. "Tell me what you were thinking about just now."

I twist my mouth and let out a sigh. "I was thinking about Seth riding his horse. But it's only because of where we are. I mean, come on." I gesture around.

"Totally busted!" Erin trills.

"Personally, I'm offended at the way you're objectifying men," Jason sniffs. "We have thoughts and feelings, too, you know."

"You're so right, Jason. Men have had such a hard time throughout history, haven't they, ladies?" Sophie says.

"Yeah, our hearts bleed for you guys," I reply as I peer out of the windscreen at the imposing building looming above us. "This place is impressive. Tonight must be a really important event."

"I bet Seth's the Prince William of show jumping," Sophie says as we climb out of the car.

"Oh, I'm sure he is," Erin confirms confidently.

"Does Prince William show jump? I thought he was a helicopter man," Jason says as he slams his door shut.

"Not literally," Sophie protests. "Come on, Christie. Get with the program."

"You see, that's the problem. I'm not one hundred percent sure what the program is," he complains.

As we walk to the building, I feel the seeds of a small smile on my lips. Hmmm, I like the sound of that. "The Prince

William of show jumping" has a certain ring to it, a ring I could get used to, even if I have a feeling Jason's right in that the real Prince William favors helicopters to horses.

"What's Seth like?" Jason asks as we walk up a flight of steps and in through the main doors.

"Oh, he's a great guy. He's really sweet and smart," I reply. *And not in love with a woman in India,* I add to myself. The vital point of difference between Seth and Alex.

"Don't forget he looks like he could be related to a movie star," Sophie says.

"Really? Which one?" Jason asks.

"Bradley Cooper," all three of us reply.

"Only without those super blue eyes of his," I add.

Jason shakes his head. "I don't get the whole women lusting after Bradley Cooper thing. He looks like a regular guy to me, not a movie star. But if that's what floats your boat, then go for it, Darce."

Sophie slinks her arm around her boyfriend's waist. "Did you just give Darcy and Seth your blessing?"

Jason grins at her. "I gave Darcy and some guy who looks like Bradley Cooper my blessing. The jury's still out on Seth, because you girls didn't want me at the Vetting. Remember?"

"You wanted to hang out with Alex!" Sophie protests, indignant.

At the mention of his name, my body stiffens. I'm not going to think about him. Tonight is all about Seth.

"It's true," Sophie says. "We put in the hard work vetting Seth while you and your new BFF bonded over drinks and a game of pool."

"That was a good night," Jason says with a far off look in his eyes. "Well, it was until Alex got a call from his ex and he left early."

My interest peaked, I ask, "He did?"

"Yup. By the look on his face he didn't exactly enjoy the reunion, either," Jason says.

I turn this new information over in my brain. I went to

Alex's apartment the morning after we vetted Seth, the night Jason's talking about. I recall him saying he needed extra caffeine, and I assumed it was from a late night out with Jason. I bet it was Chetana who called, breaking his poor heart all over again.

Sophie shakes her head. "You two guys should date. #Bromance."

"What's wrong with a couple of guys getting together over a beer or two and finding that they get on?" he protests. "Alex is a great guy."

I've had enough of this conversation. I can't think about Alex, not tonight. Not when I'm trying to focus on my relationship with Seth. I spot a desk with a line of people. "You guys? The entry is over here."

We walk toward the line of people and wait patiently until someone behind a desk looks up at me and says, "Tickets, please."

Like the designated mom I am on this trip, I pull our tickets out of my purse, and she gives us instructions on where to find our seats. Once inside the arena, I look around. It's abuzz with excited chatter, and the stage is littered with jumps of various sizes, and I feel a surge of excitement at the prospect of seeing Seth riding his horse around the course, leaping over jumps to appreciative applause.

As we take our seats, Sophie says, "Those jumps are really low, aren't they?"

"Maybe they're for ponies or something?" Erin suggests.

"I hope so. I love ponies." I look around and notice something unusual about the crowd. I tilt my head toward my friends and say, "Has anyone else noticed this place is full of tweens?"

"Oh, my God, yes! I totally noticed that," Erin replies. "I feel like we're in the Never-Never Land between moms and their eleven-year-old girls. Too young to be the moms, too old to be the kids. What is *with* that?"

I lift my shoulders. "I guess a lot of girls love horses. I know I sure did when I was a girl."

"I bet you had horse pics all over your walls, right?" Jason asks.

"Oh, Darcy was the queen of My Little Ponies, right, Darce? You told us you had all of them," Sophie says.

"I had a few, I guess." No need to give away that not only did I have all the My Little Ponies you could get, but I had the posters, the movie DVDs, the hairclips, basically all things My Little Pony. It's fair to say I was a little obsessed.

Music blares from loudspeakers, and I feel a shiver of anticipation. I'm about to see Seth ride his horse. He'll ride beautifully, probably even win, and he'll look magnificent, and I'll swoon in his arms and be "Alex who?"

"Ladies and gentlemen, boys and girls," the announcer begins, "welcome to the third annual Windsor Equestrian Horse Parade!"

We applaud as the girls in the audience go crazy with squeals of delight, half of them leaping out of their seats with joy.

Sophie nudges me. "Ah, to be a ten-year-old again."

The music starts up again and a line of girls in sparkling costumes, some dressed in equestrian clothes, others in leotards and capes and princess costumes, come running out, holding hobbyhorses.

"Oh, how cute!" Erin exclaims. "Do you think they're going to jump over those things as they hold their toys?"

I watch the girls as they line up. "I think so. You know, I had a hobbyhorse," I say as nostalgia hits me in the chest. "I would have loved to have done this when I was a kid."

"You still could," Sophie replies with a grin.

I roll my eyes. "Yeah, because it wouldn't be weird to run around on a hobbyhorse as a fully-grown woman."

"Whatever gets you going," Jason says with a waggle of his eyebrows.

I return my attention to the stage. As the MC announces each girl, they hop and prance and twirl, waving at the audience, huge grins on their faces.

Warmth spreads across my chest. "They are having the

times of their lives."

The first competitor is announced, and the auditorium falls into silence. She pauses for a moment then takes off, bobbing her hobbyhorse up and down as she leaps over each and every jump with ease. I'm certain her long legs had a lot to do with her success, possibly an unfair advantage in the world of hobbyhorsing. Once she's finished the course, she waves to the audience to excited squeals and cheers — mainly from the tweens, but I admit, we begin to get into the spirit, and whoop and shriek along with the best of them.

The next girl starts her round and is doing super well, until she bumbles one of the higher jumps and ends up flat on her face on the ground. The audience collectively holds its breath until she pops back up, a wonky smile on her face, and hobbles to the finish line.

After all the girls have completed their rounds, they ride their hobbyhorses out of the arena to much applause.

"When do you think the real show will begin?" Erin asks me.

I nod at the stage. "They're adding another level to the jumps, so I guess soon. I can't wait to see Seth."

Mr. Darcy, here I come.

The MC announces that the next round is about to begin, and I prepare myself for the real horses. Watching hobbyhorses ridden by cute kids is all very well, but it's not the reason we're here.

As the music blares, I turn to my friends and say, "This must be it."

I feel a swell of anticipation as I focus on the entrance. After what feels like long enough to sing my favorite ABBA song, a fresh batch of hobbyhorse riders gallop out onto the stage.

I crinkle my brow. "We must be stuck in the pre-show entertainment."

"I'm sure the real horses will be next. I'm sure of it," Erin says.

And that's when I see him.

He comes galloping out, his face aglow with happiness,

dressed in full equestrian clothing, looking every inch the show jumping man of my dreams. My jaw hits the floor with a clank, and I blink.

Then I blink again.

There's something very wrong with this image. Seth's horse is not a horse. In fact, it's not anything but a bit of stuffing attached to a stick. He's . . . he's riding a hobbyhorse.

No no no no no.

This cannot be happening.

A heavy brick drops down to my belly. I gape at my friends. They gape back at me, equally agog, our mouths forming a line of perfect "o's." None of us quite believe our eyes.

"But—" I begin, my mind searching for an answer, any answer, other than what has become glaringly obvious for all to see.

"Your boyfriend's horse is a kid's toy?" Sophie says, her voice riddled with incredulity.

I watch through disbelieving eyes as Seth joins the line of girls to wait his turn. Unless this is some sort of weird practice run show jumpers with actual horses do before they pull the real thing out, the evidence before us tells me the answer is a big, humiliating, and totally unexpected yes. Seth's horse is a hobbyhorse. Fin is a toy, not a real horse.

I swallow, my throat tight. Seth told me he wanted me to "meet" his hobbyhorse.

Oh. My. God.

The MC announces the first competitor, a girl of about twelve or thirteen, who takes off, bounding over the jumps with elegant ease. I look back at Seth. He beams up at me, as if him standing in a sea of girls holding stuffed toys on sticks in the middle of a horse arena is a perfectly normal thing for a twenty-something-year-old man to do. He lifts his hand and waves at me.

On automatic pilot, I wave back.

And then, his name is called, and he gallops over to the start line.

"Oh, my God," Erin mutters beneath her breath. "He's really

going to do this."

"Yup," Sophie confirms with a grim nod. She turns to me. "Did you know about this?"

I shake my head, dumbfounded, but I don't look at my friends. I can't. I built Seth's show jumping prowess up. I told them how amazing he was going to be. And now look at him.

This is like a sick dream I want to wake up from, and it's almost impossible to tear my eyes away from the surreal scene unfolding before our eyes.

As he begins his run, humiliation curls its long tendrils around me, and I shrink down in my seat. He takes the first jump, and the crowd applauds. He continues around the entire course, confidently leaping over each jump, a look of deep concentration on his face.

"Well, I'll give him something, Darcy. He's good," Jason comments.

I swallow down a rising lump. The guy I'm dating is good at riding a hobbyhorse. Now there's a thought I never thought I would have.

As I watch him leap over jumps and prance around like this is a real show jumping event, any shred of hope I was clinging onto that Seth and I could have a proper relationship floats away into the arena, replaced by the all-too-familiar feelings in the world of dating: disappointment and regret.

Chapter 20

For some reason unknown to us all, we sit through the entire performance. Maybe it's a car crash reality TV thing, or maybe our brains haven't caught up with our eyes. Who knows? But here we sit, watching as Seth and his hobbyhorse complete their first course then prance out of the arena before the next group gallops into view.

"What just happened?" Erin's eyes are huge as she looks from Sophie to Jason and then to me.

"I'm not really sure," I reply, too stunned to put my thoughts into words.

"Yeah. It was." Sophie pulls a face. "It was not what I was expecting."

"Well, I've learned something tonight," Jason says.

"What?" Sophie asks.

"Darcy's boyfriend likes to ride stuffed animals on a stick in front of tweens," he says with a laugh.

"He's not my boyfriend," I protest.

"Well, not now, he's not," Sophie says with a laugh that comes out as a pig-like snort. Her face grows serious. "Unless you want him to be?"

I shake my head. "I don't think he can come back from this as far as I'm concerned."

"Am I allowed to say that he looked really funny?" Erin presses her lips together, her eyes shining. She's working hard not to laugh. Before long, she's begun to giggle, and it spreads among us all like wildfire on a hot summer's day. All four of us clutch our sides in laughter, and people in the audience begin to turn and glare at us.

"I think we need to leave. Now." I pop out of my seat, my hand over my mouth in a vain attempt to stifle more laughter, and hurry toward the exit, trailed by my friends.

Once outside, a fresh wave of laughter rocks us. But for me, after a while, a hollow feeling begins to grow inside. I'd pinned my hopes on Seth. I thought he might be one of the good ones. Attraction is such a fragile thing. You can spend hours and hours building it up, imagining what it would be like to be with a guy, hoping he feels the same way, too. And then along comes a sharp, pointy thing that pops the bubble, and the very last thing you want to do is be within a mile of that guy.

It's fair to say any bubble I had for Seth has been well and truly popped-by a stuffed toy on the end of a stick, currently being held between his legs as he leaps over jumps.

"I think we all deserve a stiff drink after that experience," Jason announces. "Don't you?"

There's a murmur of agreement among my friends.

Although a glass of Chardonnay could help to wash away my sense of disappointment and confusion, I scrunch up my nose. "I think I need to go talk to Seth first."

"To compliment him on his show jumping skills?" Sophie asks with a grin. "Or to pet his horsey?"

"At least he was good," Erin says. "He might win the whole thing."

"Of course he will," Jason scoffs. "He's a grown man

competing against kids. There's no contest."

I scrunch my eyes shut. "Please don't remind me."

Sophie stretches out her hand. "Give me the keys. We'll wait in the car until you've talked to him."

I rummage around in my purse and pull my keys out. "Maybe he did it as a dare?" I know I'm grasping at straws here.

Erin smiles kindly at me. "You may be right, Darce. Or there could be actual living, breathing horses back there, and we're missing him riding on one right now."

"Is that a horse I see flying up there between the clouds," Jason says, his upturned face looking skyward.

"The expression is about pigs flying, Christie," Sophie says.

"I know. It was a joke. I was horsing around," he replies with an eyebrow waggle.

Erin shakes her head. "Lame."

"It's a good thing you're cute, Christie," Sophie shakes her head, "because with jokes like those, there's no way I'd be dating you otherwise."

He scoffs. "Nice."

"I'll see you back at the car, okay?" I say, interrupting their repartee.

I make my way around to the back of the arena where I'm met with the woman who took our tickets on arrival. "Can I help you?" she asks.

"I need to get backstage. Is that possible?"

"Are you one of the moms?"

"Yes, I am." I hope she doesn't notice my nervous cheek twitch.

"Okay. Go ahead." She pulls the door open, and I thank her before I step through it.

Backstage, the place is busy with people, from the kids to the parents, and a few adults in a variety of costumes. *At least Seth's not the only adult.* I spot him talking with a man dressed in equestrian hat, tails, and boots, just like he is.

He looks up at me, his brow creased in confusion. "Darcy. What are you doing back here?"

I glance at the man at his side. Luckily, he gets the hint and melts away into the crowd.

"I, ah, came to see you," I begin.

A whisper of a smile forms on his lips. "I can see that. The show's not done yet."

"I know."

"I'm in the final." He beams at me.

"That's . . . awesome." What else can I say?

"This is Fin," he says, brandishing his hobbyhorse at me. "You can pet him if you want."

Oh, this is getting weirder and weirder by the minute.

I reach out and touch Fin's synthetic mane with my fingertips before I hastily pull them away.

Suddenly, that whole weird conversation about what you see when you look at a garden spade makes sense. Seth wanted me to see a horse when I looked at his hobbyhorse. A real, living, breathing horse. I shake my head, my mind whirring. Fin's the spade.

He studies my face. "What's up?"

"I, ah, I wasn't expecting Fin to be, well, what he is." I gesture at his hobbyhorse.

He narrows his eyes. "You're not into this."

I shake my head slowly.

"You know, hobbyhorsing is a really great thing. It helps a lot of people. Kids with a lack of confidence. People suffering from depression. All sorts of things. It's helped me get over the loss of Han Solo."

I bite my lip as I recall the photograph of the beautiful Thoroughbred he showed me on our first date. "Was Han Solo like Fin?" I ask tentatively, wondering just how deep his delusion actually runs. I mean, did he photoshop himself onto an image of a horse? After what I've witnessed tonight, it's definitely not outside the realm of possibility.

"In what way?"

"In a . . . real way. You know, was he . . . alive?"

"Of course he was," he scoffs. "I'm not insane, you know."

"No. No, you're not," I say as earnestly as I can. Inside, I'm

screaming "you pretend to ride horses with a bunch of kids!" at the top of my lungs.

He stands Fin the hobbyhorse up on its end (Feet? Foot? Hoof?) and fixes me with his gaze. "I can tell you're dubious, and I get that. Really, I do. This whole world is new to you."

"That's one way to put it."

"Do you know what I'm thinking?"

The correct question should really be, do I *want* to know what he's thinking?

"What?" I ask cautiously.

"With your lovely long legs, we could compete together as a couple. Two horses, in perfect synchronicity. We would take the Hobbyhorse Couples' Competition by storm."

I widen my eyes. There's a hobbyhorse competition for couples? I shake my head. "I'm sorry, Seth. I can't see it happening. I don't think we should see one another again."

His face is aghast, like he really did not see this coming. "Are you breaking up with me?"

"I'm sorry, Seth."

"But . . . your lovely long legs."

I take a step away from him. "Sorry," I repeat before I turn around and hurry away.

"By storm, Darcy. We could take the Hobbyhorse Couples' Competition by *storm*," he calls after me.

I'm already pushing through the door, my hopes evaporated, my need to get as far away from Seth and his stuffed toy horse almost overwhelming.

— ♥ —

Erin insists on driving my car back into the city so that I can focus on de-hobbyhorse-ifying (her word, not mine, because that is so not a word, even if she insists it is). I sit back in the passenger seat and try my best to find the positive in what just happened. But really, what is the positive here? My

attraction to him was tentative at best, and the guy I've been dating likes to jump over things holding a stuffed toy on the end of a stick between his legs. I'm sure there's a hobbyhorser out there who's Seth's perfect match, but I'm not that girl. And now here I am, humiliated once again.

"He seriously asked you to compete with him?" Erin asks incredulously.

"Yup. Apparently, I have, and I quote, 'lovely long legs.'"

Jason gives a knowing nod. "Ah, the L-word trifecta of limbs. Lovely, long, and legs."

"Clever," Sophie says. "I bet he wanted you two to be the Tom Brady and Giselle Bündchen of the hobbyhorse world."

"You're only saying that because of those lovely long legs of hers," Jason quips.

"You are right," Sophie says. "Darcy's legs are lovely and long."

"Can we please quit talking about my legs, guys?" I ask. "It's not helping."

"Why not? I've heard they're lovely." Jason nudges the back of my shoulder from behind me, and I let out a puff of air.

"I guess I'm disappointed. I thought he was one of the good guys, but it turns out he was just another weirdo. I don't get it. Nothing came up when we vetted him. How did this even happen?"

"That's true. I think we might need to tighten the process," Erin says. "First that food-obsessed guy got through for Sophie, and now a hobbyhorse rider for you. Who knows what I'll end up with if this unfortunate trend continues?"

"Don't forget Davy Crockett the merman," Jason interjects. Although I'm pretty sure a grown man with a hobbyhorse habit trumps mermen right now.

"We need to find Darcy another date, stat," Jason says. "Only this time, I'll be in on the Vetting Process."

"Because you're so good at it?" Sophie challenges.

"I'm glad you noticed," he replies with a wink.

"You guys are totally right. Get back on that horse, girl." Erin realizes her blunder and adds, "Sorry, Darce."

"No more dates," I say firmly, my mind made up. "Why would I want to put myself out there once more, only to get knocked back? I'm not a masochist."

"You don't mean that." Sophie is certain. "I had those crappy experiences, but I ended up with my Prince Charming."

"Aw," Jason pulls Sophie in closer to him and plants a kiss on her lips, "I love you."

"I love you, too," Sophie murmurs in reply.

"Geez, you two. Inappropriate," Erin complains from the driver's seat. "We've got sad and lonely single ladies in the car here."

"Thanks, Erin. It's great to be referred to as sad and lonely," I grump.

Erin slows the car and backs it into a parallel park like a pro. I peer out the window. "Where are we going for a drink?"

"Cozy Cottage Café," Erin announces. "We can catch the end of the Friday Night Jam. Wine, food, and entertainment. All of which will take your mind off hobbyhorses tragically named after characters from Star Wars." She leans closer to me and adds, "Alex isn't working here tonight, so you won't have to deal with all that, too."

I give her a weak smile. "Thanks for having my back."

"Always," she replies.

We get out of the car and enter the café. Inside, the place is filled with chatter and music.

"Shall we get a table?" I glance nervously around. Even though I know he's not working tonight, I half expect Alex to jump out and laugh at me and my hobbyhorser date. Or ex-date. Whatever.

"There's one," Sophie says, immediately making her way to the back of the café where a group of people has recently vacated a table.

We follow her and take our seats.

"I'll get the drinks. Who's having what?" Jason looks at me. "Whatever you're having, Darce, I'll make it a double."

I know alcohol can't blot out the memory of my humiliation,

but I give him a weak smile. "Thanks, Jas. Chardonnay, please." Jason leaves the table, and the conversation inevitably returns to Seth the hobbyhorser.

"I thought hobbyhorses were a tween thing," Erin says.

"I saw a documentary about it once. It's big in Finland, right? OMG," Sophie exclaims. "Seth is Finnish, right?"

"Yes," I groan. "Can we not talk about it now? I'd really rather like to forget about Seth and his hobbyhorses."

"Sorry, babe," Sophie says.

The band returns to the makeshift stage, and the lead singer announces their next song. As they play the opening bars, Sophie nudges me. "Oh, no. Alex just walked in."

I don't know why I thought Alex wouldn't turn up tonight. Because of course he does. He was always going to. See me at my lowest, watch me struggle through my dashed hopes. Not that I think he'd do that anymore, not after the way we opened up to one another at the gallery this afternoon. But I did make a big deal about going to see Seth ride his horse.

With my heart thudding and my insides twisted, I watch as he strides across the floor to the counter. He looks as he always does—confident, in control, and comfortable with where he is in life. Well, other than when Chetana rears her impossibly beautiful head, that is. He looks . . . well, then I want to collect him in my arms and wipe away his heartbreak.

"Are you all right to see him? We could leave," Erin says, interrupting my thoughts.

"It's fine," I reply, even though I know it's not. "He has every right to be here."

"I'm sorry, Darce," Sophie says. "I figured he wouldn't be here if he wasn't working. I guess he was at the gallery next to High Tea."

Of course. That's where he would have been, still working on the exhibition while I found out the guy I'm dating is a weirdo. "You two are so sweet, but really, I'm a big girl. I can handle seeing Alex. We've, well, we've made our peace, I guess."

Both sets of my friends' eyebrows shoot up.

"You have?" Erin asks.

I nod. "He apologized for what he did in high school. Everything's good between us now." I sound a lot more convinced than I feel. Seeing Alex right now, knowing what a big deal I'd made of going to watch Seth show jump, could well twist the knife of mortification just that little bit more.

I don't have to wait long to find out. He and Jason arrive at our table, and Jason passes me my drink as Alex pulls up a chair and sits right next to me. I look at him out of the corner of my eye and brace myself.

"Hey, Darcy," he says gently, his features soft, his eyes...what? Kind?

I study him more closely. Yup, definitely kind. Really, I don't know why I thought he'd be anything but. I guess bad habits die hard. I've hated Alex for so long now, I'm used to expecting the worst from him. But this is the all-new Darcy and Alex Show. We're good now.

Part of me wonders whether I've been wrong about him, that maybe he's always been like this, and I've never given him a chance.

"Hey, Alex," I reply.

He places his hand on the back of my chair, his arm brushing my shoulder, and says, "I wanted to thank you again for listening to me talk about Chetana before. It really helped me. You're, well, you're a good person."

I shake my head. "Oh, no. It was nothing."

His gaze is intense when he replies, "It wasn't nothing. It meant a lot to me."

My throat tightening, I try out a smile. "We're friends now, remember?"

He returns my smile, his handsome face lit up. "I remember."

My heart squeezes, and I pick up my drink to take a sip.

"Jason told me about the horse thing."

I chew on the inside of my lip. "He did, huh?"

"It sounds like a rough night. I'm really sorry. You liked him a lot, right?"

I nod, although I know it's not true.

"I had something like that happen to me once," he continues. "Well, it didn't involve hobbyhorses, exactly, more like a girl pretending to be something she wasn't."

"That sucks."

"It did at the time, but you know what? You'll get over him."

Warmth spreads from my belly up across my chest as I look up into his soft eyes. "Thanks."

"I had to google what a hobbyhorse is, you know." He shakes his head. "What the hell is a grown man doing running around with a stick between his legs. It's for kids. And that stick is right next to some serious equipment. One wrong move . . ."

I let out a laugh. "Right?"

"See? You're laughing about it already." He takes another sip of his beer. "I finished doing what I could next door. This beer is my reward."

"You've been working there since I left?" He nods, and I glance at my work and do a quick mental calculation. "That was three and a half hours ago."

"I ducked out for pizza at about seven."

"Well, I'm glad you got to eat at least," I say, sounding like I'm his mom.

"Thanks . . . *Mom*."

We share a smile that feels so amazing, it spreads from my face right down to the tips of my toes.

He drains his bottle of beer and plunks the bottle down on the table. "Right now, I'm beat. I guess I'll see you at the gallery tomorrow."

He's leaving already? After he's been so kind to me, so un-Alex? But then, maybe this is the Alex he's always been, and I never gave him a chance? Maybe this is the guy my friends see when they tell me what a great guy he is, the guy I saw tonight at the gallery?

"But—" I clamp my mouth shut before I say anything else. A

part of me wants him to stay, the part that's thrown caution to the wind, that's tired of denying how I feel about him. The dangerous part that will only get me hurt.

He's in love with someone else.

I nod at him. "See you tomorrow."

He flashes me his smile before he says goodbye to the rest of the group and leaves our table. When he reaches the door, he turns back and gives me a quick chin lift before he disappears out of the café and onto the sidewalk. I watch the door close over behind him, a heavy, sinking feeling filling me up.

Oh, no. I recognize that feeling, and it's the last thing I could ever, *ever* want to happen. It's a total and complete disaster of epic proportions. My throat tightens as something big contracts in my chest.

I've fallen for Alex.

Chapter 21

I reach the gallery early the next day.

Back at our apartment, Erin wanted to talk about how I felt about the Seth-slash-hobbyhorse disaster and the whole "what to do about Alex" conundrum. Only he's not a conundrum, is he? He's the guy I've fallen for, the guy who lights up the room whenever he's in it. The guy I haven't been able to get out of my head since the moment I laid eyes on him at Cozy Cottage Café all that time ago.

The guy who's desperately in love with a woman he can't be with.

And where does that leave me? Up the proverbial creek with a flimsy nail file for a paddle, that's where.

I need to find somewhere to be alone with my thoughts, and since I've got to be at the gallery today anyway, I figured it was the perfect spot to escape to.

Once inside, I relish the silence. I sip my takeout Earl Grey tea from Cozy Cottage next door and survey the room. Alex has hung some of the photos already. He must have done that last night while I was in the throes of Seth-the-hobbyhorse-rider-despair. I stand in front of a collection near the gallery entrance and notice he's grouped them differently from the plan. Instead of sticking with all mountainous scenes in one area, people in the other, he's paired portraits with landscapes. It works. Being different, they don't compete with one another. Instead, they sit together in harmony.

I chew on my lip. Although I think it works beautifully, I wonder what Larissa will say. But then Alex did insist on having creative license when he agreed to exhibit, so I'm not sure she'll be able to say a whole lot.

I place my takeout cup on the polished concrete floor and sit down next to it, like Alex and I did when he told me about Chetana yesterday. Wow, was that only yesterday? Right now, it feels like a gazillion years ago. Emotionally, I've gone into overdrive. The insanity with Seth, finding peace with Alex, and then realizing the full extent of my feelings for him. It's been quite the twenty-four hours.

I take a sip of my tea, allowing the warm liquid to slip down my throat.

A pickle, that's what I'm in. A big, fat, juicy pickle. Whenever I've heard that expression before, I've always imagined someone floating around inside a gigantic jar of pickles. Well, it's me in that jar right now, and the lid is screwed on super tight. There's no way to get out.

I've fallen for a guy who chose Cora Huntington over me after our very first kiss back when we were teenagers. But it doesn't end there. Oh, no. That wouldn't be nearly enough for me and my big, juicy pickle. Fast forward to today, and that guy is in love with someone else. There. That's the winner. That's the biggest pickle in the whole freaking jar. I've got some seriously big feelings for Alex, and he's in love with a girl whose name is so whimsical and romantic and means "to be perceptive."

How fan-freaking-tastic for me.

I let out a heavy sigh, pick up my cup, and drain the final dregs of tea. From my spot on the cold floor, I look around the room. I have a lot of work to get through before the gallery opens next week. I might as well get on with some of that work. Who knows? Maybe it'll take my mind off Alex?

I push myself up off the ground and wipe the grime from my shorts. Thanks to Larissa's obsession with the color blue, I never wear it during the weekend, although right now, with the dirt on this floor, a nice, dark navy would have been a whole lot more preferable to the ill-advised white shorts I threw on this morning.

I trudge over to the tools and collect the hammer, level, pencil, tape, and hooks. Consulting the Larissa-approved plan in my notebook, I frown. If Alex has rearranged the images already hanging on the wall, how will I know what goes where now? I'm still studying my plan when the door is flung open, and Larissa comes sweeping in.

I look up at her in surprise. "Larissa. It's Sunday. What are you doing here?"

"I was in the neighborhood, and I wanted to see how the exhibition is coming along."

I spy a Cozy Cottage Café cake box in her hand before she hastily slides it into her oversized Tod's purse (to be fair, everything's oversized on Larissa, she is Hollywood petite, after all). I raise my eyebrows. In the neighborhood, huh? I smile to myself. Even an anti-sugar, anti-gluten, anti-anything delicious wellness evangelist can't resist the lure of a Cozy Cottage cake.

She runs her eyes over my outfit and crinkles her brow. "You forgo blue on the weekends?" she asks.

I glance down at my Barbie pink (ironic, remember?) singlet, white shorts, and tennis shoes. Not a smidge of blue in sight. "I like to mix it up."

"I've got on cream camisole on under this today," she says, her eyes sparkling.

"You're a rebel, Larissa."

"Blue can get a little . . ." She searches for the word.

"Blue?" I offer.

"Exactly." She wanders over to the wall Alex hung last night and studies it. I hold my breath. Although she agreed upfront to allow Alex to arrange the images any way he sees fit, when it comes to her projects, she's not exactly known for her *laissez-faire* attitude. Artistic license is very much Larissa's baby. "Darcy? This isn't what we agreed."

I take a few tentative steps closer to her. "I think it works, don't you?"

As she studies the images, she tilts her head one way and then the other. It makes her look like a confused puppy, trying to work out what her human is communicating. Food? Walkies? Fetch the ball?

By now, I'm waiting right beside her, hoping she likes it. If not, it'll mean a battle between her and Alex at worst, and at best, I'll have to rehang it all. Neither is an appealing prospect.

She turns to me and beams. "Alex Walsh is a visionary. A genius visionary."

I chortle. Alex is a lot of things, but a genius visionary? I'm not so sure.

"You like it?"

"I adore it. It speaks to me."

Ah, the ultimate seal of approval. I half expect Three Tooth Guy to open his sparsely-furnished mouth and start talking to us. But that would be silly.

I give her a relieved smile. "I'm sure Alex will be super happy to hear that."

She grips my arm with her tiny hand and says, "He is exactly what I wanted for this space, Darcy. Alex Walsh is perfect."

My heart does that weird contracting thing.

"Now, tell me. Have you got the caterers booked?" she asks, and I nod. "Everything organic, no animal products of any kind?"

"Everything is vegan, ethically sourced, organic, and local. The only way we could be any kinder to the environment is if we didn't serve people anything to eat at all. And before you ask, I've got the aura readers to act as serving staff so our guests have the option of an aura read while nibbling on their healthful snacks."

Don't get me started. The things I've got to do when I work for Larissa Monroe . . .

Larissa claps her hands together in excitement. "Wonderful. What about the technology, the music?"

"We have Phillippe playing his lute, followed by Chinchu on their mandolins and triangles, just as you wanted. I've got the PA system from the usual crowd, and your steps are ready and waiting out back."

Larissa is so small I had to get some custom-made steps for her to climb up on so that she can speak at these types of events and be seen.

"My steps! Darcy, what would I do without you? Did you have any success with the zoo?"

"They won't allow us to have any meerkats, sorry." Truth be told, I didn't even call the zoo to ask if we could have meerkats at the opening. Having been down that track with the wallaby fiasco, I already knew the answer.

Her expression is pinched. "Oh. I was sure they'd say yes after turning us down for the wallabies. But I do so love meerkats. They're so cute with their whiskers and the way they stand up like this." She does a poor imitation of a meerkat. "Oh, look. It's Alex Walsh."

Instantly, my heart squeezes as the body zings ping to life and my throat begins to dry up. There's a lot going on for me right now. I steel myself before I turn around to see Alex walking through the door.

"Come in, come in," Larissa says, although by now he's already inside the gallery with the door closed behind him.

"Err, thanks, Larissa." His eyes sweep to mine, and I say a quick "Hello." He says it back and shoots me a smile that has those darn zings darting around like they're in the Hadron Collider.

Larissa reaches up to air kiss him, but because he's so much taller than her, he needs to lean down, and even then, she barely makes it to his cheek. "Alex Walsh, I love what you've done here." She takes him by the hand and marches him over to the cluster of photographs he hung last night. His eyes flash to mine once more, then he mouths "Alex Walsh," and I'm forced to bite back a smile.

Having feelings for a guy you once spent a long time hating, have shared the two most incredible kisses of your life with, and who you've got some major feelings for now can make every moment an emotional high-speed car chase.

As he and Larissa discuss his plans for the other photos, they wander around the room with me and my trusty Labrador puppy notebook trailing behind.

"Well, that all sounds amazing to me," Larissa declares with a clap of her hands. "I can tell your synergy is working wonderfully, you two. I knew it would."

I lift my eyes to Alex's, and we share a smile. *Oh, if only she knew.*

"You two keep up the good work. Thursday is the big day. I cannot wait!" She air kisses us both—me with a lot more ease than Alex, clearly—and then she leaves in a whir of compliments and encouragement, her contraband Cozy Cottage Café cake hidden safely in her purse.

In her absence, the silence that falls around us is in stark contrast to the Larissa whirlwind, and I feel instantly awkward. I gesture at the photos he hung last night. "I, ah, like what you did here."

"Thanks." He smiles at me and it warms me right up.

I momentarily forget he's in love with someone else.

"I wanted each section to tell its own story. This," he fans his hand out of the collection of photographs, "tells the story of Three Tooth Guy, where he lives, what's important to him, his life, I guess." He points at the image of a smiling boy of about ten, holding out a milkshake. "I threw in this image of a kid at a lassi cart as a kind of an in-joke for you and me."

"You did?" I look at the image in relation to the others, and suddenly it makes sense. "I get it. Three Tooth Guy can't eat solids because he's only got three teeth."

"Exactly. And lassis are delicious. Have you ever tried one?" he asks, and I shake my head. "They're made of yogurt. My favorite is mango. I'll make you one someday."

Alex is going to make me a lassi someday? "I'd like that." I smile at him and he returns it warmly.

"We should, ah, get on with hanging these photos, I guess," he says.

I wave my notebook in the air. "I've updated the plan with what you and Larissa agreed."

"You're so organized."

I give a small shrug. "I try to be." There's no table to lay my notebook on so I stack a couple of the empty boxes and place it on top of them. "We've got twelve more sections to hang."

Alex comes to stand at my side, and we both study the revised plan. I tell myself not to do it, but I can't help myself. I breathe in his delicious scent, those Hadron Collider zings doing overtime inside.

"That all looks good to me. Let's start by moving the photos into piles, and then we can begin to hang."

We work together, and conversation begins to flow. He tells me about how he likes being back in Auckland, and how he was glad he bought his place when he did.

"Can I ask you a blunt question?"

"Darcy, most things you say to me are blunt."

"They are?"

"Yeah. It's ones of the things I like about you."

It's one of the things he likes about me. *One* of them. I wonder how long the list is. I try to suppress a massive grin, but it busts out across my face anyway. "Thanks."

"So? What's your blunt question?"

My blunt question. Right.

"How did you afford to buy your place? I don't mean for that to sound rude, it's just you're a barista, not a president of some big company."

"From this," he says with a sweep of his hands.

"From your photographs?"

He nods. "I wasn't always this high-flying, minimum wage café worker you see before you now, you know."

"High-flying, huh?"

"Oh, yeah. When it comes to making coffee, I'm the best. I can make you an Americano faster than you can say 'antidisestablishmentarianism.'"

"Antidisa-what?"

He laughs. "It's one of the longest words in the English dictionary. Didn't you study history in high school?"

"Yeah, but I don't remember anything about that."

He gives a modest shrug. "I loved history. Next to art, it was my favorite subject. And in case you want to know, antidisestablishmentarianism is a word used to describe people who were against the disestablishment of the Church of England."

"And I bet you talk about the disestablishment of the Church of England, like, a lot, right?"

His eyes dance with mischief. "Oh, yeah. *All* the time, especially when Jas and I hit the pool table. I'm very sophisticated, you know."

A giggle bubbles up and I snort. "That's what I always say about you. Alex Walsh is so sophisticated."

"See? You agree."

He's flirting with me. This feels amazing. I collect a strand of hair and twirl it around my fingers. If I'm going to flirt, I'm pulling out all the stops. "So, when are you going to make me this super-fast coffee, barista extraordinaire?"

"I'm sure we can find a time. You'll have to say the word, though. And I'm not sure how you'll get on with it. It does have twelve syllables."

"That's a lot of syllables."

"Exactly. I'm sorry, Darcy," he says with a shrug, "but I just don't think you can do it."

"Oh, you are so wrong. Challenge accepted. I will learn how to say antidis-whatever—"

"Antidisestablishmentarianism."

"Yes, that. And you will lose." I reach out and we shake

hands.

"Only, I'll win," he replies, my hand still in his.

"Sure you will."

Our gazes lock. I could almost forget the fact he's in love with someone else. I could step a little closer, I could place my hand on his arm, I could reach up and —

No. I can't do any of that. We would end up kissing and it would be absolutely wonderful, and then he'd go back to being heartbroken over another woman. Forget the nail file, I'd be up that creek with a toothpick for a paddle.

I want more from him than to be some rebound girl. I want him to feel about me the way I feel about him. But Chetana broke his heart, messed him up, and then he was sent away. It would make a sad but romantic story if I weren't the schmuck holding out for the guy.

But I guess that's all I can be to him. The schmuck. The girl he didn't choose back in high school. The girl he might like to kiss occasionally but not be with. Not really.

I shoot him the breeziest smile I can muster then turn away. I pretend to busy myself looking through my notebook, but all I can think about is how nice it would be if there was no Chetana, if I hadn't spent all this time and energy hating him, if we could be together.

And then, I feel his arms circle around my waist, and I can feel his breath tingling my neck. "Darcy," he whispers, his voice sending shivers down my spine.

I swivel around and pause for a nanosecond to look into his eyes. "I can't, Alex," I whisper, my resolve slipping.

"Why not? I figured a girl who needs to write a four-point manifesto to avoid falling for a guy must feel something for him. Something big." He brushes the hair back from my face. His touch sends a shiver down my spine. "Like I do for you."

"But . . . Chetana."

"Chetana didn't want me. And anyway, she is in India, probably married to another guy by now."

"*Married?*"

He nods slowly, his eyes momentarily closed over. "I want to be with you. You and only you. You're in here," he touches his head, "and in here." He places his hand over his heart.

I can barely believe my ears. "I am?"

A grin busts out over his handsome face. "Oh, yeah. You so are."

I reach up and push my fingers up into his hair, and he responds by pulling me into an earthshattering kiss. It's the kind of kiss I've only ever experienced with one man—the man in my arms right now.

When we finally come back up for air, after what can only be described as an utterly spectacular kiss, he presses his forehead against mine. "You know we just broke rule number two, don't you?"

Warmth spreads through my belly and a smile bursts out across my face. "I guess I'm going to have to race to rule number four as soon as I can."

"I don't remember rule number four."

"Pray."

His laugh is deep and delicious. "And what are you going to pray for, exactly?" he asks.

I pull back and lift my eyes to his, suddenly nervous. "I guess that all depends on you."

"Well, if you pray for a whole lot more kisses like that, you can definitely count me in."

"Oh, I was going to pray for a sold-out exhibition opening," I tease. "But I guess I could throw in some more kisses if I've got to."

"You're so kind."

"I'm very charitable."

"I can tell." He kisses me again, and my head begins to spin. "Did your prayers involve me asking you out on a date tonight?"

"The whole idea behind the four-point manifesto is to help me avoid you."

"Could you revise it?"

"Let me see." I throw my eyes up to the ceiling and tap my chin as though deep in thought.

"Don't leave a guy hanging here."

This time, it's my turn to pull him in and kiss him. And I make sure it's a good one, just to show him I mean business.

"I would love to go on a date with you, Alex Walsh."

"Good." And then he kisses me again. And again. In fact, we hardly get any more work done on the exhibition, we're so busy kissing and talking and simply enjoying being together.

And it is nothing short of perfection.

Chapter 22

The next few days are heavenly. We spend so much time together, getting to know one another, sharing our stories, our lives, that hating him feels like an emotion that belonged to an entirely different girl.

Today, with our work on the exhibition done, and the opening only hours away, Alex takes me to one of the places he says he loves the most in Auckland. So here we stand, me puffing a little more than I should for a walk deemed "easy" by Alex, on top of the rolling green of Mt. Eden, a dormant volcano not far from the heart of the city.

"Isn't the view here spectacular?" he says to me, his arm slung around my shoulders as we look out at the city below us and beyond to the sparkling blue of the Hauraki Gulf.

I glance up at him, and warmth spreads through me. "It is."

He looks down at me and our gazes lock for a moment before he turns to face me, pulling me against him. "I never thought this could happen, you know."

"That I'd make it up the hill?" I tease.

"Oh, I knew you could do that. You've got those lovely long legs, remember?"

I laugh. "I forgot I had those." I'd told Alex all about the hobbyhorse disaster and how Seth's biggest regret when I ended things with him seemed to be that I wouldn't become his show jumping partner with my 'lovely long legs.'

"That hobbyhorse guy was so right. You do have great legs, although I solemnly promise that I do not have any interest in you riding around on a stuffed toy at the end of a broom handle." I laugh, and he adds, "Although it would be hilarious to watch."

I nudge his arm. "I would totally rock it and you know it."

He beams at me. "I bet you would."

I stand on my tiptoes and kiss him. "So, what did you never think could happen?"

His features grow serious. "That I could feel this way about someone new. And you know what? I'm so glad it's with you, Darcy Evans."

I beam at him. "Me, too."

I press my lips together. I know it's fast, and I know I may be rushing it, but what I feel is so intense, so *huge*, I need to tell him.

"You know how people say the opposite of hate is love? It's not true. The opposite of love is indifference. It's when you really couldn't care less about a person. You don't put the energy into something as big as hating them, because they're nothing to you."

"Are you going somewhere with this?" he teases. "Or is this a general observation you feel you have to share right now?"

I laugh. "Both? You see, for years, I thought I hated you."

He shakes his head as he pushes some hair away from my face that's been blown there by the gentle breeze. "I get it. I wasn't exactly the most considerate sixteen-year-old, particularly not in ice cream parlors."

"We can agree on that. You know something? When it comes to you, I cared enough to want to hate you, when really, deep inside, I didn't hate you at all. I loved you."

"You loved me?" he whispers.

I bite my lip and nod. "I did, and I do."

His smile reaches from ear to ear. "You have no idea how good it is to hear you say that, Darcy, because I love you, too."

Before I even have the chance to process his words, he leans down, scoops me up off the ground, and twirls me around in the air. I screech with joy, happiness bursting out of me as we spin.

Me, Darcy Evans, the girl who was happy enough to simply find good guys to date, who signed up to the No More Bad Dates Pact with her friends to find her Happy For Now. I thought it would be enough. I thought there was no way I wanted anything more than to date normal, nice guys. Guys who weren't selfish or nasty or downright weird. It turns out I was wrong.

When it comes to Alex, I want the full immersion, no holds barred, take over the freaking world kind of togetherness you can only have when you've finally met The One.

"You are an unexpected joy, Darcy Evans."

I chortle. "Now who's the one who sounds like a fully-carded member of the elderly? Remember the bosom buddies conversation?"

"How could I forget? And I don't care. When I think of you, that's what I feel: joy."

"Me too."

He smiles and takes my hand in his. "Shall we walk back down together? We've only got a couple hours before we need to be at the gallery."

I return his smile, my heart full. "Sure."

We walk the whole way down holding hands, content in our newly declared love for one another. Outside my apartment, he leans out of his car window and tells me he'll see me tonight at the opening. I stand on the sidewalk and watch as he drives away, my limbs light, my chest radiating with warmth.

We're in love! I can barely believe it. Alex loves me, and I love him back. I roll our names around in my head. *Alex and Darcy. Darcy and Alex.* It's perfect. Absolutely perfect.

I walk up to the door to my building and slot in the key. And that's when I hear it. A teeny, tiny voice in the back of my head. It's been there for days. I'm sure it's not a big deal, and I keep telling myself not to even think about it for one tiny second. But still, it's right there, in the back of my head, and I can't seem to switch it off. It's this silly, niggly voice that's trying to erode my happiness. It keeps whispering loud enough for me to hear. "It's not real." It makes my insides twist painfully, and I've got to push it away, tell it I'm not listening, that Alex feels the same way about me. He does, he told me, right there on top of Mt. Eden.

And push it away I do, through getting ready in my gorgeous new dress, through driving to the gallery, through all my last-minute checks that everything's in place before people begin to arrive.

We've got the full alphabet of celebrities attending, from A to Z, as well as various movers and shakers of the wellness world. And, most important in my book, my wonderful friends and the star of the show, my love, Alex.

And you know what? Despite having to push that little voice aside, I am totally onto it. I pride myself on my organization skills, but even I'm impressed with the way I've pulled this together in such a short timeframe. I've got the technology in place, the photos are all hung and looking spectacular, the caterers are out back preparing, and the aura-readers-slash-serving-staff are busy telling one another what hue they're each sporting today and what they need to do to improve it. Who knew aura reading was a competitive sport?

After I've finalized the order for the food to be brought out, I return to the main room in the gallery. It looks completely amazing. The images are clustered so they each tell a story, just as Alex wanted. The lighting is perfect, subtly illuminating the main photo in each cluster. Alex is going to love it.

There's a knock on the door, and it pulls me out of my thoughts. I stride over to unlock it, and Larissa comes sweeping in, as she does, wearing a gorgeous dress (yes, it's blue), trailed by probably the best-looking guy I've ever seen in the flesh, dressed in a classic James Bond-style tux.

"Darcy!" She air kisses me, and I breathe in her perfume. "It looks wonderful in here. Haven't you and Alex Walsh done so well?"

I beam at the mention of his name. That's the thing when you're in love: you can't keep the happiness from seeping out. Your heart leaps at the mere mention of his name. "Thank you, Larissa. It was your vision, remember? If it wasn't for you, Alex's photographs wouldn't be on the walls right now."

She nods her blonde head sagely. "That is so true."

And it *is* true. If we hadn't gone into Cozy Cottage Café that day and seen Alex's work on the walls, if Larissa hadn't insisted on having him open her gallery, well, I'd probably still be wrapped up in my hating him. Really, I should kiss Larissa for what she's inadvertently done for us, but her makeup is perfect, and I know she'd be upset with me if I messed that up.

She places her tiny hand on her companion's arm. "Darcy, this is Adonis. He's my new personal trainer, and he absolutely adores art. Don't you, Adonis, darling?"

"I do. I love everything about the art," replies the aptly named Adonis in his deep, heavily accented voice.

Larissa beams at me. "See?"

"Great to meet you, Adonis," I say. Did his parents know he'd live up to his name when they gave it to him as a baby? Just imagine if they'd got it wrong and he looked like Mr. Bean!

He nods his perfectly proportioned head on top of his, well, Adonis-like body, and replies, "Yes."

"The photographer will be here soon," I say to him. "His name is Alex Walsh, and he's very talented. I'm sure he'd love to talk to you about his photography. Or anything else you might want to discuss with him. He's very smart and interesting and well-traveled."

That's the *other* thing when you're in love: you find every opportunity to talk about the guy. Needless to say, the caterers have heard all about what an amazing photographer and boyfriend Alex is, as have the guys who set up the PA system, the wine delivery man, even the aura-readers-slash-serving-staff, who are now all vying for the chance to read his aura.

"Yes, I like the art," Adonis says in response.

I shoot him a puzzled look. Either he doesn't understand English well or he got all the looks and not so much of the brains. I clap my hands together and say, "Well, that's just great, Adonis!"

"Darcy, darling, I need to show you something," Larissa says as she rummages around in her purse. A moment later, she pulls out the tiniest dog you could ever see. "This is my new therapy dog, Bissou." She nuzzles the squirming dog as she makes funny little baby sounds.

"You brought a puppy to the gallery opening?" I question in surprise. Art and puppies don't usually mix too well, but then this is the woman who wanted wallabies dressed as waiters here tonight, so it shouldn't really come as a surprise.

"Not any puppy. She's *Bissou*." She holds the dog out to me, and I have no choice but to take it in my hands. I place it against my chest, and it licks my neck, wagging its tiny tail.

"Oh, she's so soft and wriggly," I say as I gaze down at her cute little face. "Oh, and I can feel her rapid heartbeat against my chest." I stroke her soft fur and beam down at her. "Larissa, she's gorgeous."

"She's full of exuberance and the joy of living. I find her energy totally affirming," Larissa says, sounding very Larissa. Which makes sense, really.

I gaze down at the dog. She scrambles up, reaches out with her pink, floppy tongue, and licks me right on my nose. "Thank you, Bissou, but I guess your name does mean 'kiss' in French." She settles down a little, and I hold her close against myself.

"Oh, she must really like you," Larissa says with a motherly smile. "She's never calm like that in someone's arms unless she's—" Her features change as she trails off.

"Unless she's what?" I ask, but then it becomes obvious what Larissa means. Bissou is peeing, right on my lovely new dress. "Oh, my gosh!" I pull her away from me, and the final drips of pee land on the floor by my feet. Immediately, Bissou begins to do her puppy wriggle once more. I hand her back to Larissa and survey the damage. My gorgeous new pale blue chiffon dress has a large wet patch on it, right in the middle of my chest.

"Oh, no, Darcy," Larissa exclaims.

"I've got puppy pee on me." I stare dumbly at her.

"Can you change?" she asks.

I try to keep the edge from my voice as I reply, "I didn't expect to get peed on so I only brought what I'm wearing."

Larissa tucks Bissou against her chest. "Pop outside and talk to Anton. He can take you home to change. Problem solved." She gives me a satisfied smile.

"But it's only twenty minutes until opening. People will be arriving any minute now. I'll never get all the way across town to my apartment and back here before then."

She rummages in her purse and pulls out a set of keys and hands them to me. "My place is only five minutes away, remember? You can wear something from my wardrobe. We're about the same size."

I look from my normal-sized body to Larissa's celebrity proportioned one and scrunch up my face. "Do you have anything . . . roomie? A kaftan, maybe, or a muumuu?"

"Oh, I'm sure I do," she says with a flick of her dainty wrist. When I don't move from my spot, she adds, "You'd better go."

"Yes. Right." I give a brisk nod. I'm going on a wild goose chase to Larissa's house to try to find something in a non-size zero to wear to my boyfriend's big exhibition opening.

Fan-freaking-tastic.

"See you soon," Larissa trills before she wraps her hands around one of Adonis's bulging arms and says, "Adie, darling, come with me. I'm going to show you the images before everyone else gets here."

I glance at my watch. It's now less than twenty minutes to the official opening. A frisson of nerves rolls through me. Alex will be here any second now to enjoy his special moment, and I'll beam with pride when everyone says what an incredible photographer he is. "That's my boyfriend," I'll tell everyone, and they'll all be jealous of our obvious love. But first, I need to fix this puppy pee situation, and fast.

I rush past the squabbling aura readers, still using color as a weapon against one other, find Larissa's shiny, black car parked down the road, hop in, and instruct the somewhat bewildered Anton to get me to Larissa's place on the double. Luckily, he takes it all in stride (he does work for Larissa Monroe, after all), and before long, we're whizzing through the streets.

I sit tensely in the back and send a message to Alex. *Puppy pee disaster. Will be back at the gallery by opening.* I add *Good luck!* with a bunch of hugs and kisses before I press send. Then, I sit back and try to relax. It doesn't work. Instead, I drum my fingers against my thighs as we fly through the streets. Finally outside Larissa's building, the car slows, and I almost do a ninja roll out of the car I'm moving so fast.

Once I'm in her dressing room, which really should be renamed a "dressing floor" it's so huge, I flick through her wide assortment of dresses and skirts and jackets and blouses. Everything is teeny tiny, just like Larissa, and my nervousness turns supersonic as it aims for Mars.

And then I get a brainwave. Pregnancy clothes. Of course! Larissa's daughter is only three, she's got to have some lovely big, roomie pregnancy clothes still lurking in here somewhere. I begin to pull open drawers and rifle through them until eventually, I find a maternity bra. Yes! I'm on the scent. The next drawer down and I've hit the jackpot.

Hastily, I pull the first dress out and hold it up. It's not ideal, but with next to no time to the opening, it'll have to do. I rip off my damp dress and throw its replacement on over my head. It's roomie enough to fit my normal proportions, and I don't even bother to check my reflection in the mirror.

Dashing out the door, I glance at my watch. Seven minutes until opening! I race down to the car and instruct Anton to step on it to get me back to the gallery on time. There's no real hope I'll make it—this is New Zealand's largest city with the traffic to match, not some one-horse town where everything's closed by five o'clock—but a girl has got to try. This is Alex's big moment, and there's no way I'm going to let a splash of puppy pee get in my way of being there with him for it.

Anton tears down the street toward the gallery. We come to a pause at a red traffic light, and I can't wait any longer. I jump out and run the final two blocks, narrowly missing being plowed down by an SUV going in the other direction.

My dainty high-heeled sandals were never designed for running on a sidewalk, but where there's a will, there's a way, as the saying goes, and I reach the gallery as the final stragglers are being ticked off the guest list at the door.

I smile at the doorman as I catch my breath and follow the guests into the gallery. I scan the room, searching for Alex. I move through groups, excusing myself and saying hello to familiar faces until I find him. He's standing alone, staring at one of his photographs, his back turned to me. The man I love.

I reach out and touch his arm, and he jumps. I laugh as I roll my eyes over what he's wearing. He's in a navy jacket over a crisp white shirt and a pair of jeans, a combination I helped him chose at his place a couple of nights ago.

"Hey. You look amazing. I knew you would." I reach up and kiss him on the cheek then smooth off the smudge of lipstick I leave there.

His eyes skim over my outfit. "What the heck are you wearing?"

I glance down at my brightly colored, baggy maternity dress with its swirly pattern. On closer inspection, each swirl looks a little like a baby in the womb. Larissa once wore this? And, more to the point, *I'm* now wearing it? "I got puppy pee on me from Larissa's new dog, and I've had to borrow this," I explain.

"Yeah, I saw the dog."

I crinkle my forehead. "Are you okay?"

"Yeah, I'm good." He nods his head so fast, it looks like it could become unhinged and roll away.

What has gotten into him? Nerves. It's got to be nerves.

I rub his arms. "Look, Alex, I know you're nervous, but believe me, it'll all be okay. You've exhibited before." I peer at his face.

His jaw is locked, his eyes sunken into his head. He doesn't just look nervous, I realize with a jolt, he looks completely freaked out. "Alex?" I say breathlessly.

He glances down at me briefly, before looking away, his jaw twitching.

"What's going on?" I ask with a dash of trepidation. Okay, more than a dash.

I notice his hands balled into fists at his sides.

"I-I can't do this."

Something moves in my chest, and I place both my hands back on his stiff arms. "It'll be fine, Alex. It's just nerves, that's all. I'll be with you right throughout."

His eyes drop to mine and he mutters, "I'm sorry," before he turns and begins to walk away.

I watch as he makes his way over to the front door, pushing past people in his haste. I dash after him, through the throngs, out the door, and onto the sidewalk. I see him, about twenty feet away from me, striding down the street.

"Alex!" I call out, fear and confusion making my heart rate soar.

He stops and turns.

I rush toward him. "Where are you going?" I ask when I come to a stop in front of him, my voice breathless.

"It's too much. All of it. It's too much." He begins to pace.

"What's too much?"

"All those photographs covering the walls."

It's the photographs? Relief floods through me like an open dam. I know what's going on here. He's having a moment. I know them all too well. Larissa has them on a regular basis. I've learned all I've got to do is talk her down. And that's what I'm going to do with Alex now.

I take a step closer to him. "I want you to take a deep breath and then another. Everything will be okay. You've got to trust me."

He looks at me as though I've tried to explain quantum physics—and got it really, really wrong. "You don't get it."

"I do, Alex. Trust me. It's all going to be okay," I repeat in soothing tones.

He shakes his head. "It's more than the exhibition," he replies, and a weird feeling in my chest begins to grow.

"What do you mean?" I ask and hold my breath, every diabolical scenario playing out in my head. He doesn't love me. He wants nothing to do with me. I was just the rebound girl after all.

"I mean us," he says. "You and me. I . . . I can't do it." He shakes his head and I blink at him, not wanting to comprehend what he's saying.

"What do you mean, you can't do it?" There's a steely edge to my voice now as what he's trying to tell me begins to sink in.

His eyes glisten as he repeats the same, horrible words, "I can't do it. Darcy, I'm so, so sorry."

My hands drop from his arms, and I stare at him wide-eyed in utter shock. "You're breaking up with me?"

He nods, much slower this time, and I think I detect a hint of regret in his face, but it's gone before it's even fully formed. "It's not you, it's me."

I let out a loud "Ha!" my voice tinged with a mixture of anger and dismay. "That's the worst line in the book, Alex. Couldn't you at least try to be original?"

He raises his eyes to mine, and I see his pain. I can't feel sorry for him, I simply can't. He's breaking up with me. He's ending what we've only just begun.

I press my lips together and lock my jaw. "Why?" I ask simply, even though I know exactly why. When he doesn't respond, I ask, "Is it because of . . . Chetana?" I find it hard to say her name.

He gives me a slow nod, his jaw taut.

He's doing this to me *again*? He's leaving me for another girl? Suddenly, I feel like a complete and utter fool. Here I was, declaring my feelings for him, falling into his willing arms, expecting a fairy tale ending. But I'm just a diversion to him, aren't I? Someone fun to fool around with and have a good time.

I'm not the real deal, not for him.

"So that's it?" I ask. "We're over? You're not coming to your exhibition? You're just . . . taking off." I mimic a plane taking off into the sky with my hand.

"I can't be in that room with all those memories. Not now."

"But you've been in that room all week. With me. In fact, you kissed me in front of those memories, Alex, don't you remember? Many, many times." There's a nasty edge to my voice now, but I don't care. I feel like such an idiot allowing this to happen.

That little voice in the back of my head tells me, "I told you so."

Alex hangs his head. "I know," he murmurs. He stares at me for an uncomfortable moment. "Darcy, I never meant to hurt you."

I raise my chin and toss my hair. "No, Alex, I'm sure you didn't. Not in high school, and not now. But the thing is, you did."

Way to go, Darce. Pick the guy you hate, work out that really, you've always loved him, but make sure he's in love with someone else first for maximum effect.

"I'm sorry," he repeats before he slowly turns away from me and walks down the darkened street.

I stand and watch him leave, tears rolling down my cheeks, my heart breaking in two.

It's history repeating itself. At fourteen and now again at twenty-five. And you know what? I bet history is having a good old laugh at my expense. Only this time, it's so much worse than in high school. This time, I let him into my heart, and I can't ever imagine forgiving him for what he's done.

Chapter 23

Somehow, I manage to get through the gallery opening and then stumble through the next few days. I'm in some kind of emotionless fog. I'm numb. It's all too much for me to comprehend. Four wonderful days together and then . . . nothing. Just a long, long silence stretching out before me.

I read somewhere that to stop thinking unhelpful thoughts, you need to divert yourself away from them every time they crop up. Apparently, it's all about neural pathways or something. So, anytime my mind turns to Alex, I quickly think of something far better, like having my fingernails pulled out one by one, or having my bikini line waxed by a blindfolded technician. Both much more pleasant things than thinking about him and what he did.

I tried to carry on with my job as though nothing had happened, as though my world hadn't been turned on its head. But in the end, Larissa had someone come in and read my aura, and with a shocked expression on her face, she sent me home immediately. Apparently, a pitch-black aura with lightning rods poking out in all directions and monsoon-like rain falling on your head is not a good thing.

So, here I sit on the sofa, watching Lorelai drink endless cups of coffee in in yet another episode of *Gilmore Girls*, stewing in empty ice cream tubs and chocolate wrappers, trying my best not to succumb to the huge gulf of sadness that continually threatens to swallow me whole.

"How are you feeling, Darce?" Erin says with a hopeful look on her face. It's been a week since the gallery opening, and Erin has been tiptoeing around me, delivering my junk food and listening to me when I need to talk. She's been the best roommate and the best BFF.

I look up at her from my spot on the sofa and refocus my eyes. I wonder if there's such a thing as "Netflix Eyes," an affliction that results in the inability to focus on anything further away than your screen? I bet there is, and if it's not already a thing, I'm calling it.

"Hey," I mumble in greeting before I return my attention to Lorelai and Rory.

"Sophie's here," Erin continues and I'm forced to drag my eyes away from the screen once more to look at my other BFF. Sophie is holding a tub of something in her hands and looking down at me with soft eyes.

"Oh, Darce," she says. She sits down next to me and pulls me into a sideways hug. It's angular and weird, but I know she's only trying to show she cares.

I paste on a smile, although I know I looked wretched. "Hey, Soph."

Sophie's sent me about a gazillion messages and calls and silly memes to make me smile over the last week (didn't work), and she's visited most nights. Friends, people. That's where it's at. Forget the futile, painful search for love. Friends are our lifeblood, our sisters, there for us when we're down and out.

"I brought you some of those buttery slices you like so much from High Tea." She pushes away some empty wrappers and places the tub on the coffee table. "How are you doing? Not so good?" she ventures.

Erin sits on one of the chairs opposite us and answers for me. "I don't think you've budged from this sofa other than to go to the bathroom for days, right, babe?"

I lift one shoulder in a small shrug. It's probably barely perceptible to the naked eye, but I don't have the energy to put into it. "I forgot how good *Gilmore Girls* is."

"How could you have forgotten? You and Erin watch that show all the time," Sophie replies with a smile.

"I don't know." Do we watch *Gilmore Girls* all the time? Life before Alex feels like a distant blur to me right now. Which is crazy, right? It was really only four days we were together. That's not even a week. But then, he had been in my head and my heart for so much longer.

"Well. I'm here to get you out of the house. I know it's not our usual night for doing this, but I need you to go throw on a cute outfit and your best pair of shoes."

Why the heck would I want to go doing something like that? The thought of wearing anything other than my PJs is too daunting to contemplate. I shake my head. "No, thanks."

"No you don't," Sophie says with a shake of her head. "We're not taking no for an answer. We're going to Jojo's!" she announces as though it's the most amazing idea she's ever had, when really, it's the exact opposite.

I blink at her, my mouth open. "You want me to sing karaoke?"

"We do," Erin confirms.

It's the most preposterous thing I've heard since . . . well, since Alex told me he loved me up on the top of Mt. Eden. But there's no way I'm thinking about Alex. Quick! I need another topic, fast. Athlete's foot burning a hole in my toes . . . My hair getting singed by a fire and I've got to have it all shaved off . . . One of those painful boil-type pimples on the end of my nose, making me look like a clown . . . Yes, a nose boil. That ought to do it.

"Singing karaoke is exactly what we're saying," Sophie

replies excitedly. "Come on, Darcy. It'll be fun!"

I shake my head. "No way."

"Please?" Sophie says, doing her best impression of a cute toddler asking for more candy.

I let out a sigh and shake my head again. "I can't face it."

Erin chimes in with, "Oh, come on, girl. You need to get off this sofa sometime, and you love karaoke."

"We're both going, aren't we, Erin?" Sophie asks, and Erin nods. "And we want you there. No, forget that. We *need* you there. Say you will, Darce." She pauses before adding "Please?" again.

I look at her hopeful face. "I don't know, you guys."

"That sounds like there might be a 'yes' lurking in there," Erin says hopefully. Then she pulls out her ace card. "I don't know about you, but I feel a *Dancing Queen* moment coming on," she adds, baiting me with my favorite ABBA song.

I harrumph. "I'm in a more *The Winner Takes It All* moment over here. And newsflash: I'm not the winner."

"No talking like that," Sophie says briskly as she wrangles me out of my spot. I try to protest, but she's not listening, and she's a lot stronger than me, too. "It's time to get your *happy* ABBA on, girl. Go, get dressed. We're leaving in ten minutes."

"But—"

"No buts," she replies, sounding exactly like my mom.

"Okay, I'm going," I reply.

"Getting out will do you so much good," Erin adds.

I am not convinced. "Maybe it will."

"That's the attitude," Sophie says.

"Who knows? Maybe I'll meet someone new and forget all about Alex." My friends look at me in a peculiar way and I say, "I don't mean it. I never want to date anyone ever again."

Twenty minutes later, we're in an Uber on our way to Jojo's, and I'm feeling as excited about the prospect of singing karaoke as I am about having a colonoscopy. (Not that I'm having a colonoscopy, of course, but you know, if I ever did.

They sound completely horrible.)

At Jojo's, Sophie insists on buying us a marginally better bottle of fake champagne than we usually get on our Saturday night outings.

"You being here is a big moment, Darce, and I think we need to mark it," she says as we take our seats at a table near the stage. "And anyway, it was only $11.00 more than our usual bottle."

"No expense spared," Erin says with a sweep of her hands.

I crack a smile, but it lasts less than a second.

Sophie pours our drinks. "To Darcy." She lifts her glass. "She may be down, but she's not out, and we love her."

"Yes, we do," Erin echoes.

We clink glasses, and I take a sip. "You two are the best friends I could ever have." Tears well up in my eyes, and I sniff them back.

"We know," Sophie says with a wink.

Erin punches some numbers into the console. "Right. We are all set." She beams at me ,and I can't help but smile back. My love life might be a complete joke, but I've got my girls, and I've got the pop genius of ABBA.

Before long, we've polished off the first bottle, and we're onto our second, although we're back on the $11.00 cheaper variety, as none of us are exactly rolling in cash.

Erin grins at me as our names are announced for the next song. "We're up. It's ABBA time, girlfriend!"

I roll my eyes. "I'll get up and sing with you as long as you promise never to call me 'girlfriend' again."

By now, Erin's on her feet, grinning down at me. "Deal." She offers me her hand, I take it, and she hauls me out of my chair.

Up on the stage, the sound of Benny running his fingers down the piano signals the start of the song, and it only takes me a few seconds to push enough of my malaise firmly from my mind and surrender myself to the musical genius of ABBA. Singing ABBA songs at Jojo's is something Erin and I love to do. Sophie joins us sometimes, but we all know she's not exactly gifted in the singing department, and she's the first to admit it (howler monkey, remember?). But up on the stage tonight, we get lost in the music, doing the moves, singing together, totally hamming it up.

By the time we're done and the audience has applauded, I almost feel like the old Darcy, the version before Alex came back into my life and blew it all up. The version I so desperately want to be once more.

As I take my seat, Sophie announces that she needs to visit the ladies room, and Erin decides to go with her.

"But you only just went when we got here," I say to Erin.

"What can I say? Peanut bladder," she replies with a shrug.

"Okay. See you soon." I pick up my glass and take a sip as my friends make their way through the tables. I sit and watch the next singer do a decent job of a Shawn Mendez hit, and a moment later, the girls arrive back at the table.

"Hey, this guy's not too shabby," I say as I turn to face them. Only it's not my friends.

It's Alex.

Alex is suddenly here, appearing as though from thin air, standing in front of me at Jojo's Karaoke.

He's looking at me with electric eyes. "Darcy," he says with a look of such vulnerability that my insides twist up, and I've got to force myself to hold his gaze. Because even if I'm blindsided by his unexpected appearance, there's no way I'm letting him know how much him being here has thrown me. No way.

I clench my jaw. "What are you doing here?"

Completely uninvited, he pulls a chair out from the table and sits down next to me. I stiffen in my seat but I do not move. Jojo's is my place, and there's no way I'm giving it up for the likes of Alex Walsh.

"Darcy, I am so sorry." He reaches for my hand, and I snatch it away.

"You're sorry?" I question as my anger bubbles up inside.

"I know I hurt you. I was such an idiot. What I did to you was inexcusable, and all I can hope is that somehow you can find it in your heart to forgive me."

"You want me to forgive you?" I scoff. "Forgive you for running out on me, on the gallery opening, on all of it?"

He leans in toward me, his elbows on his knees. "Darcy, I know I messed up, really bad. Seeing all those images together at one time?" He looks down and shakes his head. "It made me think I'd left the life I wanted behind. When I left that night of the opening, I went to see Chetana. I wanted to tell her—"

"You went to *India*?" I ask, my jaw dropping to the table.

He nods.

I cross my arms and glare at him. "I suppose Chetana told you to go jump off a cliff, did she?"

"She didn't tell me to do anything. You see, Darcy, by the time I got to Delhi, I already knew I'd made a big mistake."

"You didn't see her?" My voice is breathless, and I do my best to ignore the small glimmer of hope in my heart.

He shakes his head. "I didn't need to."

"Because you found out she was already married?" I hold my breath.

"I have no clue if she's married or not. And you know what? I don't care anymore. I thought I did, but I was wrong."

My heart is thumping so hard, I can barely hear myself speak when I say, "You were wrong?"

He nods his head, his intense eyes boring holes in my skull. "I saw a girl on the plane. She must have been only about ten or so. She was holding this notebook. Do you know what it had on the cover?" he asks, and I shake my head. "A Labrador puppy."

I lift my chin. "She has good taste."

His lips lift into a smile, and I feel my heart soften a fraction. "Seeing that girl's notebook did something to me. It made me realize that I didn't love Chetana. Seeing that girl's notebook told me that it's you, Darcy. It's you."

"You hurt me," I state simply, mortified that my lip begins to tremble and my throat tightens, tears threatening to fall. "You don't do something like that to someone you love."

He has the good sense to look ashamed. "I know."

"You did the same thing you did to me in high school. You chose someone else over me."

He bites his lip and nods. "I know I did, and I want to spend a lifetime making it up to you." He's gazing at me with such love in his eyes, my heart skips a beat, maybe more. I couldn't tell you. "If you'll let me," he adds timidly. "Please let me. I-I've never felt like this about anyone before. I love you so, so much."

His words are like an explosion of sunshine. I stare at him, truly lost for words. He's sorry. He loves me. He wants to be with me.

"Darcy?" he says, peering at me questioningly. "Would you ever consider taking me back?"

I lift my eyes to his. His face is creased in worry, and when our gazes lock, hope fills his eyes. I cross my arms and raise my eyebrows at him. "You're going to have to do better than that. You'll need to show me."

"Show you?"

"You heard me, Alex. Words are cheap."

I know I'm being difficult here, but come on! This guy told me he loved me and then took off because he thought he was love with another girl. I'm not about to go throwing myself into his arms with reckless abandon. I already did that with him, and I got burned.

The look on his face morphs from incredulity to something else. "Okay. Challenge accepted. I will show you how much I love you, Darcy Evans, and then you'll know it, too."

I lift my chin. "Good."

He beams at me as though he's got some wonderful secret only he knows about. "Great."

I raise my hands in the air. "I'm sitting here, ready to be shown."

To my surprise, he gets up from his seat. "Hold that thought," he says before he turns and walks away.

I stare at his retreating figure. What the heck is he playing at? That's it? He's just leaving? Well, if that's the way he wants it, then two can play that game. I stand up and collect my purse as Erin and Sophie arrive back at the table.

"Where are you going?" Erin says in surprise.

"Home," I reply.

"But didn't you have a good conversation with . . . someone?" Sophie asks.

"No one in particular, right, Soph?" Erin says.

"No. Just anyone, really."

I look from Erin to Sophie and back again. "Did you know about Alex coming here tonight?"

They both look abashed.

Exasperated, I say, "Was this some sort of *plan* or something?"

Sophie talks first. "Look, he called me and asked me to help him. Erin and I talked about it and agreed. You've been so sad since he left, and we know how you feel about him."

My eyebrows practically jump to my hairline. "You conspired with Alex."

"You could look it like that, I suppose," Sophie replies uncertainly, her eyes darting to Erin. "We thought it was romantic."

Erin nods. "We did. He's genuine, babe. Really, he is."

I clench my teeth. So many emotions swirl around in a giant whirlpool inside. Anger, euphoria, love, hurt.

"Darce?" Erin says, peering at me.

I let out a sigh. "I know you two were only trying to help."

Their faces relax.

"So? What did he say?" Erin asks. She sits down and pats the seat of my chair.

I slump back down and tell them about why he said he left, about Chetana, about the girl's notebook on the plane. By the time I'm done, Erin has tears in her eyes, and Sophie is shaking her head at me.

"And then he just walked off?" Sophie asks and I nod.

"He loves you," Erin says, her hand on her heart. "He would have had a very good reason for doing that."

"It doesn't make any sense. Where did he go?" Sophie asks

as she scans the room.

"Who knows? Probably India," I scoff.

"Oh, Darce," Erin says. "He'll be back. I bet he left to work out how best to show you he loves you, that's all."

I harrumph.

The opening chords of a song from one of my favorite scenes in the movie *Mamma Mia* start up (the one where all the guys dance around on the beach in their skimpy shorts, although I like it purely for the music, nothing else, of course), and I look over at the stage to see who's going to perform it. It's empty.

"It looks like someone forgot they're singing this song," Erin says as she lifts her glass to her lips.

"Pity. It's a great song," I reply.

"Look." Sophie's eyes are trained on the stage.

I turn to face the stage again and spot a man in sunglasses, dressed in a white jumpsuit with the shirt open almost to his waist. He would look like he stepped straight out of an ABBA video from the '70s if it weren't for the fact he's got a significantly better body on him than either Björn or Benny ever sported. And yes, I know, that's not exactly hard.

The guy lifts the microphone to his lips and sings the opening line to *Lay All Your Love On Me*. He sounds awful. Totally tuneless, tone-deaf, the works. I thought Sophie was a terrible singer, but this guy takes the cake, the cake stand, *and* the table cloth.

I turn back to my friends. "This guy is horrible!"

"The worst!" Sophie says. "And I can say that because this guy is worse than me."

He continues to butcher the song, and then, as he launches into the chorus, imploring some poor woman to lay all her love on him, he pulls his sunglasses off and looks directly at me.

My heart skips a beat.

No! It can't be.

Alex is here, on the stage, singing an ABBA song in a terrible white '70s jumpsuit.

With my jaw dropped open, my eyes dart to my friends. They're both shooting me surprised smiles.

"That's *Alex*?" I guffaw.

"OMG. He's showing you he loves you! It's so romantic," Erin says as she gazes at him.

I turn back to watch as he continues to butcher the song. He's dancing (poorly) and moving around as though he were born to sing, although he's clearly not because he sounds like Janice from *Friends*.

Finally, when the song is over and he's left standing on the stage, looking like a complete idiot in his ABBA getup, he grins at me, and my heart softens into a mushy, gooey marshmallow.

He did that for me.

He once told me he hates karaoke, and that he'd only do it to save the world from aliens or something else equally important. With no aliens in sight, I guess the important thing in the room is . . . me.

"Darcy," he says into the microphone, "I will stand up here and sing any song you like until you take me back. Heck, I'll stand here and sing *all* the songs until you take me back."

"Take him back now!" someone from the audience calls out.

"Yeah, do it before he damages our eardrums!" someone else yells.

A bubble of laughter rises inside me, and I let out a snort. With a surge of sheer happiness, I press my hand over my mouth and watch as he steps off the stage and makes a beeline for me. In a few short strides of his long, white-jumpsuit-encased legs, he's at our table once more.

I glance quickly at my friends. Their eyes are riveted on Alex, and I can tell they didn't know this was part of the plan. I lift my own eyes to his and see the yearning written across his face.

"Did you like my song?" he asks.

"No," I laugh. "You were terrible."

"I told you I was. But I meant what I said. I'd do it again and again. For you." He reaches for my hand. "Darcy, I love you with all my heart, and I promise I will never, ever hurt you again."

Tears spring into my eyes. My heart is so full of glorious, warm sunshine, it feels like it could burst. Alex loves me. He loves me! Slowly, tentatively, I reach my hand out and place my palm against his chest. "I love you, too, Alex."

His entire face lights up, and he wraps his fingers around my hand. "You have no idea how good that sounds."

"I think I do." A giddy laugh escapes my lips.

He pulls me up to my feet and then sweeps me up in one of our incredible, mind-blowing kisses.

The audience around us cheers and hollers, and I give them a small, embarrassed wave. I take his collar in my fingers. "Where did you get this outfit?"

"See that guy over there by the well?"

I look in the direction he's pointing and see a man waving at us. "You borrowed this from him?"

"Yeah, although it's getting a bit itchy."

I laugh. "Maybe you should go get your clothes back. Who knows? That guy might actually be able to sing."

He kisses me again, and my happiness fills me from the top of my head to the tips of my toes.

Alex loves me. He's back and he wants to be with me.

The fourteen-year-old girl in me gives a squeal of delight. Alex is mine, and I'm never letting go.

Epilogue

I push through the door to Cozy Cottage High Tea and am immediately hit by the warm, inviting ambience of the place. The music, the chatter, the clink of china, and, of course, the delicious aroma of freshly baked treats. Mmmm, definitely the freshly baked treats.

I reach the podium and smile at Sophie, who greets me with a warm hug. "Hey, Soph," I say as I breathe in her perfume.

"Darce, I love the outfit! Blue be gone, right?" she says.

I glance down at my pink (Barbie, clearly) dress and cute nude peep-toe heels. Blue has run its course in the office for Darcy Evans, and now, finally, I've taken a stand. This morning, I chose an outfit from the *other* end of my closet — the one with all the colors of the rainbow — and strode confidently into the office.

"How did Larissa take it?" Sophie asks.

"Oh, she looked like she was having an aneurysm for about five full seconds until I threw in some Larissa-speak about self-realization through color experimentation. Or some such garbage. She totally bought it, and I plan on making it my plight to free the oppressed masses at work from the color blue."

I think of the way Alex described my stand as "shaking Cookie Monster off," of "rising from the Smurf ashes like a phoenix." Or some such crap. Really, the guy should go work for Larissa himself.

"Good for you for taking a stand, babe," Sophie says.

I shrug. "It's only clothes. It's not like I've found a cure for the common cold or saved the whales, or something."

"Sometimes it's not about the grand gestures. Sometimes it's about the little day-to-day things that have an impact."

I arch an eyebrow. "You're sounding very philosophical and wise, Soph."

"I *am* very philosophical and wise. You know that," she replies with a wink.

I glance around High Tea. "Is Alex here?"

"Not yet."

"You know, I used to come in here, hoping not to have to see him."

"But that was before."

I nod. Before I realized what I felt for him wasn't hate, before I knew him, before I'd even given him a chance.

"Oh, you're so loved-up, girl," Sophie says with a shake of her head. "And my cousin is exactly the same. He went all goofy when Mom asked him about you at the Mandatory McCarthy Meal on Sunday."

I try to suppress a huge grin from spreading across my face. And I fail.

"Sophie! Darcy!"

I turn to see Erin walk through the door with a gaggle of extremely well put-together women, all dressed in expensive designer clothes without a hair out of place.

I greet her with a hug. "What are you doing here?"

"I brought some of the players' girlfriends for high tea. This is Marla, Janessa, and Karli," she says, and each of the women nods and says hello to us. "They're WAGS. Wives And Girlfriends."

"We deserve this treat. Our boyfriends have been away for three weeks already this season. We need sugar," one of them says, and the others all nod their agreement.

"And we're trying to match-make Erin with one of the single guys on the team," the blonde one adds.

"Really?" I say. "How's that working out so far?" I shoot Sophie a look. We both know there's no way Erin will ever date a rugby player. She's only told us about a gazillion times.

"She's not said yes yet, but we've got the best guy lined up for her," the blonde one replies. "She'll be powerless to resist."

"Well, good luck!" I say.

Erin rolls her eyes at me and mouths, "Not gonna happen."

"I've got your table all ready, ladies," Sophie announces with a pile of menus in her hands. "If you'd like to follow me?"

As Erin and the WAGs follow Sophie to their table, I wait by the podium for my date.

"Well, hello there," says a deep, familiar voice at my side.

I turn to see Alex beaming at me, looking impossibly handsome, as he always does. Even though it's been two weeks and three days since he dressed up in a white jumpsuit and sang an ABBA song to me at Jojo's — well, I say "sang," but it was really "slaughtered beyond all recognition" if I were to be completely honest — my tummy still does a little flip whenever I lay eyes on him. Today is no different.

"Hey, you," I say as I place my hand lightly on his chest and gaze up at him.

He slinks an arm around my middle. "Hey," he replies, gazing down at me with such love in his eyes, my heart stops entirely for at least three seconds. "You look so beautiful."

"Not a Smurf in sight?"

"Not a Smurf in sight." He holds my gaze for a moment then looks up and says, "You know, I've never actually been a customer here before."

"Do you miss the pink High Tea apron, because I'm sure Soph could get you one to wear while we're eating."

"I think I'm good."

Sophie reappears and shows us to the table I requested—in the cute, romantic courtyard out the back, the place where Bailey's friends, Cassie and Will got married all that time ago.

We place our order with Natalie, our server, and then I hand Alex a sheet of paper I'd folded up and slotted into my Labrador puppy notebook. I wait with anticipation as he reads it.

After a moment, he looks from the paper up at me, his eyes wide. "You're telling me that not only did I sell all my photographs at the exhibition, but I have all these orders now, too?"

I shrug. "You're a visionary genius, remember?"

He lets out a laugh. "And quite a lot richer now, too, by the looks of things. Larissa is so right. I *am* a visionary genius." His eyes sparkle with mischief.

I grin at him. "Your modesty is your only failing."

"Oh, I know that. Cocky, remember?"

"Oh, yeah. I remember. Speaking of which, did I ever tell you I gave a speech about you at the gallery opening?"

"You did?"

"Someone had to say something after you'd taken off."

He has the good sense to look abashed. "Something I will always regret."

I give an indulgent shrug. If he hadn't come back to me within the week, I'm not sure I'd be feeling quite so generous toward him, but he did, so I do. "It all worked out in the end."

"What did you say in your speech?"

"I told everyone that although you were an excellent photographer, you were an a-grade jerk of the highest order."

He lets out a surprised laugh. "Nice. Thanks."

I nod at the paper in his hands. "It meant your photographs sold like hotcakes on the night and have continued to do so ever since."

"And you think that's because of your speech?"

"It's because everyone knows any artist worth their salt is a complete jerk."

He chuckles. "Is that so?"

"Oh, yes."

"So, it's not because I'm quite a good photographer and have been offered a bunch of work and another solo show since then?"

"Well, that too, I guess."

"Here you go, you two," Natalie, says as she deposits one of the High Tea three-tiered cake stands full of utter deliciousness on the table. "And here's your pot of tea for two," she adds.

"Thanks, Nat," Alex says.

"It's weird to have you as a customer, Alex," she replies.

"What can I say? Along with Jojo's, this is Darcy's happy place, and keeping on the right side of Darcy is very important to me right now."

"You make me sound like a terrible human being!" I protest.

"Just a little like The Hulk. 'You won't like me when I'm angry,'" he replies.

I let out a laugh as I shake my head. "See what I've got to deal with, Natalie?"

"Yeah. It must be tough dating a guy like Alex." She throws me a smile then leaves the table.

"The Hulk. Seriously?" I question.

"But much better looking, of course."

"Well, that's something, I suppose, although I think I would have preferred Wonder Woman." I beam at him.

"Remind me to get you the costume."

I giggle as I pour our tea into our delicate High Tea cups. I look up and catch Erin's eye. She's gazing at us wistfully, and I mouth the words, "your turn next."

She rolls her eyes and shakes her head, mouthing, "No way," before she turns back to the WAGs.

Alex raises his eyebrows. "Tea may be quaint, but I think I'll always be a coffee guy, you know."

"Maybe. But with me today, you're drinking tea. Earl Grey, to be precise. Remember, this is my happy place, and I'm The-Hulk-slash-Wonder-Woman."

He reaches across the table and takes my hand in his. "Well, you got me to sing karaoke, so why not drink tea, too?"

"I knew you'd come around to see things my way, Alex*ander*."

He chuckles. It's low and gets those zings fired up inside me. "The day we kissed in the kitchen and you called me 'Alexander,' I knew you had feelings for me. Feelings you did not want to have."

"I hated you," I say simply.

"Sure you did." He grins at me. "Hey, I've got something for you." He reaches into his bag and pulls out a gift. It's badly wrapped, with a lot of tape, so I know he did it himself, which has me feeling even happier than I did when I laid eyes on him only moments before.

"What is it?" I ask as I take it in my hands.

"I didn't go to all this effort wrapping it to just come out and tell you what it is. Open it."

I unwrap the gift and gaze at a color photograph of me, looking out into the lens, smiling, my eyes bright and full of love, love for the guy who took the photo. "Wow, Alex, I look—"

"Beautiful," he finishes for me.

"Well, I can't say that, exactly, but I can compliment the photographer on making me look pretty darn good. And it's in color."

He squeezes my hand and says, "My black and white days are behind me, now." We share a look, and I know he means it's because of me. I brought the color back into his life. And yes, I know that sounds as cheesy as a French *fromagerie*, but

NO MORE TERRIBLE DATES

it's the truth.

"I thought I'd hang it up in my apartment," he says. "It'll be the first of many new photographs for my bare walls."

I remember how I was struck by the lack of décor at Alex's home when I first saw it. Of course, I worked out afterwards that he'd had photos of Chetana and his time in India hung up before.

I push myself out of my chair, skim past the cake stand, and pull him in for a kiss. "I love you," I murmur.

"Me too," he replies.

This. This is what I wanted all along but never knew it. I was looking for my Happy For Now, and all I wanted to do was date a good guy. The last person on the planet I thought I would ever end up with was Alex Walsh. Yet here I am, in love and beyond happy, with the guy I thought I hated, the guy I loved all along.

THE END

Acknowledgements

I've got a few people to thank help bring this book to life. Thanks go to my fabulous critique partner, Jackie Rutherford, who tirelessly supports my writing and offers me great feedback to make my books the best they can be. You're a total rock star, Jackie!

Thank you to Sue Traynor for creating yet another gorgeous cover for me. I love it. Thanks to my editor, Karan Eleni of the Letterers Collective, for her work in getting this book ready for the big, wide world to see, and to my proof reader, Diane Michaels, whose attention to detail is second to none.

Thanks to Nadia Reagan for coming up with Larissa's name. It suits her perfectly!

To my family, thank you for being awesome and supporting me through another book.

And finally, thank you to all my readers. Without you, I couldn't do this. Keep on reading, and I will keep on writing.

About the Author

I am a bestselling author of fun, feel-good romantic comedies and chick lit. I live and love in beautiful New Zealand with my family, two scruffy dogs, and a cat who thinks he's a scruffy dog, too. He's not: he's a cat.

When I'm not penning my latest story, I can be found hiking up hills (slowly), traveling to different countries around the globe, and eating chocolate. A lot of it.

You can find me at kateokeeffe.com.

NO MORE TERRIBLE DATES

KATE O'KEEFFE